Anthony Gilbert and The Murder Room

》》》 This title is part of The Murder Room, our series dedicated to making available out-of-print or hard-to-find titles by classic crime writers.

Crime fiction has always held up a mirror to society. The Victorians were fascinated by sensational murder and the emerging science of detection; now we are obsessed with the forensic detail of violent death. And no other genre has so captivated and enthralled readers.

Vast troves of classic crime writing have for a long time been unavailable to all but the most dedicated frequenters of second-hand bookshops. The advent of digital publishing means that we are now able to bring you the backlists of a huge range of titles by classic and contemporary crime writers, some of which have been out of print for decades.

From the genteel amateur private eyes of the Golden Age and the femmes fatales of pulp fiction, to the morally ambiguous hard-boiled detectives of mid twentieth-century America and their descendants who walk our twenty-first century streets, The Murder Room has it all. **》》》**

The Murder Room
Where Criminal Minds Meet

themurderroom.com

Anthony Gilbert (1899–1973)

Anthony Gilbert was the pen name of Lucy Beatrice Malleson. Born in London, she spent all her life there, and her affection for the city is clear from the strong sense of character and place in evidence in her work. She published 69 crime novels, 51 of which featured her best known character, Arthur Crook, a vulgar London lawyer totally (and deliberately) unlike the aristocratic detectives, such as Lord Peter Wimsey, who dominated the mystery field at the time. She also wrote more than 25 radio plays, which were broadcast in Great Britain and overseas. Her thriller *The Woman in Red* (1941) was broadcast in the United States by CBS and made into a film in 1945 under the title *My Name is Julia Ross*. She was an early member of the British Detection Club, which, along with Dorothy L. Sayers, she prevented from disintegrating during World War II. Malleson published her autobiography, *Three-a-Penny*, in 1940, and wrote numerous short stories, which were published in several anthologies and in such periodicals as *Ellery Queen's Mystery Magazine* and *The Saint*. The short story 'You Can't Hang Twice' received a Queens award in 1946. She never married, and evidence of her feminism is elegantly expressed in much of her work.

By Anthony Gilbert

Scott Egerton series

Tragedy at Freyne (1927)

The Murder of Mrs
 Davenport (1928)

Death at Four Corners (1929)

The Mystery of the Open
 Window (1929)

The Night of the Fog (1930)

The Body on the Beam (1932)

The Long Shadow (1932)

The Musical Comedy
 Crime (1933)

An Old Lady Dies (1934)

The Man Who Was Too
 Clever (1935)

**Mr Crook Murder
 Mystery series**

Murder by Experts (1936)

The Man Who Wasn't
 There (1937)

Murder Has No Tongue (1937)

Treason in My Breast (1938)

The Bell of Death (1939)

Dear Dead Woman (1940)
 aka *Death Takes a Redhead*

The Vanishing Corpse (1941)
 aka *She Vanished in the Dawn*

The Woman in Red (1941)
 aka *The Mystery of the
 Woman in Red*

Death in the Blackout (1942)
 aka *The Case of the Tea-
 Cosy's Aunt*

Something Nasty in the
 Woodshed (1942)
 aka *Mystery in the Woodshed*

The Mouse Who Wouldn't
 Play Ball (1943)
 aka *30 Days to Live*

He Came by Night (1944)
 aka *Death at the Door*

The Scarlet Button (1944)
 aka *Murder Is Cheap*

A Spy for Mr Crook (1944)

The Black Stage (1945)
 aka *Murder Cheats the Bride*

Don't Open the Door (1945)
 aka *Death Lifts the Latch*

Lift Up the Lid (1945)
 aka *The Innocent Bottle*

The Spinster's Secret (1946)
 aka *By Hook or by Crook*

Death in the Wrong Room
 (1947)

Die in the Dark (1947)
 aka *The Missing Widow*

Death Knocks Three Times
 (1949)

Murder Comes Home (1950)

A Nice Cup of Tea (1950)
 aka *The Wrong Body*

Lady-Killer (1951)
Miss Pinnegar Disappears
  (1952)
  aka *A Case for Mr Crook*
Footsteps Behind Me (1953)
  aka *Black Death*
Snake in the Grass (1954)
  aka *Death Won't Wait*
Is She Dead Too? (1955)
  aka *A Question of Murder*
And Death Came Too (1956)
Riddle of a Lady (1956)
Give Death a Name (1957)
Death Against the Clock
  (1958)
Death Takes a Wife (1959)
  aka *Death Casts a Long
  Shadow*
Third Crime Lucky (1959)
  aka *Prelude to Murder*
Out for the Kill (1960)
She Shall Die (1961)
  aka *After the Verdict*
Uncertain Death (1961)
No Dust in the Attic (1962)
Ring for a Noose (1963)
The Fingerprint (1964)

The Voice (1964)
  aka *Knock, Knock! Who's
  There?*
Passenger to Nowhere (1965)
The Looking Glass Murder
  (1966)
The Visitor (1967)
Night Encounter (1968)
  aka *Murder Anonymous*
Missing from Her Home (1969)
Death Wears a Mask (1970)
  aka *Mr Crook Lifts the Mask*
Murder is a Waiting Game
  (1972)
Tenant for the Tomb (1971)
A Nice Little Killing (1974)

Standalone Novels
The Case Against Andrew
  Fane (1931)
Death in Fancy Dress (1933)
The Man in Button Boots
  (1934)
Courtier to Death (1936)
  aka *The Dover Train Mystery*
The Clock in the Hatbox
  (1939)

The Voice

Anthony Gilbert

An Orion book

Copyright © Lucy Beatrice Malleson 1964

The right of Lucy Beatrice Malleson to be identified as the author of this work has been asserted in accordance with the Copyright, Designs and Patents Act 1988.

This edition published by
The Orion Publishing Group Ltd
Orion House
5 Upper St Martin's Lane
London WC2H 9EA

An Hachette UK company
A CIP catalogue record for this book is available from the British Library

ISBN 978 1 4719 1026 5

www.orionbooks.co.uk

CHAPTER I

As I CAME up the stairs on the afternoon of the murder I could hear the telephone in my furnished flat ringing with that scornful peremptory note telephones always seem to have in an empty room.

Come on! Come on!

Tantalised, I fumbled with my key, got the door open, snatched the receiver from the hook, to hear a voice I had never heard before, crying desperately, " Are you there? Listen! Tell him it's no use. I haven't got it. He'll have to wait. I can't get it in time."

I said cautiously, " Tell who?" but I might have been a fly drowning in a milk jug. That fluid voice, with a sort of ripple in it despite the obvious panic, only repeated, " I haven't got it, I tell you. So it's no use coming round. . . . You must tell him."

And then I heard the decisive click of a receiver being replaced and in my ear the bumbling note telephones make when a line has been disconnected. I stood looking at the instrument in my hand for a minute before I remembered to hang up. Then I waited, as if expecting the bell to start again, but nothing happened; the silence was as thick as the fog beyond the window. I walked across the room and tried to peer out. There was nothing much to be seen except graduated roofs, with a slit of pavement far below, even in the sunniest weather; to-night I made out an occasional line, heard a muted

1

footstep that might have come from another world; somewhere an invisible cat mewed.

The room, shabby, and impersonal as furnished rooms are inclined to be, rang with the echo of that voice; I knew I should recognise it immediately if I heard it again. I got myself a drink out of what was described in the inventory as a likker-lokker, and glanced through some letters I'd collected on my way up. There was nothing very urgent there, nothing that couldn't wait till the morning. I poured myself a second drink, lighted a cigarette, and put through a call to a man I know called Doggett. Doggett's name matched his trade, and was doubtless intended to do so. He bred greyhounds, raced a few and sold the rest. He had built up quite a business during the five years or so he'd been on the job, had a kind of knack with animals that was almost uncanny; a tip from him could generally be relied on. I'm a natural gambler myself, the notion of clocking in and out five days a week for a regular wage has never appealed to me, so I freelance my way through life, sometimes on the up-and-up and sometimes on the skids. In a way it's the variety that makes it exciting.

Doggett, who can be as dour as a wet week-end, was full of fire to-night. He told me about a young greyhound he'd acquired that had all the makings of a champion. He's got heart as well as stamina, he explained. You can always tell. And one without the other is *no bon*. We discussed business for a bit, and before he rang off he gave me a tip—Red Maid. Never mind what the boys tell you about her chances, she's going to win, he boasted. Queen of Sheba's being tipped, but—she's not going to win. So I decided to risk a fiver on Red Maid. And I said I'd pass the word round, I had some quite useful connections. It was seven o'clock when I rang off, day drawing to its close, you might say. But, as it turned out, not my day.

The room had a cold, smoky smell, and when I opened the window I could hear a fog-horn bellowing away like some old sea-lion, calling forlornly to his cows. I hesitated about a third drink, decided against it and went out to dinner. This flat of mine was simply a pair of gloomy rooms with an ancient Victorian bathroom, cut out of a big Victorian house, the kind that planners are yearning to pull down. It wasn't even true to call it a flat, I had no individual front door, and as there was no restaurant I never ate on the premises. I even went out for my breakfast. Once no doubt the place had housed gracious living, but life had moved away from it, and it and all its neighbours—it was a terrace house, tall and smoky, with blocked up windows in the drab walls to avoid window tax—all these houses had been cut up into apartments or bed-sitters, with tenants moving in and out as nameless as ghosts. If you did meet a face on the stairs, the odds are it was one you'd never seen before.

As a rule I went along to the Chicken Parlour for my evening meal. Its disadvantage was that it wasn't licensed, but they did steaks as well as chickens, the cooking had an agreeably original tang, was within my price-range and it was never unpleasantly crowded. Also they knew me there. London's a great place for being ignored. After, I'd go along to one or more of the locals —the Horse and Mariner was my main port of call, I'd made a number of casual acquaintances there, but I wasn't quite a stranger at a number of others. I used to pass on Doggett's tips—I worked for him in various directions on a commission basis, and I had a few irons of my own in the fire, too. I'd play a game of darts, talk dogs, agree whichever Government was in power was riding the country straight into the sea, pick up any information that might be useful and so home. I'm a bachelor who's never put down roots, I'm always on the look-out for something new. Doggett, who's a mysogonist, used to say, " You're too easy-going, one of these days you'll get caught." And I used to laugh and say, That'll be the day. But that was before I met Barbie Hunter.

The Parlour was emptier than usual, thanks to the weather, I suppose, which certainly hadn't improved during the past hour. George gave me a particularly affable reception, he regards a half-empty room as a kind of personal failure. He said the chickens were fine to-night, he used to bring them round on a hot-plate and you chose your own joint. I suppose the staff had the pieces no one else wanted.

I said I fancied steak to-night, and I ordered some spaghetti while that was cooking. George, with time on his hands, stopped by the table.

" I reckon we should have a bonus hereafter," he said. " The climate we have to put up with." He put his head on one side. " Listen to that!"

You could hear the fog-horns more clearly now; the river wasn't far off, and the doleful notes went peeling through the mist. .

" There's an owl come to live in my garden," he went on. " Hoots like the Day of Judgment."

I sent the ball back over the net. " We've got a jay,

4

just visiting—I hope," I said. " Screeches like someone being murdered."

" We're cheerful to-night, aren't we?" said George, going to see about my steak.

After that I had black coffee in a pot, and it must have been nearly nine when I left the restaurant. I usually went to the Horse and Mariner—you make good contacts in a pub—but this evening I turned in the direction of the river. There was a job called the Admiral Box where I'd never been, though I'd passed it often enough. I turned into a lane not much wider than a passage, with the wall of a factory on one side; I could see a dull golden blur at the end, and that was the Admiral.

I hadn't gone many steps when I heard the car behind me, and instinctively I drew back closer against the wall. Visibility was pretty bad and the lighting was as faint as a candle-gleam; I didn't want to be the ham in the sandwich, and I could sense that it was a pretty big car. I wondered if it might be the police. It was a splendid night for crime. Then the car came closer and I knew whoever was driving it it wasn't the boys in blue. They'd never be seen in such an outfit, a real vintage model, high and smooth, a Rolls as I live. Someone had taken trouble with it, it ran as sweetly as a river, and the driver must have seen me because he slowed to a crawl, and a voice that competed very favourably with the fog-horns yelled at me. The car halted under one of the two feeble lights, so I could see the driver, and he was as much a character as the car. I heard a window wound down and then a great red face, like the moon seen through blood, was poked out.

"This your manor?" the voice bawled, and I said (cautiously) I'd been living here for a short time, passing through. but . . .

"Know a pub hereabouts that looks like a church?"

That caught me off balance. A church? Which way? I had a vision of an inn with a steeple atop to advertise its whereabouts to all and sundry. The Steeple Inn. . . .

"Stained-glass windows," offered the driver helpfully, and I came to again.

"It could be the Admiral Box," I said. "It's got sort of fancy Victorian glass in front, not specially religious, though. Hops being cut, wheat being reaped."

"What could be more religious than that? Darkish, three steps down to the bar?"

"I haven't been inside," I confessed. "It's the one at the end of the road."

"Thanks a million." The face disappeared, the car started to move; the next instant it stopped, the face reappeared.

"Not going that way yourself, I suppose?"

"Actually," I said, "I was."

He pushed the door open. "Help yourself." If I'd retained any of my original suspicions that this might be anything to do with the police they'd have died on the spot. The police will do a lot of things, but they won't go around in an out-of-date Rolls the colour of a daffodil.

"Who was he?" asked the driver cosily, as we rolled along at a funeral pace. He wasn't taking any chances.

"Who was who?"

"This Admiral Box. He must have been a nob of some kind to get his name on an inn-sign."

"Well," I told him, "the full title's The Admiral and Box. There's a painting, which you won't be able to see to-night at all, and isn't too clear even in sunlight, of an old boy with a cocked hat and his hair in a pigtail, clutching a great wooden chest, hooped with brass. Some sort of a pirate, I daresay."

"This ain't the right part of the river for pirates," said my companion. I could see at once he was right on the ball. "You'd never land the stuff."

"Oh, come, they don't have to make sense, do they?" I urged. "Inn signs, I mean. Think of The Bull and Mouth and the Swan and Pyramids. I ask you."

"What do you ask me?"

"Can you imagine a swan nesting round the Pyramids?"

"It's all according. Ever studied the cycle of nature? Things go round on a wheel. You put a contemporary swan by the Pyramids and it 'ud curl up and die, I daresay, but maybe there was once a creature called a sand swan, and it could be again. Remember the coelacanth? What with the atom bomb and all our clever young men making to the moon it 'ud never surprise me to see mastodons marching down the Kings Road—and maybe even swans nesting in the Gobi Desert. By that time all the humans 'ull be in orbit round some other planet."

I thought, I've picked a screwball all right, as he went on telling me about the other pubs he'd already visited to-night—The Cygnet and Cheese, The Halfpenny Inn, the Duck in Gum Boots—they like their pubs fancy round here, don't they? he said—he seemed to know the history of most of them.

" You'll have to park in the cul-de-sac here," I warned him as we drew near the Admiral. " Anywhere round the front counts as an obstruction."

There were only a couple of other cars and a motor-cycle parked in the cul-de-sac to-night. There was a disused fountain half-way up, three darling girls each clutching an unresponsive dolphin. It might have been quite pretty when it was working, but weather and the hooligans round about had knocked off the girls' noses and one of the dolphins' tails, and there was a sort of greenish moss growing over the bowl. No water, of course.

When we were free of the car I could see my com-panion a bit better, a roly-poly of a man wearing a ginger-coloured suit with a checked cap pulled over his eyes, which were a kind of red-brown, too. He made me think of what he'd been saying about obsolescent forms of life suddenly re-appearing. This one looked as if he'd be as much at home in a jungle as a pub. Which is saying quite something.

We pulled open the door and there were the three steps leading to the dark interior. It was obvious that business at the Admiral to-night was pretty quiet. But you could tell it was never what you might describe as a clubbable pub. I've heard them listed as ports of call or in-and-out houses, chaps dropped in on the way back from the factory, and there was a fairly new betting shop run by a man called Henry Lite not far off, and that would account for a bit more custom, but it was too far out of the way to be really homely. Mind you, I daresay quite a number of tips got passed there, and even a few plots hatched that might interest the police, but you couldn't imagine anything more than a drink or two, a few words, a nod, and so home to bed. As it happened, I couldn't have been more wrong.

The chap behind the bar looked ordinary enough, working single-handed, and not, to-night at all events, overworked. As we came in he was saying to a customer, "Television's killing the pubs and that's a fact. It's in for a few bottles (it was an off licence) and back to the box."

My companion marched up to the bar as if he'd been coming here every night for a year.

"All you need's a bit of patience," he said. "With things going the way they are, in no time you'll have the chaps swarming back to get away from the telly." He ordered a pint and said to me, "What's yours?"

I started to say this was on me, but he paid no attention. I got the impression he never paid much attention to anyone, though I found out later that was another mistake. Anyway, he paid for my whisky and the next second he was asking for another pint. The first went down in one great swallow; it's a trick I've never been able to manage myself, you just open the uvula and the stuff falls into your stomach like milk into a pail.

"Name of Ted?" he went on, and the barman said in a very formal sort of way, "That's right, sir."

"Then I'm right, too. Like a word a bit later."

This chap, Ted, seemed to freeze, and I saw he was making my original mistake. Mind you, the police are supposed to declare an interest as soon as they come in, and they can't hope to get much of a welcome. None of the brewers like the idea of their pubs being known as coppers' ports of call, and Macraes are stiffer-backed than most. Well, nothing's worse for the reputation than that.

Ginger put his hand in his pockets, and I could see Ted was expecting a warrant to emerge, but instead the chap pulled out an outsize visiting card and chucked it on the counter. I couldn't help seeing the name. Arthur Crook and an address in Bloomsbury and another in S.W.5. I looked sharply at Ted, wondering if it was going to register with him. The police would have recognised that name all right, and so would half London's underworld. I'd heard of him myself—The Criminals' Hope and the Judges' Despair was what they called him. It was obvious Ted had caught on.

" Later," he said, and went off to serve someone else.

Crook picked up the tankard and took a sup; his great red face split into a grin as wide as a door opening.

" I don't know what chaps are coming to," he told Ted when he came back up the bar, "with beer like this you should be checking 'em in through a turnstile. A lot of the stuff they give you these days," he confided, turning to me, "is half water and dirty water at that. If all the houses served beer like this there'd be so much whisky for export you wouldn't be able to sell it."

I was taking a look around. The customers were still pretty thin on the ground, but I hadn't been there long before I realised that what they lacked in quantity they made up in quality. Close behind me, two women were sitting at a table tearing strips off London Transport. Wait till you get to the spot and then ring the bell, said one. The other agreed eagerly. Same in the shops, she said, they don't want to oblige you. They both looked as fat as butter, wore imitation fur coats—in mid-

summer, by the calendar at least—and carried huge
plastic bags. It turned out they'd come from a bingo
session where both had done well. A young Indian,
dressed up to the nines, pink bow tie, bright blue suit,
checked shirt, sat up at the bar, drinking whisky and
beaming at everyone. He had that smooth gleaming
skin and warm dark eyes they so often have. I thought
if he'd come here for a pick-up he'd mistaken his mark.
He might be the little friend of all the world, but he
was drinking alone for all that. Most of those present
were middle-aged or as near as makes no difference. Next
to Ranji sat a woman, also on her lonesome, though
you'd have sworn from her appearance she was born for
company. Big and jolly-looking, handsomely curved, she
was dressed in a bright satin blouse and ear-rings like
pagodas swung in her ears. And whoever else was a
casual here she was a regular, you can always tell. She was
pushing the whisky, too; Crook, with his pint pot, must
have felt like the Lone Ranger. I went on watching the
woman; her hair was a lot brighter than nature had
intended and the rings on her fingers wouldn't have
fetched much at an auction, but she made you think of
those big cabbage roses you see on textiles, and practically
nowhere else these days. A bit full-blown, but rich,
colourful.

Crook had taken his second pint and moved over to a
table against the wall; he pulled an evening edition out
of his pocket and settled down as though he had the rest
of the night to spare. He might look dreamy enough, but
I'd overheard what he said to Ted. He was out on the
job all right, winkling some other offender out of the
clutches of the law. They said if you clocked your wife

one and hit her a bit harder than you intended, he was the only man who could persuade a jury she'd slipped and banged her head on the fireplace.

Ted was talking to the woman at the bar. "You're down to-night, Madge," he chaffed her. He put a glass on the counter. "On the house," he said.

She pushed it back. "Don't be daft, Ted. When I can't afford to pay for myself . . ."

Young Ranji here created a bit of an interlude by snapping his fingers—never popular in a bar and clearly out of place here—and saying, "Same as before and the same for the lady, too," and tossed down a note and then laid one hand on Madge's arm. He had beautiful hands, he'd never done any hard labour—and his teeth were something to notice, they'd have made his fortune on commercial television.

Madge—her other name turned out to be Gardiner— shook her head. "Thanks a million," she said, "but I'm like William Rufus there. I pay for myself."

She opened a big smart black bag and I saw the notes coiled inside, a great wad of them. She peeled one off and handed it over the bar. Ted looked in the till.

"Haven't got the silver, I suppose?" said Ted. "Everyone who's been in to-night he wanted to change a note."

She looked through her purse, then shook her head. "I haven't got it," she said. "I'm sorry, Ted, I haven't got it."

Something clicked in my brain. For an instant I was back in my flat, holding a receiver to my ear and hearing a voice say, "It's no use coming round, I haven't got it." I'd known from the start I could never mistake that

12

voice. I watched her like a hawk, playing it cool, though, asking the chap next to me if he had a tip for to-morrow's big race, mentioning Red Maid. I didn't want to attract attention, but I needn't have bothered. She didn't know I was born. I wondered what she'd say if I went over and told her, "We were having a bit of a barney on the phone say two hours back. Crete's the name, Simon Crete. Remember?"

Not that she'd remember my voice, why, she didn't get a chance to hear it, and in the state she was in I doubt if it would have registered anyway. I can't have shown any surprise because no one said, what's up mate? or paid me any attention at all. I said something to Crook in a pretty clear voice that she couldn't have failed to hear, but she didn't even turn her head. As for me, it would have taken a machine-gun to get me off the premises. How could I guess how the evening was going to end?

Meanwhile, up at the bar young India was sorting through a pocketful of change; he tossed some coins on the counter, telling Ted to give the lady back her money, the drinks were on him.

I thought Madge might shrug and accept the situation just to stop the argument, but she didn't.

She said, quite pleasantly, but as definite as a key being turned in a lock, "It's ever so kind of you, and don't think I don't appreciate it, but—well, if my friend was to turn up and find me drinking with you, well, he might not like it. Ever so jealous, see?"

This Ranji—I hadn't heard his name to date—was a real joker. He squared up and put up his fists—probably called them dukes, he was a great one for anything old English—and cried, " Pistols for two, coffee for one, is not that what you say?"

"I don't know, I'm sure," said Madge, absently. Crook was grinning all over his big red face. " I've never been in the nut-house myself." She picked up her drink and prepared to move to one of the small tables, when this young chap caught her by the wrist.

"Do not be so upstage," he declared. "It is lonely here, you should be friendly."

Madge, who clearly hadn't the least idea she'd said anything that might upset him, pushed his hand away.

"Now, look," she said, "I told you—someone I know may be coming along any minute, and what's he going to think if he finds you an me as thick as thieves?"

That really did send the balloon up. This chap had a chip on his shoulder, no doubt about it; he thought she was putting up the colour bar, though even from what I knew of Madge, I'd have said she was the last person in the place to think of such a thing.

"You will not have my drink, you will not sit beside me . . ."

Ted came along the counter. "I don't want any trouble here," he said. "You heard Mrs. Gardiner—she's expecting a friend—Bob was in some time ago," he added to Madge. "Asking for you, he was."

"Anyone else?" She didn't even pretend Bob was the one she had in mind.

"Should there be? Oh, well, perhaps he's got held up in the fog."

"Perhaps," suggested the young Indian nastily, "he has fallen in the river."

I could see Madge's face quite clearly from where I

was sitting. "Oh, no," she said, "that's not very likely." And you didn't have to be a psychologist to realise she wouldn't shed any tears if they fished him out next morning. She turned back to her neighbour to say, "Now, no offence—I don't know your name . . ."

It was like watching ice melt to see the change that came over him. She could put on the charm all right.

"I am Mr. Seringpatam Cox," said the chap proudly, and behind me I heard Crook choke into his beer.

"What do they call you at home?" she asked.

"They call me Sherry."

"Well, then, Sherry, thanks a million, but—some other night—see? I'm pretty regular—you ask Ted."

He seemed mollified and she took her glass and put herself opposite a long mirror on the wall that reflected everyone who came in. I'd noticed that whenever the door swung open she sent a quick glance over her shoulder; she was afraid all right. I didn't pay much attention to young Sherry, except to wonder he didn't look for some place where he'd find companions of his own age. How was I to guess he was going to become so important? No one, not even Crook, had an inkling of the situation that night.

I took the stool she'd vacated and Sherry and I got into conversation. He said he was a student, though it never became quite clear of what, and at the moment he was planning a book on English life and customs in the nineteen-sixties. I supposed he was getting copy for his chapter on English inns. I remember his telling me, rather primly, that in his country women didn't drink alone in pubs. He seemed to calm down somewhat, but the atmosphere of the Admiral didn't. I realised Crook felt it as much as I did. Every now and again he glanced in the long mirror as if he'd find a solution to some unknown problem, but Madge's friend didn't turn up. What did were two young madams with beehive hair-dos and heels about six inches high. The minute I saw them I decided they must have lost their way in the fog, or be pretty far out in their calculations. It didn't seem likely there'd be anything for them here. They seemed to think so, too. They let their mascara'd gaze play over all of us and you could see they wouldn't make a bid for anyone present in a jumble sale. But Sherry came to sudden new life. It was like having a young tiger at my elbow.

" You must have got the wrong address," said one of the girls.

The two bingo-women spoke almost with one voice. " Disgusting," they said. " A lady can't have a quiet drink . . ."

" Oh, is that what it is?" said the second girl. " Thought we must have stumbled into the mortuary."

" How about closing the door if you're coming in?" suggested Ted. " You know I'm not allowed to serve anyone under eighteen in this bar, so, if you're not ordering, this isn't a Rest Centre."

" Sorry we haven't brought our birth certificates," said one of the hussies.

" Your mistake," agreed Ted, smoothly.

But, whoever was glad to see the back of them, they had an electrical effect on Sherry. Springing down from his stool he showed them all his teeth; if you'd been out with him in a fog you'd never have needed a torch.

" I buy you a Coke," he offered, expansively. " Come

in, take a pew, a dirty night." He turned to Ted. "Two Cokes, and another of these." He flicked his glass with a long shining finger-nail.

Ted didn't lift a finger.

"I hope you like Cokes," said one of the girls. "We didn't come here to be insulted."

That, as Sherry himself might have remarked, put the tin lid on it. I honestly think the girl meant she wasn't the kind to be offered a soft drink, but he took it as one more insult to the colour of his skin. It actually darkened, though I didn't know they could. He started threateningly towards them, Madge, hardly raising her voice, said "Beat it, girls, there's nothing doing here." One of the fat women told the other they'd try elsewhere next time, and Sherry was only halted in his mad rush by Ted catching him by the arm, and saying, "That'll be four shillings you owe, sir." Sherry began to fumble for his wallet, the girls slipped away, everyone else returned to their drinks except Crook who called out, "It's not worth it, Ranji, take the word of a man who knows. I don't say they'd hang you, but even ten years in the cooler gives you an awful long time to repent."

Sherry paid no attention; he pushed a note at Ted, who took a long time to find the right change, then he bounced out. During the mêlée the two fat women had removed themselves. As they went one remarked to the other, "High time we were going. You never can tell with these foreigners, whip out a knife as soon as look at you."

As I said, I'd realised from the start this wasn't a cosy pub; I hadn't guessed it was all set for a Lyceum melodrama. Because that was only the beginning. Even

Crook seemed impressed. He came over to the bar for the usual reason and asked Ted, " Been here long?"

" Two years give or take a month," said Ted. " There's time I think I should have my head examined, leaving the country for this. Talk about the bright lights. . . . Trouble is, this isn't really a residential district. You get a few regulars, but mostly they come in, down a couple and off they go. Always on the rush."

" You can't complain it's not lively," suggested Crook.

" I could do with a bit less of that sort of liveliness. Mind you, it's not usually as empty as this. But the weather—and, of course, it's Wednesday."

That made perfect sense to Crook. " I suppose the factory pays out on a Thursday?"

" That's right. The boys come in here before they have to hand the whole packet over to the missus; by Wednesday they're always skint."

For a minute the tension seemed to dissolve; we stood there drinking in a kind of easy companionship; one or two chaps drifted up and joined us. But I was watching Madge Gardiner. Whoever else had relaxed, she hadn't. She watched every new-comer as if she thought he might have got a knife up his sleeve. One or two of the drinkers stopped by her table and murmured a word as they went out, but she hardly seemed to hear them. Ted went over to her once with the third whisky she'd had since our arrival, and she took it as if it were water.

" Life and soul of the party as a rule," murmured Ted, coming back.

Then he arrived—not the one she was expecting, you didn't have to be a magician to tell that—but the one who was going to set the wheels in motion, and get all our pictures in the Press. He was a young chap, no older than Sherry, and he came storming in like the wrath of God. He looked about as restful as a stick of gelignite as he stormed up to the bar and asked for Scotch on the rocks. He seemed to me too well-dressed for a man casually dropping into a pub for a pint; I wondered if he'd been stood up by a girl, which might account for his manner, or had a row with someone. He took the glass and his change and moved to the table beyond Madge's; and he walked past her as though she were invisible. Whatever was wrong with him, it was bad. Madge didn't seem to take any notice either, whoever she was expecting or fearing it wasn't this fellow. I watched them, each wrapped in a mantle of gloom, indifferent to the rest of us, two brooding explosive figures. It was like waiting for the siren when you know an air-raid's on the way.

It was Madge who broke it up; she seemed to come to a sudden decision. She threw up her head, she smiled, she turned with apparent impulse to the boy and asked for a light. It's the oldest trick in the world, of course, but it seldom fails. He groped in his pockets, produced a box of matches, and struck one. He had to get up to bring it close enough to her cigarette, and she offered him one of hers.

"No, thanks," he said. "I don't. Smoke, I mean. I just carry the matches—well, just on chance."

"Lucky for me," said Madge, lightly. I suppose his girl smoked, if he didn't, and that's why he had them.

He'd have sunk back into his mood of inspissated gloom, but Madge wasn't having that. It was as if she'd made up her mind on a certain course of action. He

19

might prefer to drink his cup of cold pizen in solitude, but he never had a chance with her.

"All on your owney-oh?" she said, and he muttered something about filling in time until his train went.

"You couldn't choose a nicer place," said Madge. I suppose she needn't have married very young to have a son of his age. "Still, no sense not being sociable. My friend won't be coming now."

He said awkwardly, "I'm sorry, what a shame!" He still hardly seemed to see her as a person.

In my ear Crook murmured, "Doesn't realise he hasn't got a chance, poor chap. Talk about snake-charmers! Oh, well, he'll learn."

I'd never met Crook before, though I knew his reputation, of course, but I could sense his keen interest in Madge Gardiner. He watched her as I'd seen Doggett watch a promising pup.

I saw Ted had noticed what was going on; rather to my surprise he looked a bit put out. Suddenly he put back his hand and switched on a radio from the back of the bar, possibly with the idea of cheering things up.

"I don't want to live for ever," snivelled a nasal voice, and Madge looked round to observe derisively, "Well, who does, for Pete's sake?"

That gave Crook his chance. "Me for one," he said, promptly. "Every day is a fresh beginning and there can't be too many of them for me."

She laughed; it was a lovely sound. "Must have become a habit," she teased him, but all her eyes were for the young chap who still hung uneasily about her table. He said in an embarrassed sort of voice, "Can I get you something to drink?" and she told him, "Well, a bit later p'r'aps. Why don't you bring yours over if you're not waiting for anyone? Oh, come on," she rallied him, "whatever it is it can't be that bad. As William Rufus has just reminded us," and she grinned at Crook, "every day is a fresh beginning and this one's nearly over. What's your name? Mine's Madge."

He seemed suddenly to make up his mind. He picked up his glass and joined her at her table, and she let out a great sigh more telling than any speech could have been. It was as if she'd been waiting for this ever since she came in.

I heard Crook say admiringly, "Marvellous, ain't it? Can't be far off retiring age, now they've got us all in the pen, but it 'ud be a deaf hippo that didn't leave its pool during a heatwave when it heard that voice. There's something to be said for looking like first cousin to an orang-utan," he went on, cheerfully. "None of the dames ever want to vamp me."

But I wasn't so sure. I'd heard a lot of stories about Crook, but the old bird who lived in the oak had nothing on him when it came to keeping his lip buttoned.

Only Ted looked disturbed. "I wish she wouldn't do it," he said to Crook, who'd come up for a refill. "I don't say this young chap isn't all right but one of these days she'll miss her step and pick a wrong 'un. She's lonely, of course, lives in some god-forsaken flat, without even a cat for company." He looked round him. "We've got one here, Bobby, she makes no end of a fuss of him, don't know where he's got to to-night. Out courting, perhaps. The fog doesn't worry them. Still, could be they don't allow animals in her flat."

"I once knew a chap who kept a cheetah in a flat,"

volunteered Crook, who was clearly never at a loss for an answer. " No dogs it said in the lease, but no one had thought of puttin' a ban on cheetahs. Friend of yours, is she?" he added, in practically the same breath, buying Ted the first drink I'd seen him accept that evening.

Ted stiffened a bit. " She's one of the regulars," he admitted. " Well, living alone, it's not natural. She'd want a bit of company."

" No Mr. Madge?"

" I understand she's a widow."

" No little Madges?" It beat me how Crook could do it so unblushingly, seeing he'd never set eyes on her before, but perhaps that mysterious sixth sense with which even the police credit him warned him that this evening was a beginning not an end.

" There was a little girl, but she lost her when she was two or three years old. Usually she's the life and soul of the party, it's not often she has to walk home alone. Well, I suppose it makes a change from the wife. Her trouble is she will believe everything she's told, and she's got a heart as big as Piccadilly Circus. One of these days, I tell her, you'll wake up and find yourself with your throat cut, and no one will be more surprised than you."

It was pretty obvious that the old black magic was working with young Colin Bruce—we didn't know his name then but everyone was going to know it pretty soon; he was a good-looking chap when he wasn't scowling, as dark as I'm fair, and they seemed to be getting along like one o'clock. I stole a glance at Crook. It was hard to tell what was going on in his mind, but if he had a heart as big as Piccadilly Circus there was a lot more than the statue of Eros in it. I suppose to a chap like that it's natural to look for the macabre in the most obvious situation, and, however popular Madge might be with the husbands, you couldn't imagine the wives taking her to their bosoms.

" Another conquest," I murmured and Crook turned sharply.

" Be your age," he said. " It's nothing to her if he's the Belvedere Apollo or the Minotaur, he's just someone, a human barrier."

" Against what?" I asked.

" How should I know? Your guess is as good as mine."

But I didn't have to guess; her voice still rang in my ears. I haven't got it—I can't get it—tell him it's no use coming round——

" But if you can't see that," Crook was going on, " you should apply for a pair of National Health glasses. What's she scared of?" he asked Ted, abruptly.

It was young Bruce and Madge all over again. At first sight Ted had seemed a bit stand-offish, as if he resented Crook's easy questions about a woman he'd never seen before; but some quality—it couldn't have been charm—in this bumptious notorious lawyer, mowed down his original opposition and he confided, " I wish I knew. Been like this quite a while now. Came in one evening looking as if she'd seen a ghost."

" That could be it," said Crook. " Nasty undependable things, ghosts. Never know where you've got 'em; even when they're in a corner they just melt away if you take a swipe at 'em."

Ted, clearly not a facetious type, continued his story unmoved.

" 'Why don't you go and see a doctor, Madge?' I said. 'Might give you some pills. Not sleeping well, see?' But I could have saved my breath. Madge likes doctors the way I like teetotallers." Then it seemed to occur to him that he was going a bit far with a stranger —not two strangers, I don't think either of them really counted me as a person, and I found that a bit galling— and he said, " You were saying something about a word —when you came in, I mean?"

I took the hint and started to move down the bar, but before I went I murmured, " I'd like a word, too, if you have the time, before the bar closes. About Mrs. Gardiner," I added.

I think that was the first time that evening either of them had really noticed me as an individual.

Though I'd moved away I could overhear the conversation, and frankly I didn't take much trouble to stay out of earshot. Talk about snake-charmers—I couldn't take my eyes off Crook. I knew his reputation, I knew an old girl like Madge Gardiner was just his cup of tea; and he was no fool; he wouldn't need the sort of phone-call I'd had to-night to realise she was in one hell of a jam, and, being Crook, he'd cast about for some way of yanking her out of it. He may have a lot of virtues, though the police don't seem to think so, but modesty isn't one of them.

But then he's accustomed to working miracles, and he expects the people he deals with to show the same ability.

Now he was leaning on the bar, explaining the nature of the help he wanted Ted to give him.

" New client of mine," said Crook. " Thought you might be able to give him an alibi for one night last week

24

when according to him he was drinking here, and according to the bogeys he was driving a souped-up wheelbarrow in connection with a break-in on a radio warehouse."

"Well, honestly, Mr. Crook." Ted seemed staggered. I thought it was a fairly tall order myself, with the chaps popping in and out like yo-yos. "Of course, if he had three eyes or something, and even then I mightn't notice. The casuals are nothing to me but a voice to order and a hand to put down the money."

"Told you a yarn about a parrot," said Crook, unmoved.

"They all tell yarns about parrots."

"Tried to get you to change a cheque."

Ted turned and indicated a card hanging behind the bar. No Cheques Cashed. "Half the chaps could afford to treat themselves to a pair of glasses," he said. "It's clear enough, isn't it? But not for them. Though if they were to find a florin in place of half-a-crown in their change, they'd notice that soon enough."

"Oh, well," murmured Crook, benignly, "try anything once."

"One of them even asked me for a sheet of paper and a stamp and said he'd make a cheque of them. Can you believe it?"

"He could, you know," said Crook. "And it 'ud bounce every bit as high as the usual kind. What night was that?"

Ted stared. "You don't mean that's the one?" He sounded as if he couldn't believe his ears. Crook didn't look surprised. Miracles are everyday affairs for him. Ted began to calculate. "Must have been Friday," he said. " I pay in of a Friday morning, Thursday being a heavy night because of pay day, see. This young chap . . ."

" You do remember he was young?"

" That's right. 'I can't take that,' I said. 'By the time I find it's a bouncer you could be in the next county'."

" Remember anything else about him?" asked Crook. " Hair? cauliflower ear? only four fingers on one hand? Anything?"

" I wouldn't know him again. Wait a minute, though. I don't suppose it 'ud help but he wore a ring, kind of scarab it was. Like me to seal the agreement with my blood?" he said.

" I knew this was going to be my lucky night," said Crook, though it's generally accepted that every night is Crook's lucky night, even those when someone tries to rub him out, because they don't succeed, see? " Now, if you'd nip down to the station," he added to Ted, and told him which one it was, " and make a statement . . ."

" You didn't say anything about going to the police," said Ted. I don't suppose he had more on his conscience than the next man, but it was clear he felt about the police as he felt about teetotallers, some principle activated them, but neither of them was any use to him.

" Any time," said Crook. " Well, you wouldn't want him to be kept at the expense of the rates, not till he's earned it."

Before Ted could put up any more objections the door was flung open and a quartet came tumbling in, and tumbling's the operative word. They hadn't been prepared for those three steps and they sounded like an advancing army. Every pub knows their sort. Start on a pub crawl at 6.30 and by 10 o'clock they hardly, as the saying goes, know their arse from their elbow. They more or less fell on the bar calling for pints, addressing Ted as Sam and bidding him make it snappy. They made rats look like a beauty chorus.

Ted could have refused to serve them, the state they were in, but he probably thought the game wouldn't be worth the candle; there were only a few minutes to go, and Crook being there may have influenced his decision. While he was drawing the pints the four stared all round them and decided to be witty at Madge's expense.

"That's a nice little boy you've got there, ma'am," said one, a big ugly chap with a scar under one eye that he never got duelling. "Doesn't favour his Mum much, though, does he?"

"I hope that's only ginger ale he's drinking," said the second. "Might cost Sam his licence . . ."

Colin started to get up, but Madge had her hand on his arm; she must have had a pretty good grip, too.

"You're not listening," she said. "I was telling you about John. Well, he was a card. Always back a grey horse, he told me. Suppose there's two grey horses in the race? I said. Well, he told me, if one of them's from the Aga Khan's stable back that, if not put your money on the one whose face you like best."

Two of the drunks started a slow hand-clap, and Colin pulled himself free.

"Can't hit a drunk man," Madge reminded him. "Here, get us one each for the road."

She opened her bag again, and there were the notes, coiled like a great snake inside. She peeled off a second note and pushed it into Colin's hand.

"Tell Ted same again. He'll know."

Colin hesitated, then someone said, "Do as the lady wants." And it wasn't one of the drunks, but Arthur Crook. Colin took the note and went up to the bar. I noticed he paid out of his own pocket, though. He had left a burberry and a pair of gloves on the table. The chap with the scar, who'd got his beer by this time, deliberately lurched against it—the table, I mean—and a lot of the beer slopped over. Something happened to Madge's face. It seemed to close up as he shoved his head down and grinned.

"You'll know me again," he said.

She snatched up the coat and gloves and tried to move, but this chap was in her way. Crook stuck out a foot in a No 10 shoe as bright as a May morning and the chap nearly fell flat on his kisser. Most of the rest of the beer shot over his own suit. He turned, looking uglier than ever.

"You want to look out," he said belligerently. "You could do yourself a lot of harm, an old man like you. Might have broken my leg," he added.

"Want Ted to send for an ambulance?" asked Crook. "Might be a good idea any road." He turned to Madge. "You won't want to sit among the dregs," he said, and he picked up the coat and the gloves and put them on a stool by the bar. She snapped out of that moment of naked terror with a speed Crook himself couldn't have bettered. Like an actress, passing from one cue to the next.

"You got anything for me, Ted?" she inquired, and Ted told her, "All packed up and ready behind the bar. How you going to get them home?"

"My friend here will carry them for me, won't you, sweetie?" she said. If Colin was startled he recovered himself pretty quickly. I was hovering on the outskirts myself, ready to offer if he had a pressing engagement, but it wasn't necessary. I was realising why it was she seldom had to walk back alone. That smile, that voice, made you forget age and avoirdupois and the colour of her hair. Ted got a cloth and mopped up the table, two of the drunks shambled off to the Gents, one of the others demanded another pint.

"Not in my bar," said Ted, firmly. "And I don't want to see you here again, what's more."

"You got to serve us," said one of the men.

"Don't you start telling me what I can do in my own bar," Ted told him. It looked for a minute as if it was going to be a free-for-all. It was amusing to see how the few remaining drinkers slammed down their glasses and got out, muttering, " 'Night, Ted," as they went.

"It's the law," the drunk insisted.

"I'm the law," said Crook, and that stopped everything. The one or two who were left vanished like magic.

"Let's see your warrant," one drunk demanded. Crook put his hand in his pocket, the two chaps came back from the Gents, picked up the situation and looked round for the hats they'd left behind a couple of pubs back.

"Bloody coppers' pub," sneered one, as they went out. Madge and the young chap had disappeared; I hadn't even seen them go.

"Out by the back, I expect," murmured Ted. "I

put up some bottles for her; she knows her way around here all right."

He picked up a coin one of the four had passed to him and rang it on the counter. Dud, he said, too dud even to be counterfeit. Then he asked, " Any more orders? You don't have to worry about that clock, there's five minutes to go yet. It's a trick you soon learn, put it on a few minutes, then if there's any argument you're still within your time."

I came to a lightning decision. " That woman," I said. " Mrs. Gardiner."

"Well?"

Crook turned to me. " You're on," he said, " but make it snappy. We don't want Ted to lose his licence. Can't get beer like this every day of the week, more's the pity."

"It's about Mrs. Gardiner," I said. " You may not believe me, but I swear she's the woman whose voice I heard on my phone to-night."

And I told them about the call.

Ted looked startled. " I don't see how you can be sure."

" Could you forget that voice?" I challenged Crook. " Oh, I know it sounds like the craziest coincidence, those two particular lines getting tangled and me getting the message, but—the instant I heard her speak . . ."

Ted was still looking sceptical, but Crook swallowed it all as if it were the most natural thing in the world. Perhaps to him it was.

" No hint who he might be?"

I just shook my head. " Just tell him . . ."

Ted interpolated suddenly, " I suppose it couldn't have

been *Jim*—there is a chap here, he's seen her home once or twice . . ."

"This is someone she was petrified of," I said. "And no—I'm certain it was *him*. She said it twice. I started to ask who he was, but she hung up on me."

"Not giving you a hint what it was he's got to wait for?"

I looked surprised. "Well, money, I suppose. Isn't it usually?"

"Don't follow," said Crook. "Might be secret info., a key, plan of a house, photo even, some incriminating document—the choice is wide-open."

His voice had warmed, he looked like that chap in Raymond Chandler's book who'd eaten two tigers for breakfast.

"She didn't seem exactly short of the ready to-night," Ted reminded us.

"It's all according. Five pounds could be a haul to one man and peanuts to another."

"I'd say she hadn't much less than fifty quid in that bag," was Ted's shrewd comment. "I wanted to tell her to keep it buttoned up. I can't be answerable for every chap who drops in, and we get some queer customers here, being so near the river, and the only pub worth its name for half a mile. There's a couple of ale-houses, you wouldn't have to be very particular not to fancy them. And it's a dark road to the Mansions."

"She's got young Galahad with her," Crook reminded him.

"We don't know what he was doing here to-night."

"I do like a chap who looks on the gloomy side," approved Crook. "From what I could see she was doing

the Gioconda act, not him. And not for his *beaux yeux*,"
he added, briskly, in a voice that would have made a
French canary drop off its perch, " but just for the company. So—she ain't sure if X is going to take the hint,
and keep off the grass."

"Why didn't she ring him herself?" Ted wondered
aloud, but Crook, as usual had an answer for that.

"Maybe he ain't on the phone. Or he's got one of
these bossy wives that take all the calls and start to
wonder, possibly with a poker, why hubby's having himself a ball with a strange dame."

"One thing," I said "we know whoever it was didn't
come."

Crook looked startled for the first time that evening.
"How do you make that out?"

"Well," I pointed out reasonably, " she'd have recognised him. And it's clear she didn't."

"Who says she's got to recognise him? Ain't you
never read these accounts of kidnapping? How often
does the chap who does the blackmailing surface in person? No, he puts through a call, you'll find, he writes a
no-name letter telling the victim where to leave the ransom money and/or what'll happen if it's short, he warns
him to make himself scarce before X comes along to
collect—and to keep away from the rozzers—that's the
usual pattern," he wound up blithely, " and you're talking to the man who knows."

"Take it easy, Mr. Crook," objected Ted. " Madge
isn't a criminal."

"Nor was Oliver Twist, but he went through the
window of someone else's house for all that. There's
times when you don't have much choice between taking

orders and taking a short cut to the churchyard. It could be a case of more people knowing Tom Fool than Tom Fool knows."

"She doesn't look good for a packet," murmured Ted. "Those Mansions are nothing specially classy, and I happen to know she goes out obliging three days a week to help out."

"Like I said, it don't have to be money." Crook drained his tankard and set it on the bar. "Well, a very interesting evening. You won't forget about going to the police about young Ron Turner, will you, Ted?"

"Oh, him!" said Ted, as if he'd forgotten his existence as most likely he had. "If you're right, Mr. Crook, I hope Madge has the sense to bolt her door to-night. And talking of doors, it's time I bolted mine, if I'm not to lose my licence. I'll go along about that young chap in the morning," he added, rather grudgingly.

"Is this always the way of it?" I asked Crook, as we turned towards the cul-de-sac where he'd parked his car. "I mean, do you pick up a case in every strange pub you go to?"

"What's all this about a case?" You might have sworn Crook's amazement was genuine. "The time I start worrying about some other chap's affairs is when I'm paid to do it."

But I wasn't deceived.

: :   : :

There was no sign of Madge and her escort as we turned into the cul-de-sac where the big yellow Rolls was now the only car to be seen. The fog had cleared a little, but it was a demmed moist unpleasant night. Crook didn't offer me a lift back, but that didn't surprise me either. Clocks might never have been invented so far as he was concerned, he worked as long as the work was there, and if he got back and found a client waiting on the doorstep it 'ud be for him like the beginning of the day. A good friend and a pitiless enemy—that's what they said about him. If Madge Gardiner had known her onions she'd have picked on him instead of young Bruce.

The horns were still honking away as I stood watching him drive off. Practically no one was about, though here and there a blur of light showed behind a closed window. Leaving the cul-de-sac I saw a tall dark blur, which was Mayflower Mansions, where Madge lived. There were lights at a few windows. I stopped to light a cigarette, I wasn't in any special hurry. Even if it had been worth waiting for a bus, and it wasn't, not the comparatively short distance I had to go, most of them would have stopped running by now. A little blue car ran past me and a man got out and went into the flats. A motor-cycle zoomed past at the other end, gathering speed as it went, going much too fast for safety in such weather. But motor-cyclists seldom seem to have heard of the speed limit; I heard it zooming away into the distance; that and the persistent fog-horn were the only sounds I heard; even the gulls were quiet now. I thought about Madge Gardiner and the young chap who'd gone home with her; he'd gone readily enough and yet I swear he had someone very different in mind when he came bursting into the Admiral.

The rain, that had stopped earlier, had begun again before I reached my flat; although it was latish the old girl from the ground floor—Miss Muffett, if you can believe it—was standing on the doorstep rootling in a bag nearly the size of a pantechnicon for her latch-key. I wondered what on earth she was doing out and about at this hour and in this weather; she didn't look much of a night-bird.

She turned, and even in the fog I could see her beam. "Oh, Mr. Crete, how fortunate. I do believe I've left my key behind, I was just wondering if I dared try and get in through a window."

The sills of the ground floor were pretty wide, but to reach them you had to cross a gulf from the front steps, with a drop to the basement if you missed your footing. I produced my key and opened the door.

"I wouldn't advise it," I said. "Can you get in now?"

"Oh, yes, I always hang a key in the broom cupboard." She whipped open the door and showed me. "I do hate fog, don't you? It makes me think of boats on the river, poor people drowning. My father was a rector in Dockland, he remembered one night when a boat was cut in two in the dark—such an awful death." She shivered. "So cold."

"You could be run down by a lorry on terra firma," I told her soothingly. "So messy. You want to be careful."

"Oh, I am," she insisted. "I always wear a white mac. They say drivers can see that, it warns them. I suppose it was silly of me to go out on such a night, but I did want to see that film at the Classic, and they change the programme to-morrow. And, of course, the buses had stopped running, which could be a blessing, couldn't it?" She was making ineffectual stabs at the lock with her key; I took it from her and opened the door.

"How cold you are!" she said. "I do hope you'll

have a nice hot drink. I drink Chocolatina myself, so comforting and with Vitamin B included."

I thought for a moment she was going to give me a lecture on Vitamin B and I'd had just about as much to-night as I could take.

" It's nice to be back," she smiled. " At least under your own roof you know you're *safe*."

She scurried into her flat like a mouse scurrying into its hole. It never seems to go through the mouse's mind that the cat may have got there first.

As I went upstairs I heard a clock somewhere chime the half-hour. Thirty minutes to go to the new day.

CHAPTER II

THAT WAS WEDNESDAY.

I didn't go along to the Admiral again till Friday and found the place practically unrecognisable. It was packed with chaps drinking, smoking, arguing, comparing bets and muttering in corners. I got the impression it was the sort of pub where quite a lot of on-the-side transactions might be put through, I mean it wasn't a clubbable pub like the Horse and Mariner where you met the same types night after night. I looked round me but I didn't recognise a soul. Young Bruce wasn't there, no reason why he should be, of course, and nor was Crook : Sherry drifted in after a while, with a girl in tow, but they didn't stay long. I wondered what he was doing in England anyway. I didn't altogether go for that student lark. He looked as if he might be any speculator's prey, but you can never be certain, appearances are so deceptive. When Ted passed me my pint he didn't even look up, and probably wouldn't have recognised me if he had. I drifted off and soon I got into conversation with a chap who had a tip for the three o'clock next day that he said was a dead snip. I don't go for the horses much, I said, dogs now . . . I passed on another of Doggett's tips, Mighty Runner, a youngster who was beginning to show high promise. Actually Doggett had bred him but had sold him recently to one of the larger combines, keeping a small part of him, which showed how much he believed in his chances.

"Not in a million years," said my companion, "not unless all the others are hobbled. Black Prince 'ull win hands down."

(In point of fact, he didn't. And Mighty Runner came in first.)

My companion had departed and I was thinking of calling it a day when the door banged open and Crook came in like a tidal wave. The crowd had thinned considerably, the married men going back to their wives and the younger chaps moving off to their private pleasures elsewhere. Well, I thought, I might as well have one more for the road, so I moved over to the bar as Crook got his first pint. He didn't swallow it wholesale as he'd done before, I wondered if he only put on this performance the first time he visited a pub. He stood there tasting it, and looking round. He recognised me and nodded approval of the fact that to-night I, too, was drinking beer. When Ted had a free moment Crook said cheerfully, " Just looked in to say thank you for putting in a word for young Ron Taylor." And I remembered the chap with the scarab ring, who told a yarn about a parrot and tried to cash a home-made cheque. "Grateful, were they? At the station, I mean?"

"What do you think?" asked Ted. "Surprised— yes. Funny, wasn't it, I should remember about the ring? No one been jogging my memory of course, and would I recognise it again? And out one came, not the real McCoy, of course. Do you mind? I asked. Who do you think you're kidding? Even when I remembered the chap made out the cheque with his left hand they didn't really like it."

"Well, you can't please everyone," said Crook. "Ron's old Mum would buy you a medal if she could."

"Better save her dollars for the day they take young Ron for breaking and entering," suggested Ted, gloomily. "I don't know why you bothered, Mr. Crook. Really I don't. That chap 'ull be behind bars within three months, you mark my words."

"His Mum thinks he was led astray. Any cleaning that gets done in my flat she does," he added.

"The things mothers will kid themselves." Ted brought my pint and held out his hand for the money.

"I wanted Ron to come along and say Ta for himself," Crook went on, and Ted leaned over the bar to say earnestly, "Do me a favour, Mr. Crook. You keep him away from here. I don't want a lot of teds in my bar, the drunks are bad enough."

Talking of drunks seemed to put a new idea into Crook's head. Looking round, he asked, "Where's Lady Bountiful to-night?"

"Madge? Funny thing, she hasn't been in the last two nights. Got a cold maybe."

"Or doing her drinking elsewhere," suggested Crook.

Ted looked shocked. "She wouldn't do that, Mr. Crook. This is Madge's port of call. She's not one of the easy come, easy go lot."

"Still, if she's got the idea it might be some other fellow's port of call too, she might think it smart to do her drinking elsewhere, just for the time being, that is. She was stiff with panic Wednesday, and well you know it. Seen any more of young Galahad?"

Ted said No and didn't expect to, and ten minutes later Bruce came in. Call it coincidence, if you like, but it's the sort of thing that always happens to Crook; he pulls them out of a hat like rabbits. The young chap came up to the bar, nodded to Crook, saw me without recognising me, and asked for half of mild. When Ted had drawn it he said—Bruce, I mean—"I suppose you didn't find one of my gloves lying about when you were clearing up the bar last Wednesday night?"

"You didn't drop it here," Ted told him.

"Oh, well, I thought . . ." he mumbled something about it being a new pair.

"Tried the L.P.O. at Baker Street?" Crook asked.

And he said yes, but it wasn't there. "I suppose no one would bother much about a single glove."

"You might have dropped it in Mrs. Gardiner's flat," I suggested.

"Well, but in that case, wouldn't she have brought it round? I mean, she'd know it was mine."

"Well, she might," Ted agreed, "only she hasn't been round the last couple of nights."

"Happen to mention she might be going away or anything?" asked Crook, casually, turning to Bruce. Bruce frowned.

"Not to me. I only stayed a few minutes. But she was in no end of a stew. I mean, when we got back, first of all she wanted me to have a drink. I said no, I had to catch a train, and anyway," he added candidly, "I'd overstepped my whisky ration for one night as it was. Then she said well, would I wait a minute, she wanted to be sure the neighbour's cat hadn't got in. She had an allergy about cats, and this one had got in once before, and she was like Lord Roberts . . ."

"Who are you kidding?" demanded Ted. "Madge was crazy about cats. She'd sit with Bobby on her lap here half the evening."

Bruce looked impatient. "Well, of course it wasn't a cat she was afraid of, even I realised that. I'm only telling you what she said. Anyway, there was a picture of her on the mantelpiece with a little girl, not much more than a baby, and a cat. So I knew she was pulling my leg. But—she was afraid of something. She went into all the rooms, well, it's a small flat, but she kept opening doors and slamming them and presently she came back and said it was all right, there wasn't any cat. I asked her if she was sure she'd looked under the bed—well, I don't like being taken for a ride any more than anyone else—and she suddenly flamed up. Listen to Mr. Smartie, she said. She'd had another drink while she was looking, I could hear the clink of glass in the kitchen, so I said, Well, if you're in trouble why don't you go to the police?"

"You've missed your vocation," said Crook. "You should have been in the Diplomatic Service. When people like Madge Gardiner want any assistance from the police, they get it direct without any advice from you or me."

"She didn't tell you anything?" said Ted, slowly.

"No. She noticed me looking at the photographs, and she said that was her daughter and that was her grandson . . ."

"What are you talking about?" demanded Ted. "Madge hasn't got a daughter, she had a little kid, but she died . . ."

"That must have been another one. There were several photographs, at all ages, and a couple of this little boy."

"Any pictures of hubby?" Crook asked.

"I didn't see any."

"Well, p'raps he didn't take well."

"She hadn't seen him in a dog's age, she told me that herself," said Ted.

"Same way she told you she hadn't got a little girl," suggested Crook, and for a moment I had a glimpse of how tough he'd be in opposition.

Ted didn't take offence. "Maybe there was a divorce and he got the kid—poor Madge, it hasn't been much of a velvet path for her. She came up the hard way, you know—started in a pierrot show run by her people, got picked up by a talent spotter and got a little act in one of the halls—never made the big dates—Pally or anything like that—but she played the provinces a lot—I suppose somewhere along the line she met Gardiner. She doesn't say much about him."

"You haven't seen her again, I suppose?" Crook asked Bruce and he stared.

"Well, of course not. This isn't really my part of the world. I only happened to be here because I had a snap invitation to see a nuclear scientist who's been over from the States—that's my job too—and I particularly wanted to see this chap, and he was leaving on a night plane. That left me with time to burn, I saw this place and I turned in."

"I was wondering if you'd thought of asking her if she found the glove," Crook explained.

" Well, but if she found it wouldn't she have brought it here?" demanded Bruce for the second time.

" She'd know you weren't a regular, wouldn't she? What's the real reason?"

I thought for a minute Bruce wasn't going to reply. Then he said, " There's a woman, lives across the landing, got a nose an elephant might envy. She was watching at a crack of the door as I came up. Madge—Mrs. Gardiner—says she's always on at her about how nice it must be to have so many brothers and all so devoted."

: " Old cow !" said Ted.

" And you're afraid the girl-friend may start putting two and two together?"

" Not the girl-friend so much as Mrs. Lizzie Costello. You know, there was nothing I could have done for her, I'd carried the thing home, there was no one in the flat, I heard her shoot the bolt as I went down the stairs, and yet—I have the feeling I let her down in some way, that she expected something of me." His eyes glared defiance to us to suggest the usual thing she might have in mind. Though I don't think any of us were thinking of the obvious. What Madge Gardiner had wanted was some assurance of security from young Bruce that he couldn't give her. I put into words the thought that must have been in every mind.

" If anything had happened, if she'd been taken ill, say, surely she'd have rung someone, the doctor, a neighbour."

" Always assuming she's got a phone and the strength to reach it," capped Crook.

" How about milk bottles? newspapers? They'd accumulate and someone would notice."

" Madge doesn't take a paper, only an evening edition to see what's won the 3.30. Still, you have a point there," Ted allowed. " If anything was wrong Lizzie Costello 'ud know. She never misses a trick. I've heard Madge say she was half afraid to take her teeth out at night in case Lizzie was peering through the transom. Mrs. *Sunday News* she calls her." He turned to Bruce. " You can take your oath on one thing. She'll know the exact minute you came and the exact minute you left. A loss to the Civil Service really. You married?"

" No," said Bruce, shortly. " Do you mind?"

" You make the most of it," Ted advised him. " The day's not far off when bachelors 'ull be classed as luxuries and taken off the menu."

Bruce turned rather pointedly to Crook. " I heard her shoot the bolt behind her when I'd gone," he said again. You could see he was a do-gooder type, that wants to carry the whole world's burden if it means breaking his back. Because, after all, an old totty like Madge Gardiner wasn't really his responsibility. " Well, sorry about the glove, it's not that important."

He nodded to us all and made off. Crook's curious glance followed him.

" But important enough to bring him a goodish way from his home," he suggested. " And I'll tell you something else. Either of you hear him say he didn't stop long that night?"

We both agreed.

" And how far is it from where Madge Gardiner hangs out to Bagshott Street?"

" Six minutes—for a chap that age. Seven maybe," said Ted.

" Well, I spied him with my little eyes belting into Bagshott Street at 11.30 on Wednesday, as if the peelers were after him. Probably afraid of missing the last train. And it didn't look as if he'd been enjoying himself either."

" That's why you asked him about the L.P.O.?" I discovered.

Crook nodded. Nothing else of interest happened that night.

: :   : :

Sunday was D-Day. Sunday in a town can be a pretty drab affair. The pubs don't open till 12 o'clock, and if you're not the psalm-singing type or go in for hiking or one of the modish sports, and if, on top of all that, you don't even own a car, there's not much to do. I've often passed a London pub shortly before opening time on a Sunday morning and been amazed at the types you find waiting for the clock to strike. So, when I arrived at the Admiral a little after opening-time that Sunday it didn't surprise me to find a more—I suppose genteel is the word I have in mind—gathering than I'd seen there hitherto. This lot hadn't come for the odd drink and out again. This was where they met their chums once a week, they tended less to stand at the bar and instead swooped on tables, and sat round chatting and buying each other rounds. Of course, a fair number were husbands who'd been shooed out of the house while Lovey dished up the Sunday beef. Take the dog in the park, you could hear the wives saying. There were a lot of dogs in the Admiral that morning.

I got my drink and found myself standing by a tall, thin type who was clearly making half a pint go as far as possible. He broke into a diatribe about the Test match. Our bowlers were being flogged to every corner of the field, and you imagined he winced every time the scorers chalked up a boundary. You find his sort in every pub, particularly at week-ends. Bachelor or widower, living thin, nothing much to look forward to, existing on a pension; sometimes eked out by National Assistance, thirsting in both senses of the word, both for the stuff and for the company with whom to drink it. Bright-eyed, civil, not pushing but always hoping to be asked What's yours? and always knowing the answer. This time I said it, and he looked to see what I was drinking and then said a pint of brown, if it's all the same to you. He knew his onions so far as cricket was concerned, went right back, in knowledge at least, to old Dr. Grace, and probably pretty near him in actual experience. I didn't grudge it him, you never know which way the wheel will turn, and it gave me an excuse for hanging around in case anything should be cooking. He told me he'd played for Wellington and only just missed getting his Blue at Cambridge. He asked if I was a cricket enthusiast and I said dogs were more in my line, and of course he thought I meant hounds; he knew a lot about them, too. He was speculating whether I was good for a second pint when a new-comer came in, not exactly bursting in but endued with such a sense of purpose that mine weren't the only eyes that slewed round in his direction. It was obvious from Ted's expression that he was a stranger here, but he was no more different than Crook had been at a first visit. He didn't even pretend to look round for any buddies, just ordered a drink and then said, " Is your name Ted?"

46

"Well?" said Ted. "What if it is?"

"If so you're the man who may be able to help me. I believe you're a friend of Mrs. Madge Gardiner."

"Are you the police?" asked Ted, bluntly, and the chap said, "What on earth put that notion into your mind? No." He fished out a business card and put it on the counter—again like Crook. "My wife is Mrs. Gardiner's daughter."

Ted didn't even look at the card, he just pushed it back across the counter.

"I'm afraid there's some mistake," he said, "the Mrs. Gardiner I know hasn't got a daughter. She lost her little girl when she was only two or three years old."

The chap let the card lie. "I suppose that's one way of putting it," he said. "Do you mind telling me when you last saw Mrs. Gardiner? I've been round to her flat in reply to a letter I found waiting for me when I got home—I've been in Amsterdam with my wife for the past week—and it was fairly urgent, the matter about which she wrote me, I mean. But I can't get any reply."

"Then I suppose she's out," said Ted. "Anyway, sir, you've got hold of the wrong Mrs. Gardiner."

"I don't think so." He put his hand in his pocket again, and pulled out a large blue envelope addressed in an excitable feminine hand. "Would you know her writing?"

Ted looked a bit shaken. "That looks like hers," he admitted. "It's funny, I've known her two years and she's never mentioned a married daughter."

"The circumstances are a bit unusual," the man admitted. He behaved as though he confronted this type of crisis every day of the week. "Mrs. Gardiner gave her daughter for adoption when she was very young. We only met—by chance—comparatively recently, but whatever the law may say in my eyes she's still Clare's mother. And I think she's in trouble. She spoke of you once or twice . . ."

" I wouldn't know about that," said Ted, wooden as ever. " Sorry, Mr.——" he glanced at the card—" Mr. Chapple, but I don't see what I can do."

" Just give me a little information," said the chap and his voice was as hard as a vice. Ted had started to move away, now he stopped dead. " I'm telling you, Mrs. Gardiner wanted my assistance, she wrote, she telephoned to my office, but I only got her letter this morning. We had a shocking air passage, couldn't come down at London Airport at all, and I didn't look through the correspondence my secretary had forwarded until this morning, and then I found this. I telephoned at once, but there was no answer; I went round to see her, and she didn't open the door. Her neighbour over the way—I don't know the lady's name——"

" Mrs. Costello," said Ted impassively.

" She's neither seen nor heard anything of her since Wednesday night. She heard her come in with a friend . . ."

I was rooted by this time. The friend, of course, would be Colin Bruce.

" And she says she heard the friend leave about 11.15. Since then there hasn't been a sound, though normally the wireless plays all day."

" Then it looks as if she's gone away," muttered Ted, but his tone didn't carry much conviction.

"Without this Mrs. Costello noticing? I should imagine it's like living opposite the *Sunday News* having her across the landing. In any case, she wouldn't go without making a further effort to see me. Her business sounded critical."

"As a matter of fact," acknowledged Ted, "she hasn't been in here since Wednesday. And she didn't seem her usual self." He glanced up and recognised me at last. "This gentleman was here, he noticed it."

Chapple turned to me. "You know her?"

"I saw her for the first time Wednesday night, but it stuck out a mile, her being in trouble about something, I mean. Not that she said anything . . ."

"There was a young chap here, carried some parcels back for her," Ted volunteered. "We haven't seen hide nor hair since."

"That settles it," said Chapple. "I'm going to get the police. There's something very wrong . . ."

"If you're thinking Madge would do anything crazy you're mistaken," Ted assured him. "Like turning on the gas or anything, I mean."

"There has to be some reason."

Ted said to me, "Perhaps, sir, you'd best tell the gentleman what you told us, about the phone call, that is." So I did.

Chapple made a point no one else had made to date. "You mean, she was under the impression that she'd warned X it was no use coming round, whereas in fact . . . he wouldn't know she hadn't got whatever it was, and he could have gone round . . ."

"She bolted the door behind Bruce, though," I said.

"She could unbolt it, I suppose," was Chapple's dry comment.

"Ah, but would she? If she thought it was her enemy . . ."

"With a woman like—what did you say her name was?—Costello—just across the way?"

"That's true," Ted admitted, "if she'd known anything we should have heard. Did you say you rang her bell, sir? Lizzie's, I mean."

"She must have heard me, she came out; she said she was anxious . . ."

Ted went to serve some new-comers and we stood waiting beside the bar. When he came back he said to Chapple, "I was thinking, if your wife is outside, she might prefer to wait—there's a room behind the bar . . ."

"My wife isn't with me," said Chapple. "She doesn't know about Mrs. Gardiner being her mother. She thinks she was a war orphan adopted by a childless couple . . ."

"It doesn't sound like Madge," Ted burst out. "She always seemed so fond of kids."

"Yes," agreed Chapple. He didn't say another word and we all felt a bit uncomfortable. I said it was my turn for a round, and the cricketing near-Blue who'd been waiting on the verge of the group, without taking any part in the conversation and possibly not even hearing it, contrived to get himself included. Then he backed a few steps—he was a nice old boy, a bit pathetic really.

I fancy we were all convinced that this mysterious and until now undreamed-of daughter was the hub of the affair, but Chapple volunteered no further information.

What he had said, however, seemed to have impressed Ted.

" I've got an idea, sir," he offered, " before you get the police, I mean." Obviously nobody wanted the police dragged in if there was any alternative. It certainly wouldn't do Ted any good. Brewers never like to have their houses associated with the law, not on the wrong side of it, and Macraes—the Admiral was a Macrae house—are fussier than most. " If Madge is all right it wouldn't do her good to have them around . . ." We all agreed without a word said that the less one had to do with the police the better. Ted moved away into the other bar; we all sipped our beer. Oddly enough, no one round us seemed to have the least notion that anything unusual had been going on. Suddenly Chapple said, " It doesn't make sense, does it? That I should be away that one week . . ." And then Ted came in, followed by a thin fair little chap with a long pointed nose and very pale sharp blue eyes.

" This is Charlie, sir," he said. " Charlie, doesn't Madge get her milk from you?"

" When she has any," agreed Charlie, winking cheerfully. " Not that I could buy much more than bootlaces on the commission I get from her. Half a pint now and again and a pint on Saturdays. She likes her tea of a Sunday, does Madge, and she likes it milky. Then there's that cat from downstairs, like a mother to it she is . . . Should have had kids of her own."

Chapple said sharply, " Did she get any milk yesterday?" and Charlie said, " Well, now you come to mention it, she didn't. Not since Tuesday, I believe."

He didn't question Chapple's right to be interested, I suppose Ted had briefed him during their minute together. "I was thinking," he went on, "if Lizzie hasn't seen her—there was my Auntie May, she was about Madge's age, had a stroke, just fell down and no one found her for three days. Still, Ted's right, sir, if she should be staying put for her own reasons and you go calling the police in, she'll have your blood. They won't like it in the Mansions either, a very stuck-up lot there. Ted, has Alfie been along yet?"

"Alfie'll be working," said Ted. "He has a round-the-clock job," he added for Chapple's benefit. "Locksmith. Lady comes back of a Sunday morning and finds she's left her key the wrong side of the door. Rings Alfie's firm and they send someone round—twenty-four hours a day, fifty-two weeks a year. Including Christmas."

"This is his free day, though," Charlie insisted. "Told me to look out for him. He'll be coming along from the Catholic church any minute now. Goes to the twelve o'clock and cheers himself up with a drink afterwards. He'd do the job for you, if you took the responsibility." But his voice sounded doubtful. "If he knew who you were," he added, a bit lamely.

"I'm the nearest thing to a next-of-kin Mrs. Gardiner has," Chapple assured him.

Charlie went to watch the street for Alfie's arrival, and Chapple handed round his cigarette-case.

"No, thank you, sir," said Ted. "I don't." But the rest of us did; even the old cricketing chap managed to get one. Chapple saw through him at once, and ordered another round. The old boy knew the rules, took his half-pint and sheered off. Ted was busy at the bar, Chapple and I kept up the appearance of conversation. It occurred to me no one had mentioned Crook, and I thought how put out he'd be to be out in the cold. Still, he might nose his way in yet; there's no telling with a chap like that. Mrs. Chapple's name wasn't mentioned. Chapple must have done a good job to keep Madge's existence a secret from her, I reflected. Of course, I know it's the usual thing, when a child's given for adoption, for the legitimate parents to fade out. At last Charlie came back with Alfie in tow; he was a little dark chap with black hair like porcupine spikes standing up all over his head. Ted had a pint waiting for him.

"Here, what's this in aid of?" Alfie enquired. "It's not my birthday."

"Didn't Charlie tell you?" asked Ted. "We've got a job for you. Emergency."

Alfie, who had grabbed the tankard, set it down untasted. "Now, wait a minute, mate," he said. "I'm no blackleg. If you ring the guv'nor he'll send someone pronto. Shouldn't be long."

"It's Madge," said Ted. The word was like a spell that never fails.

"What's about Madge?"

"We don't know. But no one's set eyes on her, nor heard her, since Wednesday night, when she was in here; and in a pretty taking, too."

"She's no right to be living alone," said Alfie, angrily. "What sort of a society have we got that lets old folk live by themselves?"

"Who are you calling old?" asked Ted, genuinely surprised.

"Well, I reckon she's earned a break. Not since Wednesday, eh?"

"That's right."

"Just let me get outside this," Alfie said, "and I'll nip along and get my tools. And if any interfering copper pushes his long nose in, I look to you to pull it for me," he added to Chapple.

"I'll do that," Chapple assured him, gravely, and off the little man flashed. Charlie, leaning against the bar, said in reverent tones, "Poor Madge! Poor old cow!" in a voice that even Queen Victoria could hardly have jibbed at. All this time the other drinkers had appeared completely engrossed in their own conversations. We were like a little group on an island cut off from everyone else. Then Alfie came back and he and Chapple departed; you could see Alfie was the type that never has to tell anyone he's as good a man as you are, Gunga Din, because it would never occur to him anyone would think different. I could see my old cricketing bore polishing up another yarn of the 'eighties, so I pulled my Sunday paper out of my pocket and moved over to another table against the wall that was mysteriously unoccupied. Sitting there I was as invisible as if I wore a fairy cloak. Come hell or high water I planned to stop there till we had some news or the pub closed, whichever was the earlier. A lot of time passed. Neither Chapple nor Alfie returned; the husbands and dogs started to go home, the crowd thinned. Ted said to the near-Blue, "Anything more I can get for you, sir?" and the old chap looked round, saw no hope for it, and returned brightly, "Well, just a half before I toddle back to the Sunday joint. My landlady's a stickler for punctuality."

Afterwards I saw him sitting on a bench near the river eating something out of a paper bag; in the light his coat looked almost as green as the grass. I supposed he rang the changes on the pubs every Sunday, for fear of finding the " No Entry " sign up if he stuck to the one for too long. Charlie, who'd stopped where he was, was just saying, " If I don't get back soon Hilda 'ull have my scalp for her tea," when the door burst open and a little black beetle of a woman almost fell down the three steps. She tottered to the bar and ordered a black velvet. If she'd taken out her curlers that was her sole concession to Sunday. Like a little witch she was; I looked round for the black cat.

" If my husband could see me," she gasped. " Never mind, I need it, my Gawd, do I need it? That poor Madge Gardiner!"

I came up to the bar for a refill as Ted asked, " What's happened to her then? Fallen downstairs?"

" In a flat? Don't talk silly. Well, didn't he come here, that chap who called this morning? I told him the Admiral—though, mind you, I didn't think he'd find her here. I mean, three whole days and never a murmur out of her."

Ted said in the same good-natured voice, but tight as a drum under that surface composure, " Don't keep it to yourself, Lizzie. What's happened to Madge?"

And she said, dramatically, " She's dead. Murdered. The police are there now."

Ted didn't speak for a moment; he put out his hand and it closed round the whisky bottle. He poured out the stiffest drink I'd ever seen and swallowed it at a gulp. Not that I blamed him. I felt the same way myself.

" Mind you," Mrs. Costello went on, " she's only got herself to thank. The times I warned her. You'll get the flats a bad name, I told her, and you won't be doing yourself any good either. And that Wednesday, a chap young enough to be her son . . ."

" You saw him then?"

" Not to say see, just that he was young, well, you could tell that from the way he came up the stairs. Went down a bit less lightly, though, and no wonder. Couldn't get away fast enough if you ask me. I suppose they had one or two . . ."

" Mean to say they didn't ask you in?" said Ted, with tremendous irony. His powers of recuperation were amazing, or perhaps this was the news he'd anticipated all along.

" My husband's teetotal, I daren't have a drop on the premises. Local preacher down at the Cut, I thought you knew."

It appeared that being an (unpaid) preacher in the service of the Lord was a full-time job, and Lizzie went out office cleaning to keep the pair of them. That's what I like about a pub, you meet all sorts.

" Heard him go about 11.15 it 'ud be," Lizzie went on. " I'd been cleaning myself in the bathroom. Of course, if I'd had any idea . . ." She drained the glass and looked at it hopefully. Ted refilled it without a word.

" Didn't hear anything, then?"

She had to admit that was so. She told us about Chapple's visit that morning—might have known Madge is never on the move of a Sunday before 12 o'clock, she observed. Still, I told him come here—and then him and Alfie came back, and Alfie got the door opened, and then I heard him come flying out of the flat like a bat out of hell. There was a bobby in the hall having a quiet smoke. They often do of a Sunday, where the sergeant won't spot them. You'd best come up, copper, he called. You're wanted. After that, they came one and all, photographers, finger-print chaps, a doctor. Won't do the flats any good having police cars hurtling round. Came to my place presently. Did I know Madge? Well, I told them, I live opposite, don't I? The daft questions men will ask. Had I heard anything? Was I sure? This young chap I saw on Wednesday, would I know him again? Well, of course I wouldn't."

"How was it?" asked Ted, keeping his head and going to the root of the matter. "Or didn't you get that?"

"Of course I got it. She'd been slugged, a brass candlestick, her own, mark you. What a liberty! Still, you would think with all you read in the papers and all you see on the telly a woman like her, living alone, would have too much sense to leave lethal weapons lying about. Putting temptation in the way, you could call it."

"I was always telling her she'd take one chance too many one of these days," Ted muttered, "but I never thought that young fellow—he didn't look the type." (I could almost hear Crook telling him there was no such thing as a type—murderers and V.C.s, they come all shapes and sizes.) "I'll have to be going," Lizzie went on, regretfully. "Just thought I should steady my nerves. If my old chap starts about the demon rum and look what it leads to, there'll be another murder in the Mansions, and this time I'll get *my* picture in the papers."

At the door she turned to say, " Think they'll ever find out who the young chap was?"

" I wouldn't be surprised," Ted told her. " He was in Friday night, asking about a glove he'd lost."

" What's that?" Lizzie exclaimed. " Here, you'd best get round to the police right away. You see, when they moved the body they found a glove lying underneath it."

CHAPTER III

Soon AFTER Mrs. Costello had reluctantly departed Alfie came back. He hadn't got a lot to add to what Lizzie had told us. Chapple had asked him to accompany him into the flat and they'd found Madge in the living-room, sprawled on the carpet.

" And that didn't happen this morning," said Alfie. He had shot out and called up the policeman, who had telephoned the local station; then they'd all waited for a higher authority. Madge's big black handbag had been lying on the carpet nearby, wide open and empty; drawers and a cupboard had been opened and ransacked, and the clothes torn off the bed.

" What he thought he'd find there . . ." said Alfie, in gloomy tones.

Ted and I agreed it might be a way of dressing the stage to give the impression the murder had been for gain.

" Where's Mr. Chapple?" asked Ted, and Alfie said he'd gone down to the station with the sergeant.

" Sergeant?"

" Yes, well, the Chief Inspector was off having his lunch, but they left a message. What I want to know, Ted, is how could anyone hate Madge like that?"

: :   : :

We didn't see Chapple again that day, but the police arrived to talk to Ted, and Charlie volunteered to look after the bar. Business was slackening off and Ted said he wouldn't be long. He couldn't tell them anything they didn't know already, except about the glove.

" Sent them away with a nice assortment of fleas in their ears," he informed us on his return. " I don't know who the chap was, I said, why not ask Mr. Crook? You should have seen their faces fall. Nearly cracked the lino."

" Not Arthur Crook?" said Charlie, disbelievingly.

" The same. He was here both times the young fellow came in."

" What's he doing in these parts?"

" He couldn't just be having a quiet drink, I suppose?" said Ted.

" Be your age," said Charlie. " This isn't his manor."

" He saw the chap making for the subway at 11.30 on Wednesday night," Ted amplified.

" Well, that fits," Alfie agreed. " Lizzie said she heard him go about 11.15."

" He told us he was only there a few minutes," I put in. " No sense jumping to conclusions. She could have had another visitor."

" With the door bolted?"

" What's that about the door being bolted?" asked Alfie. " Not when we got there."

" See what that means?" I said.

" It's only his word she ever bolted it," Alfie pointed out.

" If she didn't how would he know about the bolt?" I inquired. I was like the snake when the charmer starts to play, however much it 'ud like to slither away somewhere cool and have a kip, it has to stop on, going through the motions.

"How can they be sure even it was Wednesday it happened?" Ted went on.

"The bottles were still unpacked in the basket."

"What was she wearing?" I said.

"How'd I know? Something shiny, greenish, I think. Tell you the truth I felt pretty green myself. Didn't properly look."

"No one saw her after Wednesday," Ted reminded us. "If this chap hadn't come along asking questions it could have been a week before she was found."

They were still nattering when I left. That evening there was a message on the radio, the usual thing. The body of an elderly woman, Mrs. Madge Gardiner, aged about 60, was found in her flat (address supplied) around noon. Police were anxious to interview a young man, first name believed to be Colin, who might be able to assist them. They repeated it next morning, so either he hadn't heard or was lying doggo—you could take your choice.

The "heavies" only gave the news a paragraph on one of the inside pages. After all, what was one elderly woman more or less to them? The *Echo* and the *Argus* had a little more respect for the dead and their readers' natural curiosity. WOMAN FOUND MURDERED and DEAD WOMAN THREE DAYS IN FLAT, they reported. It was left to the *Record* to bring out its big guns. It was a dullish period for the Press, nothing out of the way to report; that is, there were the usual rumours of war in the East, demonstrations against violence in the West, strikes, losses in public enterprise, crime figures rising, and, of course, the weather, but these were everyday topics and too big to have any personal application, except possibly the last, and we'd got tired of that. But a violent death in a London flat is homely, intimate even. Not that it would ever happen to you or me—imagination seldom stretches that far—but the party on the floor above—all manner of queer sounds coming from there, all very mysterious, which is always true somehow of activities in the flat above yours, wherever you lived—you tell yourself you'd never be surprised to learn that something pretty rum was going on there.

Yes, the *Record,* which prides itself on knowing the public taste, really went to town on Madge. What a reporter wants, one of them once told me, is a hook on which to hang a topic, and in this case the topic was poor unfortunate Madge Gardiner.

They ran a big picture on the front page and a headline—Mystery Man sought by the Police; and another smaller picture of the Admiral Box, which proved remarkably good for trade, all manner of strangers turning up in the hope of a tit-bit that evening. To top everything up nicely the editor ran a leader—Who Cares?—dealing with the tragic problem of old people living alone. No one in their senses, of course, could have thought of Madge as an old person, she had far too much vitality and go, but the chap spread himself all right. According to him, our senior citizens were all neglected, unwanted, under-financed, misunderstood and, in general, short-changed. And he had a second headline—What's Known about This One? He instanced various cases of old folk living on their lonesome coming to a sticky end, falling down liftshafts, collapsing in single rooms without a telephone, unnoticed, unmissed.

" One of the Independent Companies will pick that

up," I heard a man say at the Hay Wain, where I'd dropped in at lunch-time for a pint, just to get the general feeling of the affair. " Might get a correspondence going, with a couple of letters written in the office; the rest 'ull follow like ants on a sugar trail."

On the six o'clock news we heard the announcer say that Colin Bruce, the man wanted in connection with the Gardiner murder, had been to the station and made a statement.

The details were released next day.

According to this statement, Bruce knew nothing of Madge's death until he saw the *Record* on Monday morning. He'd been away for the week-end, attending some kind of conference in connection with his job, which had to do with nuclear physics. He stayed on a bit on the Monday to talk to the lecturer, and nearly missed his train. A porter bundled him into a carriage just as the train started to move, and he found himself alone with an elderly battle-axe who stopped him smoking, stopped him whistling and eventually offered him her newspaper to prevent him fidgeting. It was one of those old-fashioned carriages that don't communicate, so he was landed with her till the next stop, which was almost an hour away. And when he picked up the paper, intending to use it mainly as a screen, the first thing he saw was Madge Gardiner's face staring into his. The next thing he recalled was the Battle-axe asking him if he felt all right, adding that women like that got everything they deserved, and putting temptation in people's way was as much a sin as yielding to it. What he really wanted, Colin said, was a tot of brandy and a bit of peace, but in the circumstances he got neither.

When he alighted at Paddington he was noticed by a young constable, who had been posted there to look out for members of a fur-thieving gang who'd pulled off a coup the night before and were believed to be splitting up in all directions. This chap saw Colin enter a phone booth, talk two or three minutes and then, still carrying a handcase, bolt into the street and board a 27 bus. He got in touch with his superiors but by the time they could contact the bus their suspect had vanished. He surfaced at the police station around 2 o'clock, and explained he'd only learned about Madge that morning.

They didn't give him a red-carpet reception by any means. Before they listened to his story they wanted to know why he hadn't come to them direct.

They told him he'd been seen telephoning on arrival, and he said he'd rung up the lab. where he worked to say he'd be delayed.

" And the 27 bus—that wouldn't bring you anywhere near here."

He admitted he'd called to see a friend, but wouldn't give the friend's name. Their original idea was that he'd bolted home, possibly to cover his tracks, but he flummoxed them by saying he had digs at Parkshot Royal, near his work. He'd gone to see a friend to explain he wouldn't be able to keep an appointment for that evening.

" Is your friend not on the telephone, Mr. Bruce?"

All he could say to that was that he preferred to conduct the interview by word of mouth. When they started to get tough with him he got tough back. Crook said afterwards, " That should have shown them he was innocent; guilty men play it smooth, anyway to start with, except those who break down right away." Apparently they let that ride for the time being and he told them his story, which was the same as the one I'd heard in the Admiral on the Friday evening. He insisted that Madge was all right when he left the flat, and he'd heard her shoot the bolt. Asked why he'd waited so long to come forward, he said he came as soon as he heard. He'd not listened to the wireless news on Sunday or early Monday morning. Then Chief Inspector Scott, who was in charge of the case, asked him if he'd lost a glove recently, and he said yes, and he described it. "You mean it's been found?" he said. And Scott let him have it, full strength. It had been found all right, though it wasn't in very good shape any more. He produced it, Bruce didn't make any bones about identifying it; anyhow, he had the second glove. Scott told him where his chaps had found it. In the murder flat.

Bruce took the news with surprising calm. "I imagined I might have dropped it there," he said. "I asked at the Admiral if she'd found it and brought it back."

"You asked at the Admiral?" said Scott, very, very gently. (Bruce told us all this when he came to the pub that night and was greeted with about as much warmth as a ghost or a policeman himself.) "But you didn't really expect to find it there?"

"I thought if Mrs. Gardiner had found it she'd probably take it back."

"You didn't think of calling at her flat?"

"I work all day, outside that area. I gathered she was generally to be found at the Admiral in the evening, it seemed the sensible place to call."

"You could have telephoned her."

"I didn't even realise she was on the phone. There was no instrument in the only room I saw."

(Subsequently it was shown that Madge's telephone had been installed beside her bed.)

"I asked Scott if he was trying to tie me up with the murder," Bruce went on, and when Crook heard that he said in his outspoken way, This chap can give points to the Holy Innocents. "He said I was a perfectly free agent, I'd made my statement of my own free will, he'd told me I didn't have to answer questions and I'd raised no objections—well, why on earth should I?—I could walk out that minute if I liked, but there were one or two other points. Had I noticed, for instance, what she had in her bag when we were in the Admiral? I said it was stuffed with notes, anyone there could have seen it. He asked if I objected to having my finger-prints taken for elimination purposes and I said of course not, but all I remembered handling was the photograph on the mantelpiece, the one of her and the little girl. I told them that was all I knew."

What he didn't know then was that Scott had obtained a search warrant to examine Bruce's rooms. What they expected to find there I can't, of course, say. What they did find, tucked under the lining paper of a drawer, was about forty pounds in single notes. When he was asked if he could explain their presence he said they were his savings. When they asked why he hadn't banked them he said because they were a special fund. When they asked him what they were for, he said, that was his business. His landlady hadn't known about them, no one had known about them; he'd been saving for quite some time. It was such an absurd story it could be true, but apparently the police didn't think so. They had found that Madge Gardiner had withdrawn fifty pounds, all the money she possessed, from her account the day before her death; that was the money we had all seen in her handbag. When the bag was found again it was empty, and a sum not very dissimilar from that which was missing suddenly appeared in Colin Bruce's room. Apparently Bruce said that if he'd been crazy enough to steal money he'd have banked it, but there was a simple answer to that. He might have found it difficult to explain how he came by it. If what he earned—and everything in this connection soon became public property—was typical of the money paid to young nuclear scientists, it's a wonder the country has any at all. And an unexpected sum of forty pounds would take some explaining away. Even if he'd claimed to have backed a winner, and he never put forward any such claim, he'd have been asked to supply details. What with the money and the glove the police seemed to think they had sufficient evidence to apply for a warrant and a couple of days later everyone knew Colin Bruce had been arrested for Madge Gardiner's murder.

"He's an innocent all right," said Crook. " Couldn't even drum up a good reason why he only caught the last train. Had things on his mind and went walking by the river! In this weather—I ask you."

I noticed he didn't say he didn't believe it.

: :   : :

Someone once observed that an engaged girl is about as exciting as a rice pudding at a Lord Mayor's banquet, and much the same thing could be said about an arrested man. So long as people could speculate on the identity of Madge Gardiner's murderer, her name was on everyone's lips. The police had interviewed everyone they could trace who had been at the Admiral that night, without getting much forrader. There seemed no escaping the fact that young Bruce was the last to see her. They'd decided she had been killed on the Wednesday, partly because of Mrs. Costello's evidence, partly because they'd found a tear-off calendar in the dead woman's flat still showing Wednesday—women are creatures of habit, said Chief Inspector Scott, she probably tore off a leaf when she put the kettle on in the morning and this hadn't been torn off after that date—and also because Madge's wireless, which came on first thing in the morning and stayed on solid all day until she went to the Admiral, hadn't been heard since the six o'clock news on Wednesday. As for motive, well, as Crook said, it isn't essential, it's like putting fruit into a cake, it's more tasty with it, but you can get by with just the plain ingredients. Anyway, everyone had his own explanation. The two most favoured were that Bruce had made a pass at her, she'd repulsed him, possibly even laughed at him, seeing the difference in their ages, and he'd lost his head and hit out; or that she'd made overtures to him, he'd tried to make a bolt for it, there'd been words, a row, and he'd lost his head. On the whole, the former was the favourite solution. You can knock a man down, even put the boot in, and he may forgive you, but offend his sexual pride and you're asking for a quick ticket to the churchyard. All Bruce had said, according to our information, was a repetition of his original story. Of course, he pleaded Not Guilty.

I believe there was quite a big turn-out at Madge's

funeral—I didn't go myself, but Ted got a stand-in for once and a number of regulars put in an appearance. Then the matter seemed to be closed. Bruce was a stranger, no one cared much what happened to him. Murder plus theft is still a captial crime, and if he was proved guilty there wasn't going to be much sympathy for him. Ted summed up the general view when he said, " I hope he hangs as high as Haman."

And then into the picture breezed Barbie Hunter, like a wind blowing from all four corners of the earth at the same time; she nearly blew the Admiral off its foundations, and she was quite prepared to do the same for the Metropolitan Police Force (C.I.D.)

I met her, as indeed I met all the protagonists in this affair, in the Admiral. Bruce had been brought before a magistrate and remanded in custody, and so far as I was concerned you might have thought that was the end of the case. Then one evening, forty-eight hours after news of the arrest, I was sitting with two dog-fanciers—Jenks and Snell were the names if that's of any interest to you, though they don't really come into the story at all—talking about a tip my friend, Doggett, had given me. He may take a little time to find his feet, Doggett had said —meaning the dog, that is—but pretty soon he's going to be a gold-mine. And then Barbie marched in, half avenging fury and half the most beautiful girl I'd ever seen. Up to this date there'd been no mention of any female in Bruce's life, no photos of his old mum, nursie, sister, girl-friend, not even a dog; he didn't seem to have any intimate connections at all. Or if he had he was keeping them dark. So that this astounding girl burst on us with all the surprise of Halley's Comet. The bar was reasonably full, and I swear mine wasn't the only voice that faltered, the only eyes that slewed round in her direction and found they couldn't slew back again. She'd have been a sensation in any bar, coming in alone like that, and the Admiral's not the sort of pub where women do come by themselves. There'd been Madge, of course, but she was a law to herself, but the women, when they came at all without a male escort, came in pairs, like the bingo couple on my first night. Mostly they dropped in with reluctant husbands, or stayed for a quick one with the boy-friend before going on somewhere a bit more lively. I'm not a woman so I can only say her clothes looked as if they'd been built on her, though they were simple enough—a black suit, a plain white blouse, a small half crescent of diamonds in her lapel. She had lovely legs and her stockings did very little to conceal them, narrow shoes, long gloves wrinkling over her wrists, no hat on her butter-coloured hair that she wore almost as far as her shoulders. Ted, characteristically, gave her a pretty cool welcome. He never approved of women who drank on their own. I run a pub, not a pick-up shop, he said. This girl gave one sweeping comprehensive glance round the bar, dismissed us all as casually as if we'd been blades of grass hoping to be trodden underfoot by her shining high-heeled shoe, and walked over to Ted. I couldn't hear what she was asking him, whatever it was it gave him no pleasure. I saw him shake his head. He looked at the girl as if she was a bee or something walking over his hand; he wanted to shake it off, but didn't like to shake too hard because bees can sting. The girl wasn't having any of that. She said another piece, Ted talked back, she opened one of her hands in a curiously appealing gesture, Ted looked round the bar and seemed to indicate the table where I was sitting. I didn't believe it, of course, and I looked over my shoulder. The next instant she was threading her way through and stopped beside me.

" Are you Mr. Crete?" she asked. " The barman says you may be able to help me. I don't want to break up your conversation now, but when you've got a minute to spare . . ." She nodded and carried the little glass in her hand to a table against the wall. Either she didn't realise everyone was watching her or she didn't give a damn.

" Come on, Nick," said Jenks with a grin. " You won't get any more sense out of Simon here to-night. Brown Bess isn't the only bitch . . ."

I was suddenly furiously angry. Nick (Snell) started to get up. " Be seeing you, boy," he said, " and that tip of yours better be good. This ain't a Latin country and the police can be quite nasty about chaps going around without a shirt on their back."

They indulged in a little more clumsy wit and then sloped off; they stopped at the bar for a word with Ted, but he didn't give them sufficient change to pay their bus-fares home. The door hadn't closed behind them before the girl was sitting at my table.

" I'm sorry if I broke up your party," she said, coolly, "but this is urgent. The barman tells me you know Mr. Crook."

My heart sank so abruptly I almost expected to hear it splash in my entrails; then I thought, if you can't be the rose it's better to be the thorn on the rose's stem than nothing, so I said, Yes, I did. She said, " Then you can give me an introduction to him. I want his help, but I can't just ring him up out of the blue and tell him so."

That was precisely what she could have done with Crook, but there was no need to let her know that. I said " Do you feel like giving me any idea why . . . I mean, he's bound to ask."

She said, " I'm the girl who's going to marry Colin Bruce when he's been cleared of this ridiculous charge, and I'm told Mr. Crook is the best man to do it. He knows a lot of the facts already."

I thought whatever the police may feel about this, Crook will give three rousing cheers. He likes to follow every case through to the last chapter.

" Bruce didn't mention he was engaged," I told her, and she said, " Well, it's unofficial. He's as stubborn as Carter's mule, whoever that remarkable beast may have been, and he wouldn't agree to an open engagement until he could afford to put a ring on my finger and a roof over my head. But it seems to me the sooner he has someone to look after him, the better. Anyone but the police would realise that carrying an old harridan's parcels for her is just the sort of idiotic thing Colin would do. How soon can you contact him—Mr. Crook, I mean?"

I tried to copy her composure. " No time like the present," I said. " Wait here, I might be able to get him on the phone."

" At this hour of the evening?"

" Oh, time doesn't mean a thing to him," I said. " What's that you're drinking? I'll tell Ted to send along another."

When I told Ted I'd like to use his phone he said, " I don't want Mr. Crook making trouble for me here. Macraes have created enough as it is."

" You tell them to try and keep him out," I retorted, " and if your phone's so blasted private there's one up the road."

So then he said it was all right to use his. There was no reply from Crook's office so I tried his home address, and he had the receiver off almost before the bell started to ring.

" Where are you?" he inquired. No asking who I was, he's got the memory of an elephant. " O.K., stop there. The Superb and I will be with you in five minutes. Young lady got a name, by the way? Well, try and nail it before I get there. It's always a disadvantage to have to start a conversation with Miss."

" He doesn't lose any time, does he?" said the girl admiringly. But you could see she wasn't really surprised; she was like Crook in that. If she wanted a thing she took for granted she'd get it. What she wanted was Crook now and Bruce later, and she gave you the impression she was going to get them both. She told me her name was Barbara Hunter, commonly known as Barbie, she was twenty-three and lived with her mother in Kensington. She'd known Colin quite a while, and had had a date with him for the fatal Wednesday evening. When he ditched her at short notice she took umbrage—not surprising really, but now she was blaming herself. Because he'd explained he had to see this chap and would ring her later if he could get away in time, and when the telephone rang she'd let it ring.

" If I'd answered it Colin would never have come here and never have met this Madge Gardiner," she pointed out. " Once he met her you could be sure he'd fall into any trouble that was going. Why should she pick on him to take her home? Oh, I'm not surprised they found Don Quixote crazy, the pity is they didn't lock him up before he'd wrecked some perfectly good windmills."

I could see Crook was going to love her and I was right. He came faster than you'd have thought possible, that car of his was more like a flying carpet.

" How come you heard of me, sugar?" he asked, as cosy as a fairy-tale. So she said she'd approached her own family lawyer in connection with Bruce's defence, " and Mr. Anson said his firm didn't handle this sort of case, and what I needed was a last ditcher like you, and I remembered seeing in one of the evening editions that you were here the night it all happened, so I came down to try and find someone who could put us in touch."

" Would I be wrong," asked Crook, " if I suggested the visit he paid on his return from his week-end conference was to you?"

" You would not. He came to say that there was likely to be trouble, and he didn't want me involved. He said once my name was mentioned, as it probably would be, once it got round that we were engaged, there'd be reporters on the doorstep and in the dust-bins and hiding under the kitchen sink."

" He knows his onions, that young man of yours. Come to that, so does your family lawyer. Anson of Fletcher Anson and Pole? I though as much. They do like to keep their hands clean and say what you like, murder may be a thrill to the masses, but it's never anything but dirty."

He looked down at his own hands, big and strong, with reddish hair on the backs. You could see he'd never had a manicure in his life.

" Of course, that's what he was saving the money for, the ring," Barbie went on, " though the vultures could have his liver before he'd tell the police. I can't think why women want to marry men at all, they're such fools. I suppose it's because there's nothing else for them to marry."

" He's innocent, you know," she went on a minute later.

" If I take on the case you're darned tooting he's innocent, that's the only kind I ever represent. And if you ain't happy about the present position I'd say the police ain't exactly overjoyed. I mean, the jury's composed of twelve good men and true, like you and me, sugar, only maybe not so bright, and they're going to ask some very awkward questions. F'r instance, is it likely, they'll ask, that he should suddenly light into her with a candlestick, a woman he'd never seen before in his natural, mark you . . ."

" They may not believe that," she interrupted.

" *I* believe it. And I was there, wasn't I? It's what they call irony, here was he all of a dither because of you, there was she, ditto because of the unknown enemy— why, if they'd met in the street the next day they wouldn't most likely have recognised each other."

" They're saying he might have tried—tried——"

" To get payment on the nail? Forget it, sugar. Why, Madge could have eaten two Colin Bruces for breakfast. And since it don't seem likely he'd want anything she had to offer—wouldn't even take a drink from her in her place, remember, and that's borne out, because there were no dirty glasses and the drying-up cloth was as dry as a bone—yes, I know about the money, but less than forty pounds ain't worth it, not these days with the £ worth about seven-and-sixpence. And I know about Burke and Hare," he added. " They're always quoted as committin' murder for something like six pounds, but six pounds was six pounds in those days and anyway it was their profession. No, jurymen generally look at a situation from an intensely individual standpoint. Here's a decent young chap, nothing against him, meets this old girl for the first time, well, if she does suggest a little affectionate dalliance, and we don't know that she did, would *I* bang the old moppet with a brass candlestick? I tooting well wouldn't, so most likely this chap wouldn't either. Mind you, most of them wouldn't have carried her basket back in the first place. Too scared of the wife with the flaming poker. Still, someone dotted her, and our only way of convincing everyone, not just a court of law, your intended ain't guilty is to fix the blame where it belongs."

" You must tell me what I can do to help," said Barbie, eagerly. " I'll do anything."

" I'll tell you what you can do," Crook agreed. " You can play like you're the Tar Baby that lay low and said nuffin. And that's gospel. Once it gets out that you'd given him the frozen mitt you're going to have a lot of bright young chaps going psychological on you. Not the murdering type, perhaps, they'll say, but he started the evening with a grievance against the sex, and he took it out on poor old Madge Gardiner. By the way, does he know you're pulling me in?"

" How could he? I've only just made sure of it myself. I told my mother I was going to ask you."

" H'm. Now the money in the drawer—what makes you so tooting sure it was for the ring?"

" It has to be," replied Barbie, earnestly. " Anything else—income tax or a car or—or a record-player, only he doesn't want one—he'd have told the police. But he was so keen on keeping my name out of it . . ."

" That he did his best to get himself pulled in? He's going to be a helpful sort of client, I must say. Now how about the glove? That's something else he's got to explain away."

" Anyone can drop a glove," she defended him, instantly.

" Not in the flat of a dame who's got herself murdered. That's arrant carelessness."

" If he thought he'd left it there, would he have come round to the Admiral, and drawn attention to the fact that he'd lost it?"

" Depends how cagey he is. When they find the glove they're going to remember he's the one who saw her home. He'll be asked does he recognise it? Has he missed one? No, no, askin' was just what a guilty man who knew his onions would do."

" You don't miss a trick, do you?" said Barbie. " Well, where do you start?"

Crook was away like a show jumper over the first fence.

" If she had a local enemy that chap over there," he indicated Ted, " would likely know about it. You can't keep much from the fellow behind the bar."

" According to what he said, he didn't know she had a daughter living, let alone married," I put in a bit diffid-ently. I didn't want Crook to say, " Thanks for the intro and don't let us keep you." More than anything on earth at that moment I wanted to stay where I was in the middle of the picture.

"Well, in a sense she hadn't," Crook pointed out. "If you have a fur coat and you give it away, well, you haven't got a fur coat any more. That don't mean the fur coat don't exist any longer, just that it don't belong to you. And the same with Madge Gardiner's little girl."

"Was she at the funeral, I wonder? The daughter, I mean."

Crook looked surprised. "Asking me? Couldn't say, I'm sure. I wasn't there. Seeing she didn't know the dead woman was her Mum I'd say it wasn't likely. The man we want now, the only man, bar the murderer, who can really help us at this stage, is Chapple himself. He's the one she turned to when she was in trouble, and the instant he read her letter he came beetling round to hold her hand."

Barbie's eyes sparkled. "Do we know where he was on Wednesday night?" I could see we weren't going to have a dull moment on this case.

"Yes, sugar, we do," Crook assured her. "He was in Amsterdam with Mrs. C. And if you've any cagey notions about him nipping back like they do on the telly, hitting his ma-in-law over the head and being tucked up with wifie first thing the next morning, you can forget it. Some people call it immoral to tell kids fairy-tales, but they're nothing to what their elders are prepared to swallow. For once, the weather on the Continong was even worse than we had it here—and our Wednesday night was no picnic."

"Well then, he's out. How about Madge's husband? Is he dead or something? I thought whenever someone died of murder the first suspect was the husband or wife."

"And half the time that's the answer," Crook assured her. "Still, there have to be exceptions or there wouldn't be rules. This time they seem to have picked on the boy-friend—line of least resistance, of course, but what do you expect?"

"Didn't they even look for the husband?" Barbie pursued.

"Why should they? She's given out for years that she's a widow—now, there's a point—wonder if she's been drawing the pension all these years. Anyway, no one seems to have set eyes on him, and there's a young chap on the scene, all of a tizz from the instant he bursts into the Admiral, here's a mysterious store of bank notes in his room—and the police are like me, they outgrew fairy stories a long time ago—you can't hardly blame them for taking what's dumped into their fat blue laps. It's the job of the defence to winkle out X, the real criminal, and that, sugar, is just what we're going to do. Come to think of it, we don't know anything about her yet, not even if Gardiner is her real name."

"There's Somerset House," suggested Barbie, looking as eager as a hound on the trail. "They ought to be able to help."

"Always assuming we know what we're looking for. The weakness is that, though they can prove you were born (unless it was to someone's interest to suppress the fact, and that 'ud only be if you weren't going to stay alive long enough to justify the bus fare) they can't prove you're dead. Listen, sugar. You're Barbara Hunter—right? And sometime in the not too distant future you're going to be Barbara Bruce—you hope, and the records 'ull show both facts. But say, for a lady's private reasons, the day dawns when you decide to call yourself Barbara Smith, without goin' through the formality of a deed-poll, and when you snuff it that's the name the neighbours know you by—well, what happened to Barbara Bruce? She's dead all right—in a way you could say she died when you decided to switch monikers—but that name ain't going to appear on the records—not unless someone's got suspicious."

" They must have a lot of loose ends up there," suggested Barbie, scornfully.

" They do, of course, though not so many as you might imagine. A lot of digging's done to try and establish identity where there's any doubt, no family, see, but if there's no relatives interested and no documents found in the possession of the deceased—there's dentists, of course, sometimes they can help—but even they ain't infallible. You just remember the newspaper reports that have come your way—unknown bodies fished out of the river, whose own mothers wouldn't know them, victims of fire—who was the chap burned in Rouse's car?—no one knows to this day. Corpses are discovered in old workings, washed up by the tide—there was that skeleton discovered in a tree some years back—female, that's about as far as they got with that one—and the dead losses to humanity (he was graver at that moment than I'd hitherto seen him), the junkies who've got right to the bottom of the hill, the meth. drinkers of Spitalfields—they all had names and histories once, but even they often don't remember them now. Take my word for it, there's going to be some nasty shocks when all the graves are opened and the sea gives up the dead that are in it."

" Couldn't Mr. Chapple help?" Barbie urged. " After all, he married her daughter; even if she changed her name when she was adopted, as I suppose she did, her original certificate would be at Somerset House, and that would give the name of her real parents."

" It don't work out that way," said Crook. " When a child's adopted the original birth certificate is removed from the record and a new one substituted. The original ain't destroyed, but it's put on a special file and can only be seen on order of the court, and they ain't easy to come by. Say that fictitious character of my childhood, the rich uncle from Australia, should suddenly surface (on a death certificate, that is) and it can be shown he left a will bequeathing his all to his next-of-kin, and the next-of-kin proved to be an adopted child, then the records could be examined, I suppose, so as not to deprive the legatee of his or her fortune . . ."

" Always supposing the new parents wanted to claim it."

Crook shook his head in disbelief. ". Sugar," he told her, " they always want to claim it. Well, why not? It belongs to the child, and why give the Government any more than they take by force already? A lot will depend, of course, on how much Mummy Number Two told her prospective son-in-law—did he happen to mention how he met up with Number One? Well, never mind, I dare-say I can find that out for myself. *If* she gave him any hints then we've got a starting-point."

" She can't have been much of a mother to sign her own child away," cried Barbie, impetuously.

" I daresay she had her reasons. They could even have been good ones. She didn't look to me like a woman who'd be easy frightened—and take my word, she was scared rigid that night, wasn't she?" he added to me.

I agreed. "But if she was being blackmailed surely that's what you'd expect."

"Do you suppose she was being blackmailed on the daughter's account?" inquired Barbie.

"Well, she was asking the husband for help; your guess is as good as mine. Wonder what the chap's hold over her was. If you don't give me whatever it is I want I'll tell your daughter who her mother really is? Don't make sense to me. Why should she mind the girl knowing? No, there's more to it than that. If Chapple can give us the real mother's name—you know, we're like those things that go round and round in circles in the dark, we're getting nowhere."

"I was thinking," said Barbie. "This money the police think Colin took and hid in his room—why shouldn't she have given it to this mysterious visitor?"

"In that case," returned Crook, reasonably, "why should he have slammed her on the head? Besides, we haven't proved yet there was another visitor."

"Well, of course there was. There has to be." Barbie's eyes looked like those of the dog in the fairy-story, as large as cart-wheels. "Someone killed her."

"I said proof, sugar. What you and me know ain't worth a button in a court of law till we can prove it."

"And there's another thing," Barbie pursued—she was as single-minded as the crow that flies direct from A to B. "In blackmail cases I thought it was always the blackmailer who got murdered. Unless, of course, you're suggesting that Mrs. Gardiner . . ."

"I only saw that woman once," said Crook, "but take

my word for it, sugar, she was no blackmailer. Blackmailers don't sit around shaking in their shoes."

" And yet she was murdered."

Crook took the wind out of both our sails by remarking, " We don't even know that for sure. It could be manslaughter, and don't tell me that's the same thing, because it's as different from murder as chalk from cheese. Murder has to be of intent, a deliberate act, like when a chap breaks in to rob and steal and is disturbed by the owner. He can say he only meant to knock the fellow out, but he was prepared for violence, and if that violence ends in X's death, then it's murder. But it could be he only went round to ginger her up a little—don't think you can play silly boggers with me, if the lady 'ull excuse my language—and she lost her head. You keep off, she tells him, and picks up the first thing that came to hand —to wit, the candlestick. A chap with murder in mind generally takes his own weapon along with him or uses his hands. He can't count on there being a candlestick or whatever conveniently close."

" If he'd been in the flat before he'd know about it being there, though," Barbie insisted. It was like a running fight, and Barbie would run till she dropped; and even from the ground she'd put out a hand and grab her opponent's ankle and bring him down as well.

" Well, but, sugar, you know as well as me that because a lady has a candlestick on her mantelpiece on Tuesday, that's no proof it'll be there on Tuesday week. You know what the ladies are. Never so happy as when they're changing the place around, so that when you come back in the small hours, (so husbands have assured me) creepin' on all fours so as not to wake the ever-loving, they find 'emselves tryin' to go to bed in the wardrobe. That candlestick could have been put in another room, gone to be lacquered, been popped with Uncle Joe—anything. And say this chap sees red—it's a genuine illusion, you know, I wish I had a pony for every chap who's told me the air really does turn red, though it don't go for much in a court of law—juries don't like to see husbands getting away with it, mostly being husbands themselves who've never resorted to the blunt instrument or the doctored dose of salts. You might think it 'ud make 'em more sympathetic, knowing here's another chap who bore the burden in the heat of the day and it was too much for him, but it don't work out like that. Now, say she came for him with the candlestick, or started to yell blue murder, and he, not wanting to be identified with Blackmailers Anonymous, snatched at the first thing that came to hand to shut her mouth—a good lawyer might be able to swing self-defence. Mind you, the missing bank-notes 'ud be against him. Trouble is, now the weapon's been wiped clean of fingerprints there can't be any actual proof."

" What was the point of him coming round anyway if she'd told him there wouldn't be any money?" Barbie wanted to know.

" But she hadn't told him," I pointed out. " She'd told someone whom she thought was X, and she never gave me a chance to explain about the mistake."

" You have something there," Crook agreed handsomely. " Still, she must have known or believed she knew, who she was letting in."

" Why do you say believed?"

" A chap could ring your bell, sugar, and say into the

talking machine—I bet you have one in your house—
This is Mr. Crook here. Or this is Simon Crete—but it
don't have to be Arthur Crook or Simon Crete. For
instance . . . with a sudden change of voice he mimicked,
' Let me in, dear, there's something you ought to know.
The police . . .'" I nearly jumped out of my skin. It
was Lizzie Costello to the life. "Or maybe—' Mr.
Costello's had one of his turns, dear, like a raging beast
he is, I got to phone the doctor . . .' She'd know about
Madge having a phone, and it's long odds against most of
the tenants of that block having a private line."

"She was afraid he might turn up at the Admiral,"
I mused, and Crook took me up as sharp as a gimlet.

" Not if he had the sense he was born with he wouldn't.
She had friends there. Murderers ain't normally the
world's bravest men. Anyone threatening Madge in public might go home with a few less teeth and fingers than
he started out with. Too bad Mrs. C. was splashing like a
porpoise at the time Bruce says he was making his getaway. I suppose she wasn't used to Madge's visitors leaving so prompt. There's this step she says she heard at
11.15. Not that it had to come from Madge's flat, of
course, there's plenty of others living in the building."

I remembered the blue car that had run noiselessly up
to the front door. " I don't suppose the driver had anything to do with it," I confessed. " He'd hardly have left
the car standing in the drive if he had . . ."

" What time was this?"

" Oh—say 10.45. Not long after I left the Admiral,
anyway."

" Didn't get the number, of course? Well, why should
you? Make?"

"One of the Archer group," I said. I don't own a car myself at the moment, but I'm pretty handy with them, I even worked in a garage for a short time for the rent's sake. "An Archer Minor, I'd say. Of course, the light wasn't very good . . ."

"Probably find he's a tenant and in the clear," Crook agreed. "Still, no harm asking. You know, sugar, your young man likes to play it the hard way. Just look at the facts. He swears he left the building at 10.45."

"If Colin says he left at 10.45, that's the time he did leave," flashed Barbie; it occured to me the Amazons could have made good use of her.

"But next time he surfaces it's 11.30, and he ain't above ten minutes' walk from the Mansions. You can't blame the police if they ain't members of the Magicians' Circle. You give them two and two and they'll make four nine times out of ten. Mind you, he could have been visiting someone else, I suppose." But you could see he didn't believe it. "Any of the locals stay open after half-past ten?"

"There's the Horse and Mariner," I said. "That doesn't close till 11. Only it's in the opposite direction from Bagshott Street, and didn't he say that night that this wasn't his line of country, he just happened to be in the neighbourhood because of this American scientist?"

"Sure did," agreed Crook. "Still, could be his bump of locality's not too well developed. Who was the chap who didn't know a hawk from a handsaw? I've met plenty who didn't know north from south. Still, forty-five minutes to reach the station's pretty poor going."

"I suppose that chap in the pub, the one who was

chucking his beer all over Madge, he couldn't somehow be involved?" I suggested.

Crook stared and I felt a fool.

" It was her expression when she looked down at him. She was—revolted . . ."

" Maybe Mr. Madge indulged and she don't like the past being brought back. No, I don't see how it could have been him. In the state he was he could never have climbed a flight of stairs. Well, if Holmes here has no other bright suggestions we'll have one for the road, and I'll pop round for a word with my client—just make sure he don't remember anything he forgot to mention to the police. Then I'll get in touch with Mr. Chapple— Madge's little girl did very well for herself there, by the way. Wheatcroft and Chapple ain't a firm to be sneezed at. If I was to go calling there they'd expect me to go to the back door. Well, like I said, I'll see if his little candle can throw any beams, and . . ."

" You will keep in touch," pleaded Barbie. " I'll be so anxious."

" Not any more you won't," promised Crook. " I only work for the innocent, remember. Mind you, if you had any sense, you'd go into a nursing home for the next couple of weeks or get yourself picked up for shop-lifting, any place where you could count on bein' looked after, and where the Press ain't allowed to come calling. But, seeing dames never do take good advice, I don't doubt you'll stop at home, and be a sittin' duck for all the long noses in the country."

" I have a job," said Barbie, casually. (She worked for one of the independent television companies, she told me later.) " And anyway, my mother wouldn't like me to be picked up for shop-lifting."

" Well, like I said, I hadn't really any hopes," said Crook. Then up he bounced as if it were nine o'clock in the morning instead of nine o'clock at night. " I'll give you a ring when there's anything to report, in the meantime mum's the word."

And, having drained his one for the road, he went bouncing off like a great rubber ball.

" I must be going, too," said Barbie. She smiled in a practised sort of way and said, " Thanks for the introduction, I should think Colin was bound to be all right now, shouldn't you, with Mr. Crook on the war-path?" (Don't ask me how Crook does it, he rolls 'em all over like bunny-rabbits. One word and they're dead sure he'll floor the whole C.I.D. by the end of the week.)

" I'd like to keep in touch," I suggested humbly. " There might be something I could do."

She turned sharply. " There isn't anything you haven't told Mr. Crook, is there?"

" Well, of course not. Only—there's no such thing as an inconsiderable detail to him, and if some trifle came my way that didn't appear important to me . . ." I hoped to goodness she wasn't going to ask me what sort of trifle I had in mind, as I hadn't the least idea myself. I just wanted an excuse to keep in touch.

She seemed to be thinking along different lines. " It's a dangerous job," she said, suddenly.

" Being murdered?"

She shook her head impatiently. " Being Mr. Crook. Don't they say it's the first murder that's important? After that, you've comparatively little to lose, so can afford to take chances. I do hope he'll be careful and remember that Colin and his life depend on him."

"Crook 'ull take care of himself for his own sake," I assured her. "He's been doing it for a good many years now."

Suddenly she smiled. "And, of course, we have you on our side as well."

I could see what she meant. Even if Crook's bumped off, she was thinking, there'll still be someone in the know. I don't think it went through her mind that I might be in danger, too. She was out on a limb for Bruce and she'd hang on like grim death, and so long as said death didn't touch him—well, it would be a pity but she'd be able to bear it. Still, half a loaf's better than no bread, and you can't blame a man for fighting for his own hand. She wasn't altogether in the clear herself. Knowing too much can be just as dangerous as knowing too little.

CHAPTER IV

IN THE CIRCUMSTANCES Crook must have found it a bit ironical that I should be the next person to fit a bit into the jigsaw. For some days absolutely nothing happened, not a line from Crook, not so much as a call from Barbie. I couldn't be sure if they were going ahead and leaving me out or if nothing really had happened. I dropped into the Admiral and casually asked Ted if Crook had been along, to hear that he hadn't, the information being given in the voice of a man who's glad to be able to say No. I caught a glimpse of Sherry, but he was deep in conversation with someone else and I didn't stay long. Then I did something that I knew would make Crook turn puce with rage when he heard, but there's a limit to a man's patience and I wanted to get things moving, so without a by-your-leave I trotted round to the Mansions and called on Lizzie Costello. I let her think I was from the Press, and she said she'd already told all she knew, and that wasn't much.

" I told the old one just the same," she said.

" What old one would that be?"

" The one like a red bear. Isn't he one of your lot?"

I immediately recognised this as a description of Crook. " But that was some time ago," I urged. " There might have been developments."

" The only developments there've been have been in Mr. Costello," she told me. " He seems to have forgotten he's a lay minister of the gospel and he's going round like

a roaring lion, with me for the lamb." Anything less
lamb-like than Lizzie with her curlers rampant and her
nose as sharp as a potato knife I could hardly imagine.
"Anyone might think you were afraid of the police, I
tell him. If you've got a clear conscience why should
you worry? Mind you," she added, " he never did see eye
to eye with Madge. Tried to vamp him, I daresay, not
her fault just her nature, any man with a bit of fun in
him would have been highly amused. But not Mr.
Costello, with his talk about the daughters of Babylon
and other words I wouldn't demean myself to repeat.
How come you know so much about them? I ask him,
seeing you're so tooting respectable. All the same," she
came closer and her voice dropped confidentially, " did
he find out about that chap, the one that came calling?"

I had to play this one off the cuff. " Well, not positively," I said, " but he's got a line out."

Mrs. Costello heaved a sigh of comprehension. " Can't
blame him if he is foxed," she said, generously. " I mean,
Madge having all those boy friends. That's what riles
Mr. Costello. Thought you were all for sweetness and
light, I tell him, but when you get a bit of it across the
landing anyone 'ud think it was a cup of cold pizen. Not
that I blame him, really," she added—she was a most
accommodating woman—" some people get religion like
others get polio, some get cured, some don't."

" This chap we were talking of," I urged. She nodded
and the curlers on her forehead bounced like little balls.
" Came just the once, did he?"

" That's right. Mind you, I don't think he had anything to do with it, I mean it wasn't him came back with
her that night. This one was a different cup of tea. Little

dark chap, big hands, black hair, mostly out of a bottle, talk about women being vain. Found him down by the keyhole like a human croquet-hoop. Excuse me. I said. Never saw anyone straighten up so fast. If it's Mrs. Gardiner you want, I told him, she's out. I'd just seen Madge turn into the Admiral, but I wasn't going to tell him that. Well, he asked me, short and nasty, how about Mr. Gardiner? Oh, Madge keeps him in a cupboard, I told him. Bed-ridden, see. No one round here's ever set eyes on him. Between you and me, dear" added Lizzie, "I've sometimes wondered if there ever was any such person. Who shall I say called? I asked him. Madge 'ull want to know."

"What did he say?"

"Tell her it's her friend from the west country. I'll write. Mind you, this was before the murder and he never surfaced again, you can take my word for that, I'd know if he had."

I believed her. "And you told this ginger chap about him?"

"That's right. Don't you fellows divvy your information? He said, That's a funny thing, seeing he was her friend, did he come to the funeral? Well, dear, I hadn't thought about it before, but it's true, he didn't. Mind you, there was plenty did, but not that one."

"You're sure you'd have known him again?" I murmured. "I mean, just seeing him the once."

"I'd have known him," Lizzie assured me, grimly. "I mean, he passed the remark himself. You'll know me again, he said."

"And—you hadn't seen him before?"

She shook her head and once more the curlers flew.

" He was a stranger hereabout. I mean, fancy him asking about Mr. Gardiner."

She went into squeals of laughter. I thought she probably had been fond of Madge in her own way, but nothing could detract from the kind of pride she felt in having lived so close to a woman who'd got herself murdered, finding herself sought out by the Press and now by me.

She couldn't tell me any more, and I went off.

The letter arrived twenty-four hours later.

It came on the afternoon post, while I was out. I found it lying on the hall-table, smeary and grubby-looking. These flats are pretty makeshift, no separate letter-boxes, for instance; the first person out after the postman's called gathers and sorts the mail, and in this house it's practically always Miss Muffett. I used to think she sat at the window watching for the man, though I never once saw a letter addressed to her in all the time I was there. I suppose she had collected them before I got there, or perhaps she simply didn't get any. She was a bundle of curiosity, always peeping from behind curtains, and with her ear at any available key-hole. It occurred to me once that if she'd ever married she was the kind of wife who ends up as the subject of a coroner's enquiry. I could just see her steaming open a letter addressed to her husband, and then fastening it again, but being a bit of a bungler the odds are she'd betray herself, and sooner or later she'd be found strangled or batted over the head as poor Madge had been.

The envelope was very carefully laid on top of two others, also addressed to me. I rather expected to hear the door of the ground floor flat click open, but perhaps

Miss Muffett was at the telephone passing on the glad news—the most extraordinary person has come to live in the flat upstairs, gets anonymous letters, no, of course I haven't opened them, but anyone can see what they are. By this time her imagination would have supplied three or four to bolster up her case.

Any policeman would have known the communication for what it was, the cheap envelope, the address in sprawling capitals obviously intended to deceive—the enclosure was as hackneyed as the rest.

> Look out Mr. Crete you take a friends advice and keep away from what dont concern you that goes for the girl too. Pass it on.

It was signed—Well-Wisher. The postmark was Earl's Court, not far from where I myself live. The obvious deduction was that it had been sent by someone with an interest in the Gardiner case, presumably not on Bruce's side. The correct thing, I know, is to take an anonymous letter to the police or else destroy it and forget about it. There seemed very little sense taking this to the police, since they already believed they had the right man under lock and key, and, like all experts, don't like to have their judgment questioned. The obvious thing was to pass it on to Crook, but I had another idea. It would, I decided, prove an admirable Open Sesame to re-opening negotiations with Barbie Hunter. If she and Crook had any idea of letting my interests lie fallow here was a chance to persuade her to change her mind. Anyway, I decided to risk it.

I didn't ring up to announce my coming, I just went round about six o'clock when I thought she might be back from work. The house in which she and Mrs. Hunter had a flat was in a quiet Kensington street, planted with trees, with window-boxes on practically every sill and great pots of shrubs and flowering plants in the stone areas of the basements. No. 14 had a blue door decorated with a silver dolphin and a charming bow window, painted white. There was the inevitable queue of cars along the kerb, but even they had a more spruce and affluent look than the jalopies that sprawled in the gutters in my street.

The door was opened by a small trim woman whom I realised at once was Barbie's mother. There was no particular physical likeness, but the quality of her voice, the quick fluid movements, the decision, the general air of anticipation and resolve proclaimed her identity.

" She isn't back," she said at once. You could see she was always telling men that Barbie wasn't available. " Is she expecting you?"

" Not precisely," I said, and mentioned my name. " The fact is, there's been a development in the Gardiner affair, I thought she'd wish to know." The words were jolted out of me in a series of staccato jerks.

" Oh, you're Simon. I've heard her speak of you. Come in, won't you?"

There was a brightness about the interior of the flat that matched the outside; I liked at once the gay simplicity of the room no one would be permitted to call a lounge, with its low-built bookcase, the Mexican pottery bowl with its vivid red and yellow motif, the defiant brightness of the scatter cushions on the brown linen covers of the sofa and chairs. Everything seemed to cry aloud of Barbie.

" I was wondering," I said, " if Barbie had had one of these."

I held out my letter. Mrs. Hunter didn't take it, though she recognised it at once for what it was.

" Oh, no," she said in a remote sort of voice, " she'd have told me if she had. Does that mention her?"

" In a way. I'd like you to read it."

She handled the envelope with extreme distaste. " I've never seen one before," she admitted. " Have you shown it to the police?"

" I don't think they'd be particularly interested. I'm going to take it along to Crook. They must come a dime a dozen to him."

She handed the envelope back, then opened a cupboard and brought out some sherry.

" My husband used to say criminals were mostly people of limited mentality," she remarked, filling a glass and handing it to me. " What on earth does the writer of that letter think he's accomplished? It's just a waste of a threepenny stamp. He can't suppose his threats will stop Barbie going ahead."

" I'm sure it won't," I agreed. " In any case, it's too late, now Crook's on the job. It won't stop me either," I added, coolly. " Bruce is a very lucky chap."

" To be arrested for something he didn't do? As a matter of fact, I think he's a very silly one. I warn my daughter she'll spend her life running after him with a dustpan and brush picking up the pieces once they're married. He's not really a practical person at all, apart from his work. I believe he's very good at that."

" Surely it could be that he's had bad luck?" I urged.

" A practical person would have made sure he'd got both his gloves with him before he left the flat. Quite apart from everything else, gloves don't grow on trees. And if he marries Barbie, or rather if she marries him, that's about the size of it, he'll grow increasingly helpless."

" Perhaps she'll be practical enough for two," I suggested.

She gave me an odd look. " Women should be taken care of, not be expected to carry the baby all the time. However, I might as well talk to a stone wall as try and make Barbie see sense."

" Crook would agree with you," I told her. " You know he tried to persuade her to go into a nursing home or something till the affair's cleared up."

" Ridiculous!" declared Mrs. Hunter, obviously linking Crook and Bruce together as impractical creatures. " When anyone could come along during visiting hours, claiming to be a colleague or something, and leave a box of poisoned chocolates or some doctored champagne."

I thought she and Crook would make a good pair; they both knew all the answers.

"Anyway, why should she be in any particular danger?" her mother went on. " She's not in a position to do the real murderer any harm. If this Mr. Crook's all he's cracked up to be he won't give her any information till he's got the whole affair wrapped up."

" I don't think that's what the letter-writer has in

mind," I offered. " But she could be a useful hostage."

" Oh, dear," said Mrs. Hunter. " Cops and robbers. But surely he knows—or she knows, there's nothing to indicate sex, is there?—Mr. Crook wouldn't let that stand in his light. From what I've heard of him he may be a pirate, but he certainly isn't an appeaser."

She took my glass back and refilled it.

" Such a pity this Mrs. Gardiner can't know what's being done on her behalf."

I looked astounded. " How on earth would it help her?"

" I suppose actually it wouldn't. But—you can't be absolutely sure. Look how anxious people are about posthumous fame. You read autobiographies by literary figures who should know better, hoping they'll be read two or three generations hence, when even the royalties can't matter to them then, bequeathing their manuscripts to museums. It's human vanity, I suppose." She changed the subject with bewildering speed. " I do wish I could remember who this woman reminds me of."

This was a development that had never occurred to me. " Mrs. Gardiner?"

" If that's her real name. Mind you, it doesn't ring any bells, and I have the feeling it was a long time ago, but from the instant I saw her picture in the paper I've had a conviction I've seen her somewhere, some time. Not anyone I knew intimately—I suppose it could be someone I worked with in the war in which case I'd never recall her name—or someone I met in a hotel?" She looked at me questioningly. " And she was younger then. And I don't stay in English hotels."

" I doubt if you'd have met her abroad," I said. " I
can hardly picture her even in the country."

" It's so exasperating. Like remembering someone's
name or the title of a play—it's on the tip of your tongue,
but it won't pop out."

" You never went to the Admiral?"

" I didn't even know there was such a place until all
this started; Barbie and I do our drinking at home, I
suppose it sounds absurd but I've hardly ever been inside a London public-house, so where on earth could I
have run across a gin-sodden old hag . . ."

" She wasn't a gin-sodden old hag," I cried. " I never
saw her when she was young, but I should imagine she
might have been quite something in her stage-days, a sort
of Marie Lloyd Junior—what is it, Mrs. Hunter?"

" That's it," cried Mrs. Hunter. " I mean that's where
I saw her. Fancy my not remembering! But it's such a
long time ago, before Barbie's time altogether."

" Then you have got a clue?"

" Yes. Mind you, I still don't remember her name,
anyway she probably wouldn't have used her own on the
stage, they hardly ever do, do they?—but I know where
I saw her. Twenty-five years ago," she added. " No
wonder I didn't remember her. She hasn't really changed
so much as just grown older. She had something then
and I suppose she had it still, if what they say about her
and her attractions are true. It was the Castle Theatre at
Kew. You won't remember it, I expect, it was bombed
out in the war, and never rebuilt, at least they've rebuilt
flats on the site, I understand. But Cyril and I—that's
my husband—used to go every week. Sometimes it was
repertory but mostly it was a sort of revue, musical show

—I don't know the professional description—anyway that's where we used to see her. They changed the programme every week and we used to go on Saturdays. They specialised in new names, quite a number of well-known artistes have graduated from the Castle. I remember Cyril saying, If that woman sticks to it you'll see her name in bright lights in Piccadilly one of these days. She had something, a sort of *joie de vivre*. When suddenly she stopped appearing it was as if a light was missing from a cluster—do you know what I mean?"

"Yes," I said. "She was like that, I understand, almost to the end. The life and soul of the party Ted called her. He was the barman at the Admiral, you know. Is, I mean. I don't know why I used the past tense. You're quite sure you can't remember her name?"

"Quite sure," said Mrs. Hunter, "but it doesn't matter, there must be records or something. Your wonderful Mr. Crook will unearth those."

"No one's come forward who remembered her," I pointed out. "When was this?"

"Between the wars— I suppose it would be from 1936 for about two years. Then she just faded out. I remember we thought she might be having a baby. And then in 1938 we had Barbie and then came the war and that took Cyril—I haven't really thought about her since. How strange to think of coming across her again in these circumstances."

"I gather she was doing domestic work to help out her pension or whatever these last few years. She must have been round about sixty."

Then the telephone rang and Mrs. Hunter went to answer it. When she came back she said, "That was

Barbie. I didn't tell her about your being here, when she's on the job she's as single-minded as a crocodile after its prey. But when she comes back—have we got your telephone number?"

I gave it to her, and my address. " It's a furnished flat," I explained, " and I'm out a lot, so if you don't get an answer the first time don't imagine I've left."

I saw a new suspicion flash into her face. " You're nothing to do with the Press?"

" No. Though Mrs. Costello thinks I am. I'm a free-lance in life—it has its points."

She didn't ask any more questions, I don't think she was particularly interested in me. She did add before I left, "I suppose you're a bachelor?" "Well, yes," I admitted, "I have to plead guilty. One of these days, I suppose, I shall have to kiss the rod like anyone else."

I tried to ring Crook's office from a call-box, but he was out and I left a message with a very aloof-sounding chap called Parsons.

" Mrs. Gardiner had an engagement for about two years before the war at the Castle Theatre, Kew," this character repeated without a grain of enthusiasm. " I'll see Mr. Crook gets the message. Anything else?"

" Well, yes," I said, piqued by his reception of my in-formation. " You might tell him, just for the record, I've had an anonymous letter warning me off the grass and suggesting that Miss Hunter follows suit."

I didn't wait for his comment; I rang off.

A dreary sort of drizzling rain had begun while I was drinking sherry with Mrs. Hunter, and now it was thickening into a steady downpour. A chap sheltering under an adjacent shop-front came forward as I left the box to know if I could give him three pennies for a three-penny-piece. I hesitated for a moment. It's an old trick, as old as the light-for-a-fag set-up. While you're fumbling in your pocket for change the chap taps you in the bread-basket and helps himself to your wallet before you've got your breath back. However, this chap seemed on the up-and-up, took his coppers, thanked me and vanished inside the phone-box. I walked along, stung by the miserable rain, until I saw a pub called The Daisy Chain that advertised snacks at the bar. I went in to find the place fairly full, but two or three spare stools up at the bar, so I hung my coat on a peg and joined the queue. You can never be sure when you may not make a useful contact in a strange pub. The snacks were good and substantial and even Crook would have passed the beer. I bought myself a second pint, got into conversation with the chap next door about the state of British politics—it was one of the crisis periods that kept recurring all that year—and came out to find the rain had thinned. I had a sneaking hope that Barbie might have turned up and got her mother's message and think it worth while contacting me, so I hastened back, but no joy. The phone was as silent as graves are popularly (and sometimes erroneously) supposed to be until just after 11, when Crook came through. He sounded as chipper as Saturday morning.

"You're a dark horse," he greeted me. "Still, that's the kind I usually back. Now, about Madge. I've put on a man to go round looking for info., first thing in the morning. If Madge was working regularly at the Castle she'd be bound to have a London agent, and though they've probably changed a good deal since the war, the personnel, I mean, if we're lucky we should be able to turn up someone who recognises her picture. The police are being very civil," he added in the voice of a man who refuses to be bowled over no matter how huge a miracle may appear, " let me have one of the photos when she was young, and we've had it blown up. Rogers 'ull be taking it around. By the way, Bill said something about a letter."

" That's right," I agreed. " The usual gypsy's warning. Only this one happens to mention Barbie, too. Wait a minute, I'll get it, it's in my coat pocket."

Only when I went to look it wasn't.

I stood there for a moment, with the receiver dangling from my table, till I heard Crook's voice shouting through the ether.

" Well," he said when I picked up the receiver again, " I thought it must have turned into a snake and mistaken you for Cleopatra."

So I told him. " I swear I had it when I went into The Daisy Chain," I said. " I hung my coat on a peg near the door . . ."

" Never abandon your coat in a strange pub," said Crook, in reproachful tones. " Too simple for a chap who knows what he's looking for to slip his hand in and gain possession, you're spouting away like Niagara up at the counter—were you, by the way?"

" Well, I was," I admitted. " But to no one I'd ever seen before. You know how it is. Anyway, how would anyone know it was in my pocket?"

" A good question," said Crook. " Happen to notice the chap who asked you for change?"

I could hear myself gasp. "You're not suggesting that he . . ."

"Ain't suggesting anything, just considerin' possibilities. Well, you remember what it said, I suppose? Not that a non-existent letter can be put in as evidence."

"Mrs. Hunter saw it," I put in eagerly. "I took it round—I told her I was going to bring it along and show you."

"Anyone else?" asked Crook.

"Well, you can bet your bottom dollar the old girl on my ground floor saw it, though even she could hardly read through an opaque envelope. Of course," I added, "there could be another."

"Up to you," said Crook in oracular tones. "A nod's as good as a wink to a blind horse. Of course, if you pulled it out of your pocket with your gloves or the evening paper . . ."

But I was quite sure I hadn't lost it that way.

"Got your address on it?" Crook went on. "Well, of course it had. That narrows the field a bit. Be sure to let me know if some conscientious cuss picks it up and sends it back."

He rang off and I stayed beside the telephone, but though I waited till half-past midnight Barbie never came through.

She rang next morning, though, "Mother told me about Mrs. Gardiner," she said. "What's Mr. Crook done about it?"

"Give him a chance," I urged. "He only knew last night."

"I thought he was the kind that moved faster than _at,_" said Barbie, ungratefully. "I'd ring him myself, but I've tried him every day and last time he told me I could stop wasting my coppers, when there was anything to report he'd let me know. What's more," she added, " he had the nerve to say that probably prison was quite a rest-cure for Colin. No need for him to be anxious now I'm on the ball, he said. I reckon he's been bounced half off his bonce by his well-wishers."

" He's probably used to being given a free hand," I said cautiously.

" Monarch of all he surveys. I know. Still, it's you and Mother who've got the ball rolling."

She rang off and I felt cheered; I was sure now that, so far as she was concerned, I was definitely " in."

CHAPTER V

THERE WAS another silence that seemed endless. Then Crook rang up. He'd got some info. at last on the late Madge Gardiner, and he'd be imparting it to his client, Miss B. Hunter, that evening at his office. If I was interested I was welcome to come along.

I didn't need a second invitation.

And if we'd had to wait it was certainly something worth waiting for. Even Barbie had to admit that. I'd wanted to pick her up at her studio and take her to tea or something, but she said she'd come direct—they were working outside the London area that week—and if there was time she'd have a bone with me afterwards. So we all met at 123 Bloomsbury Street.

" We have to hand it to Sherlock Holmes here," said Crook, when he'd settled us in the two most uncomfortable chairs in the metropolis, " he put me on the trail all right."

" Thank Mrs. Hunter," I murmured.

" Did it help?" demanded Barbie, practically.

" Well, what do you think, sugar? Once I got a line on her I had this chap go the round of the agencies. Like I said, not many of the old crowd are still functioning, but at last he got wind of an old boy called Percy Cutbill. He's out of the rat race now, but he was a real pushover for the job in his day. Lives in two rooms in Streatham and he can't ever be short of wallpaper. You never saw such a place." (I realised with a shock that Crook had gone down in person.) " Photos, framed letters, telegrams, obituaries, the lot. He's pushing eighty if he's a day and pushing pretty hard, but he's still got plenty up in the attics." He tapped his own forehead meaningly. " Well, he saw the photo and he recognised it. ' Fancy Margery Gay turning up after all these years,' he said. ' Where for Pete's sake did you get that?' And off he went into a spiel about the dear old days. I remember her coming in like it was yesterday, he said. He's an immense old boy, with rolls of yellow-white curls and a face like a tiger. I could see at once she had something. Now, let's see, what was she calling herself in those days? I do remember saying no one with a monniker like that will ever top the bill, you want something a bit frisky and gay, and she said, That's it, Mr. Cutbill. Margery Gay. Smart as a whip, she was. Too bad she should have died like that. If she could have stuck to it she'd have reached the top. He leaned over and pulled a picture down from the wall, and there she was, Margery Gay, 1938, great big sprawling signature, great big beaming smile. She had the right temperament, he said, and then a long spiel about temperament and talent and the relationship between the two. I wouldn't have interrupted him for all the beer in the brewery. A happy marriage, he said, about the only kind there is. Well, you know how it is, they always dress it up with a bit of parsley round the dish. I got a word in there, not easy, though, talk about an elephant going through the eye of a needle. How about marriage? I asked. Any talk of a husband? And he grinned all over his big red face—he's been a lad in his time, you take my word for it—and he told me, They were all married, boy

—Boy! Me!—with or without the ring. Nothing to me, only some of them wanted to be billed in a double act and that's every agent's headache. One half's always twice as good as the other, and you have to carry the can for the lame dog. Left us to have a baby, the old chap went on. A little girl, I heard. She never came back. Of course, there was the war. I saw the bit in the paper about her, I've got it somewhere. And out came a thing as big as the Domesday Book and he went through it like a mouse through cheese. Here it is, he said, and there it was—all four lines of it."

Barbie and I stared at him. " Four lines?" said Barbie. " That's absurd."

" Lucky in a war to get that much," Crook assured her. " Seeing she'd been out of the picture for about six years. Naturally, it was only the local Press, she didn't rate the national . . ."

" Who are we talking about?" I interrupted.

" Margery Gay, of course. Music-hall artiste killed by flying bomb. Date 1944. Shakes you a bit, don't it?"

I leaned back and said nothing. Barbie gasped, " You mean we've been following the wrong trail all this time?"

" Someone has to be wrong, don't they?" Crook agreed sympathetically. "And seeing it can't be us it has to be old Percy Cutbill. Not that it's his fault, he only went on what he saw in the paper."

" But why should anyone think she was dead if she wasn't?"

" I'm coming to that," said Crook. "You don't remember the V.1.s, of course," he assured Barbie. " And I suppose you were in the Forces or something," he added to me.

" Do you mind?" I murmured. "I was at school . . ."

Crook didn't pay the least attention. " Funny," he said. " I remember that raid. A Sunday afternoon it was. We hadn't really got used to the fly-bombs then, they only started coming over early that year, why, chaps used to turn out and stand on the pavement and look up when they went by. Like great big kids' toys they looked, all bright and silver in the sunlight. Only when the light started flashing in their tails you went to ground pronto. Literally to ground, I mean. The number of suits—and they were on coupons then, remember—that were ruined by their owners dropping down in the nearest gutter or pelting for those little sheds that passed for shelters 'ud set up a tailor in Clarges Street. I went to look and then I realised it was coming down any second—once the light stopped flashing your guardian angel had to be pretty direct on the ball if you weren't going to have the hat goin' round for a personal wreath in the next day or two—I remember I had a big wardrobe in my room— bought it off the pavement in Camden Town for a quid dear knows how many years before, and, believe it or not, I was inside like a flash. The things I do for England! Then I heard the crash. It seemed to go on for ever, as if London Bridge really was falling down at last. And then I found I was stuck. Blast, you see. Blast was the great enemy of the day. Staggering the number of bodies you found after the big raids, no injury that you could see, just caught the blast, specially in narrow streets, the breath literally sucked out of them. And that same blast had jammed the door of my prison. Well, I thought, this must be the cheapest coffin in England. Still, I huffed and I puffed and suddenly the door burst open and there

I was sprawling on my fanny like some darn great beetle. And when I looked out of the window—you never saw such dereliction." He put such force into the word I felt myself shudder. "Great blocks of flats smashed like kids' toys, furniture blasted into the street, glass everywhere, it was like a bomb exploding in the Crystal Palace. Plane had come down in a square, see, and the blast couldn't get out, round and round it went . . ." I looked at Barbie, she was as enthralled as I. He rushed along like a river in full spate, using up a week's energy for a normal man, painting a picture for us we'd never seen in our lives. You could almost smell the stink of the bomb, the burning, hear the cries and the crumble of great stones. And he looked such a common-place down-to-earth sort of cuss in his appalling bright brown suiting.

"I suppose Madge was in London in the area at the time," said Barbie, who kept her head admirably, "and someone reported her dead. Why didn't she contradict the rumour?"

"Because those raids were a godsend to a few, gave them a chance to disappear and start all over again somewhere else. Say you were AWOL, with the M.P.s looking for you, and the report went round that you'd been seen vanishing into a shelter on the night of a big raid, and say that shelter got a direct hit—a number of them did, there was one near me, under the street it was, the authorities opened it next morning, took one look and shut it up again. No one walking over it nowadays realises he's walking over a communal grave. Or you could have been seen thereabouts and never surfaced again and it 'ud be reasonable to suppose you dived for safety and —well, hit your head on the bottom."

" But I thought everyone had identity cards and ration books. How could they manage without them?" Barbie was the most practical creature I had ever met.

" So they did, sugar, and very lucky for the Black Marketeers, too. There was a big sale for fake ration books, same like passports for refugees after the war. I know more than one chap who was able to retire after the war on his profits. Mind you, you had to know the ropes, dodge in and out of the Man Power Act like the famous wireworm through a three-pronged fork. Or there were the stolen books, of course; and the chaps who surged into the Town Hall after a big raid claiming all documents had been destroyed. They started 'em off with emergency cards, but if you knew your onions you could often get a duplicate, I knew chaps who had three and four . . ."

He brooded a minute, then shook himself to say, " But that ain't what Madge did. She just swopped identities with a lady called Gardiner who caught her packet that afternoon. It seems she was living in a hostel there and working at a factory in Fulham, and that was a place that took a beating too. We've traced a Mrs. Brett who was living there at the time, bright as a new sixpence even now, lodging with a married son in Bath. She remembers someone called Madge, no one bothered with surnames there, she said, but she'd been on the music-hall stage, used to give them a song sometimes, had lost a husband and a little girl but didn't want to talk about it. Well, there's nothing unusual about that in a war. Mrs. Brett has a nice turn of phrase. Sunday afternoon she said, and we were having a nice game of gin rummy, didn't really know about the plane till the house started to come down over us; when I come round again there I was with my head under a chair and my son-in-law (home on leave he was, did you ever?) lying dead beside me, and I called upon my God to save me and He heard!" The old woman's triumphant voice rang through the room. " Mrs. B. was carted off to a hospital and kept there a couple of days and when she came back she started calling the rota. What happened to Daisy? Belle? Amelia? Madge? Well, they told her, Madge was among those who'd just disappeared. There were corpses under those ruins the Recording Angel 'ud have been hard put to give a name to. And if there weren't relatives coming up and joining the queues to see if they could identify this one or that—streets all roped off, W.V.S. sitting at little tables taking particulars—well, your name went down on the roll of honour. And Madge—her name was Daniels then, I'm coming to that in a minute—was never seen again by any of them. They found her hand-bag with its ration book and identity card, and they were handed in when no one claimed them, and—there were four lines in the local rag."

" And she became Mrs. Gardiner, who really had been killed in the raid?"

" I see you're right on the ball, sugar."

" But wasn't it awfully risky?"

" Everything's risky, even getting born. And she had her reasons. It wasn't Margery Gay she was buryin' but Madge Daniels. And why should she want her to go on existin'? As for Mrs. G., Mrs. Brett remembers her, a proper gloombird she said, no wonder hubby had opted for a better land some years earlier, two sons in the Far East, one never came back and by the time the other did the raid was ancient history. She was one of those they identified, only thing they didn't find was her ration book, etc. Found Madge's though, and seeing she never surfaced it was reasonable to assume she never would."

" I suppose you're going to tell us why she wanted to adopt a dead woman's personality," I suggested. "As Barbie says, it was pretty chancy."

" You're holding the stick at the wrong end," Crook assured. "She didn't want to adopt a dead woman's identity, she wanted to lose her own. And as for it being risky . . ." he leaned backwards and picked up Volume 2 of the London Telephone Directory, " just look at these —columns and columns, all Gardiners if they don't all spell it the same way. No, provided she went far enough afield she was in the clear. She had to call herself someone because of identification papers, so she produced Mrs. G.'s. She didn't have to have a photo and she only had to mention the raid and no one would ask questions, it was happening all the time. The morning after a raid the main London stations were like a Cup Final, the L.C.C. coping with one lot, particularly Mums and kids who'd probably been evacuated once and now found they couldn't take London any more, and the others who were travellin' under their own steam, going to friends or relations or just taking a chance. Madge wouldn't stand out in that crowd; she'd just have to remember who she was, and that'ud take all she knew at first. There was no difficulty about getting a job, though you couldn't always take the one you wanted. Still, the authorities wouldn't be on Madge's tail, not in either name, since the real Mrs. G. was dead. Mind you, getting around the country was no picnic in those days, trains mightn't run, might run to quite a different destination from the one they were meant for, sometimes they stopped half-way and turned everyone out, and you waited for another to come along—to anywhere. Still, I daresay it didn't matter much to her where she went. She'd given the little girl away . . ."

"What about her husband? You said her real name was Daniels."

I was interested in this bit, too. "That's right. Mrs. Foreman, that is Clare's official Mum, told Chapple that the girl was adopted, but was really her sister's child. She couldn't keep her, she said, husband deserted and never came back, she had to get work and the work was in the cities. Mrs. F. and hubby were comfortably-off but no family and no prospects. Madge took the little girl down to the country to stay with her sister when the raids started; and when the dam burst Mrs. F. offered to adopt the little girl."

"What dam?"

"We managed to track Madge down through the sister; she'd been a Miss Lighterman, which is a nice unusual name, so all we had to do was find another Miss Lighterman—assuming they were true sisters which, praise the pigs, they were, first name Margaret or Margery—and there she was. Married Joseph Carter Daniels in 1936, had a little girl christened Maureen Clare in 1938. In 1940 Daniels was picked up by the Army, no question of reserved occupation, work never seems to have appealed to him, and he went AWOL the following year when the regiment was due to be sent overseas—after Pearl Harbour, that was. That put Madge in a spot. A deserter's wife can't claim army allowances, she had to find work, so back she came to the Smoke, leaving the child with Mr. and Mrs. Phineas Foreman. Then at the beginning of '42 Daniels surfaced, facing a charge of wilful murder. He'd been having him a ball with a W.A.A.C.—we didn't call them W.R.A.C.s then, she'd overplayed her hand, there'd been a punch-up, and she got the worst of it. Mind you, she wasn't much loss to the Forces, they wouldn't have kept her long anyway, not the condition she was in, but knocking out pregnant women never gets you much sympathy in this country. There was never any actual proof the child was his, there was a nice batch to choose from—but that isn't why he went for her with a meat-axe—metaphorically, of course. She knew or she found out he was a deserter. Well, he probably had no ration book, was living on the Black Market and anything he could scrounge, and there were a lot of ways if you knew the road in; anyhow, she seems to have threatened him— you do as I say or I'll turn you in. You could almost call it suicide, and his counsel called it manslaughter, but the judge wouldn't wear either of those. Daniels stood trial for murder, Madge refused to give evidence, and the judge put on the black cap. But the jury added a strong recommendation to mercy. Could be they thought there was enough death going on overseas without adding even one more, or they believed him when he said he never meant to do her a mortal injury, she came for him and he hit back and he

was stronger—anyway, there was an eleventh-hour re-
prieve, and he went to Foxville, the big West Country
prison."

I drew in a sharp breath. Tell her it's the one from the
West Country, the stranger had told Lizzie Costello. Just
in time I remembered that Crook knew nothing of that
visit, and I held my tongue.

"And that's when Madge gave up her little girl?"
Barbie was saying, and Crook was telling her Yes. It
couldn't, he pointed out, be very pleasant to have to tell
your daughter that her father was doing a life sentence
for murder.

"Not that it is life these days," he added. "Twelve
to thirteen years at most. Provided you behave yourself,
that is. Which he didn't."

"But when she was grown up wouldn't she want to
know?" Barbie insisted. "Wouldn't Mrs. Foreman tell
her?"

"Grow up, sugar," Crook admonished her. "Where
was the sense in giving her a fresh start if she's got to
learn the truth just when it matters most she shouldn't
know it? No, Maureen Daniels was dead and buried,
and there wasn't a thing to be said against nice, pretty
Clare Foreman. She was christened Maureen—Mrs. F.
did tell Chapple that—but she thought the name a bit
common, and used her second one. She never even knew
she had an auntie, and officially since 1944 she hasn't.
The real mother gives up all her rights, no surreptitious
peeking, no phone calls to Mum Number Two, it's slam
the door and on your way."

"Wouldn't Daniels have to sign the consent form,
too?" I asked.

" That wouldn't hurt him. According to what Mrs. F. told Chapple, and she must have got it from Madge, he never showed an atom of intcrest in the kid, didn't even support her. Madge did a double job. No, he wouldn't know who the adoptive mother was, the real one would see to that, and luckily he was where he couldn't muscle in."

" And how much does Chapple know now?"

" I fancy Madge was going to put him in the picture, only someone prevented her. Any more questions?"

" Yes," I said. " How did he come to know her at all? He'd have been told she was killed in an air-raid. Or was the sister in the secret all along?"

" As to that," said Crook, " your guess is as good as mine, but Madge didn't strike me as the sort of woman to do anything by halves. Still, it was her gave the show away. Chapple told me as much. It seems that Mrs. F. passed in her dinner-pail about a year ago, and Madge went to the funeral. I daresay she'd been like the people in the hymn watching from afar, she could get the news of the marriage from the local paper—they lived in a fairly remote country place and Phineas Foreman was quite a big frog in a little pond. His daughter's wedding 'ud be news, so Madge would know who her girl had married, and she'd hear when the sister died. I suppose she thought the funeral 'ud give her a legitimate chance of setting eyes on Clare again. Anyway, the Chapples went to the funeral as chief mourners, and there Madge was, looking about as unobtrusive as a unicorn in a string of pet poodles. I suppose she kidded herself there was no likelihood of her being recognised, she'd just trail along with the anonymous crowd that generally gathers at a local interment. Only it turned out to be a rotten day and there wasn't much of a crowd, and you could hardly fail to notice her, a big woman swathed in black—she'd even robbed a museum somewhere for a black-edged handkerchief—acting like Niobe. It was that more than her appearance that caught Chapple's interest. He said you could see she really cared, possibly the only one there who did—barring the girl herself, one assumes. There they were standing round the pit, rain starting to fall, parson snuffling through the responses, clay all sticky-gold—Chapple's got a nice turn of phrase—box going down a bit jerkily, and Madge just standing there with the tears pouring faster than the rain. No wonder she nailed his attention. And when it was over she just went on standing, looking around like the prophet Elijah waiting for a fiery chariot to take her back to the station and the charioteer seemed to have lost his way. Well, Chapple did the civil, asked if he could give her a lift anywhere seeing her car hadn't arrived, and she went with him like a bird—a big dazed bird. In the car I suppose she felt some sort of explanation was necessary, so she choked out something about it being her only sister, the last of her generation, and then little Mrs. C. ups and says, My mother didn't have a sister; she was killed in the war. Madge seems to have kept her head to the extent of not giving the show away, just mumbled something about them thinking it best this way, getting married again—old Phineas was a starchy type—well, of course there's marriage and marriage, three kinds really, Church, register office and marriage in the sight of God, and the Chapples seem to have taken it for granted that

Madge's union was the last kind. Only *he* was on the ball, knowing that Clare had been adopted by her own aunt. Seems to have acted like a gent, too. When he set her down he gave her his business card, told her to get in touch with him at the office if there was anything he could do."

" And she did?"

" Well, have a heart, sugar, she was human. What would you have done? Pussy was out of the sack anyway. Mind you, she didn't tell him about Daniels, just that she'd married a no-good, overfond of the bottle, a war deserter, hadn't set eyes on him in twenty years. And at that time it could have been true."

" Do we know where he is now?"

" We've a good idea where he was not long since. Lizzie's description of the nameless visitor to the Mansions ties up with what we know about Daniels. How did he find her?" He shrugged his big shoulders. " He came out in '58, lost his remission on account of an escape attempt in 1950, during which a warder got beaten up. As to where he is now—well, all I can tell you is he ain't back in the pen."

" How can you be sure?" asked Barbie. " Couldn't he be using another name?"

" It don't matter how many names you choose, you can change the shape of your face and the colour of your hair, but you can never alter your dabs. If he'd been picked up in any name the authorities would have made the check and nailed him."

" But doesn't the Home Office keep a record of prisoners?"

" He ain't been a prisoner since '58, they've got no more power over him, so long as he keeps his nose clean, than they have over you or me."

" Perhaps he's going straight." Barbie sounded quite prim.

" They tell you water can run uphill, but you don't often see it doing it. He'd be about 55 now, he was a bit younger than Madge, he'd spent over sixteen years in quod, and he don't seem to have had a regular trade even before that. He'd chucked the army without H.M.'s permission, he messed around with a girl and put her down for the count, he helped to deprive a warder of the sight of one eye while in captivity—one way and another he don't sound the sort of chap you'd rush to put on your pay-roll, even if he did come to you hat in hand. Mind you, I don't say he even tried, but you have to admit that life, even for reformed criminals, is hard. What's he got when he comes out of chokey? A lot of good advice, the chaplain's blessing, five bob and an introduction to the Labour Exchange. He can't draw the dole till he's got an address, he can't get an address till he can put down a week's rent, he ain't got any stamps on his card, he won't even get National Assistance till he's got somewhere to live. You can call it reaping where he sowed if you like, but it's a precious barren harvest. Odds are he's been living on his wits—we know he has one buddy because of the skewwhiff phone call that came to Simon—Tell him I haven't got it meaning the blackmail money. How he met up with Madge again—well, you know what they say, sooner or later everyone comes to London. Odds are he'd come beetling back to the Smoke, they mostly do. Up to that time he must have thought he was a widower, Madge was officially dead, remember. And even if you're in durance vile you're still next-of-kin when your wife snuffs it. Remember, Simon," he turned to me —during this period of explanation they'd mostly behaved as though I wasn't there—" that chap, Ted, said Madge came in one evening looking as if she'd seen a ghost. And not the only one. It must have been a bit of a shock to him, too, banging up against her again, when he'd thought her in the grave for nearly twenty years."

" I don't see how you can be sure he'd know her again?" objected Barbie.

" Your Mum recognised her picture, didn't she, and she hadn't seen her for even longer. Anyway, so husbands always assure me, wives don't change, they just develop, often for the worse, but they're the same person grown older. And Madge isn't one you'd easily forget. Mind you, he played it cagey, coming round to Mayflower Mansions to get the lay of the land. Y'see, he wouldn't even know what name she was using, and I daresay he thought it might be useful to have a little of the gen. before he went calling there. Mrs. C. gave him the name—Gardiner—and the fact that there wasn't any Mr. G."

" But surely he couldn't have made any claim on her after all that time?"

" She was his wife, sugar. The old ball and chain. She'd made a new life for herself, and I daresay it occurred to him it might be worth her while to pay him off to keep him quiet. And then, of course, there was the girl."

" But he wouldn't *know* anything about her."

" After talking for twenty minutes to Madge he would. Like getting pennies out of a kid's money-box getting info. from her. He'd only have to mention his daughter and she'd be up in arms. We haven't got a daughter, you agreed to the arrangement yourself. Anyway, she's married and safe, got a little boy and a good husband, right out of our world—oh, I can just hear her, and every word a nail in her own coffin. Mind you, there were pictures of the little boy in the flat, Chapple got those for her, she's never seen him in the flesh, of course. The situation was cut to measure for him. Unless Madge helped him out he'd find the girl and tell her the truth. You might say it was unlikely he'd succeed, but it wasn't impossible. Why, there may even have been a letter from Chapple in the flat, anything."

" He can't have known surely, or he'd have gone to Chapple direct," Barbie urged.

" Well," said Crook, thoughtfully, " no coward soul (I trust) is mine, but I'd think a long while before I'd try any blackmailing tricks in that direction. He's as tough as the Rock of Gibraltar."

" He couldn't do anything, though, without his wife finding out."

" She's going to find out now anyway. Even Chapple sees that."

Barbie threw herself back with an impatient gesture. " It's all such a waste," she cried, " all this adopting and covering up, it can't change the truth. Whatever happens she's still the daughter of a man who served a sentence for murder, all they've done is make a phony of her."

" You're tough, sugar," said Crook, " but it might

shake even you down to learn a thing like that about your own father. He died in the war, didn't he?"

" That's right."

" Suppose someone could prove to you that his story was the same as Joe Daniels, would you thank them? Or if you were your mother would you let your girl know the truth?"

There was a moment's complete silence. Then she said, " I think sometimes how unfair it is that I should never have known him, he was killed when I was about four, but when I think what some people have to bear— no, I suppose you're right. But she's got to know now."

" She's a woman now, she's got a husband—kids are defenceless. And you have to recall," he added, jumping back a few paragraphs, " Madge was living in a bit of a glasshouse herself. Borrowing someone else's name, using someone else's documents, causing a false entry to be made in the register—you can probably get life for that— no, she'd turn over every flat stone in sight in the hopes of finding the fairy gold—I fancy she kept Chapple to the last—threatening her was like taking pennies out of a blind man's hat." He waited a moment to let that sink in, then turned to me and said, " No more letters, I take it?"

" Letters?" said Barbie. " Oh, you mean the anonymous one you showed to Mother. It's funny, she isn't easy to shock, but that appalled her. What made you take it round?"

" Good thing he did," said Crook, " seeing it vanished so soon afterwards. I don't say even your mum's word would convince the police that letter ever existed, but it's convinced me."

" You mean, it was stolen? Who on earth would want it?"

" The chap who wrote it, perhaps."

"Because of finger-prints? But surely there'd be far too many to be any use to anyone. The postman, the sorter, the collector, anyone who might have handled it before it came into Simon's possession. Or can you identify hand-writing if the words are all printed?"

"I ain't an expert," confessed Crook, "but there could have been something. Hang on to any others that come like grim death. The first is usually just a warning, Keep off the Grass, there could be a concealed bomb. Odds are it's just plain ordinary lawn, but you can't be a hundred per cent sure, can you?"

" There's one aspect of the case we haven't considered," I put in, wondering if Crook would blast me off the earth for making the suggestion. "We're all taking for granted that Madge was killed by a black-mailer, but there isn't, as you say, a hundred per cent proof that that's so. She was flashing her money about in the bar that night like nobody's business, someone might have thought he'd like a share . . . Oh, all right," I added to the bleak silence that followed my words. " It was just an idea."

" You go on having ideas," Crook encouraged me. " You can't ever have too many."

" Anyway she wouldn't have opened her door to any Tom, Dick or Harry in the state she was in that night," Barbie urged.

" The police didn't see the state she was in," Crook pointed out, " and don't forget, we're the Colin Bruce

Defence Committee, working strictly on hunches. Still, not to worry. Sooner or later our chap will get just that bit too clever that lands nearly every criminal in the net and then we'll have him. Like that." He opened and shut his enormous fist. Mrs. Costello had said Daniels— the mysterious visitor, that is—had big hands, too.

CHAPTER VI·

WE DIDN'T STAY with Crook much longer. Barbie agreed to come and have some food with me, after which I couldn't get away fast enough.

"It's so hard to remember that he has other cases on his mind," she told me, thoughtfully. "Don't let's take a taxi, let's walk a little way."

I was afraid there might be some palaver about having to ring Mummy, but she didn't mention Mrs. Hunter, not then. But during dinner I learnt quite a bit about herself. Mr. Hunter—Captain Hunter he'd been then—was killed on D-Day, and Mummy had coped, pretty successfully come to that. Gone to work, given Barbie a decent education and, above all, never made her feel she ought to be grateful.

"Gratitude," said Barbie. "The most horrible of all the virtues. Making other people feel—what's that American word?—obligated. People should do things for love or else leave them alone. And, of course, mostly they do. Love of the other person, like Madge giving up her little girl—or love of yourself. And if you've done it for love of yourself why should you expect anyone's gratitude? I'm not putting myself out for Colin, I'm doing it for me, because without Colin what have I?"

I might have said she had a good deal, her work that she loved, her future, home, mother—the lot. But I let it ride. As for Mrs. Hunter—well, said Barbie, she's got into the way of thinking of Colin as the son she and

Daddy didn't have. I didn't say anything to that, either. If I was honest with myself I'd have to admit I was in this for no unselfish reason. Only most people are less candid about their motives.

After dinner I thought we might have gone on somewhere, but she said she had to go back; she'd be rehearsing the whole day to-morrow, and she had a lot to tell her mother.

" I'll keep in touch," she promised, as the taxi stopped at her door. She didn't even ask me in, she had too much to do. I let the taxi go and started walking aimlessly in the direction of my flat. It seemed to me that at this moment I was living on two separate planes of existence, had almost become two different people. There was Barbie's Simon, who'd only been in existence about a fortnight, who was so new he was still something of a stranger to me. Living on your own develops an egocentric mentality; I'd known girls in the past, of course, but they were like shadows passing across a scene, vanishing and leaving no trace behind. Barbie was the first who seemed to live in three dimensions. Hitherto I hadn't had to consider anyone but myself, and though I couldn't pretend my position here was a disinterested one, Barbie had managed to complicate it in a way I wouldn't have believed possible two weeks ago. On a different level, but at the same period in time, was the Simon Crete known to the people among whom I worked, Doggett, the chaps at the Horse and Mariner, innumerable other contacts upon whom I relied for a living. The further I got from Barbie's flat the remoter her Simon seemed to become. Even then I suppose I knew he hadn't got a permanent existence. I thought of us always as being together now; to-morrow was like a room with the blinds drawn and me standing on the other side of the glass.

Remembering the more familiar Simon turned my steps in the direction of the Horse and Mariner. There was a chap I'd met there, called Tom Fraser, who had asked me if I knew where he could acquire a new young dog for a smallish track he ran on the outskirts of the city. I'd inquired of Doggett who claimed to have just the job.

" If ever I had a potential champion through my hands Lefty is it," he had told me. " If I kept him myself I'd get four times what I'm asking in a year from now." But he never seemed able to sustain his interest to that pitch.

When I turned into the Horse and Mariner the place was pretty full and blue with tobacco smoke. I saw Tom with a chap I didn't know sitting against the far wall and I went over to join them. They were discussing to-morrow's chances. Queen of Sheba was their fancy and she was a good bitch, but I knew, barring a miracle, she wouldn't win.

" You want to put your money on Mickey Rooney," I said. " By the way, about that dog you wanted. My pal's got one that might suit."

I gave him the details.

" Where is he now?" Tom asked.

" Doggett's got him, of course."

Tom winked and nudged his companion with his elbow. " Listen to him," he said. " Butter wouldn't melt in his mouth, would it? He almost makes you believe there is such a chap."

I was so astounded that for a minute I couldn't speak. "Are you suggesting . . .?"

"Ever hear of Mrs. 'Arris?" asked Tom. "Well, if this pal of yours is so knowledgeable, why don't we ever see him? Don't tell me he never comes to the Smoke?"

He did, of course, but not very often. He didn't need to, with me on the spot.

"If you don't believe me," I said, "why don't you go down and collect Lefty yourself? You'll want to look him over anyway."

"Lefty?"

"The dog."

"What made him give a brute a name like that?"

"What's wrong with it?"

"It's unlucky, mate, that's what it is. Ever heard of a play called *Waiting for Lefty*? Well, I ask you."

"I don't get to the theatre much these days," I said. "Too pricey."

"This was a long while ago. My Dad (they'd call him a fellow-traveller these days, I suppose, but he was just a red-flag waver then), he used to talk about it. All about a lot of taxi-drivers beefing about their wrongs. Why don't they get in and do something about it? my Dad shouted. He was all for action, direct as you make it."

"With a bomb?" I suggested, and he nodded.

"Though my old lady was the bomb in our house. Not surprising Dad curled up and passed in his checks before he was fifty. Mind you, he wasn't eating too well in the 'thirties. Still, this is the age of progress, isn't it?"

"If you're going down in the morning," I said, "I'd better let Doggett know."

He asked softly, " What 'ud happen if I went without any warning?"

" He might be out, of course."

" But if you give him the say-so he'll get time to materialise." He turned to the tall man beside him, who'd practically not uttered to date. " Tell me, Harry, did you ever hear of a man born when he was—how old is this chap, anyway?"

I thought a moment. " About fifty-four or five, I suppose."

" Well, born middle-aged." He was grinning as he spoke.

Frink—that was Harry's other name and he was abnormally tall, how tall I didn't realise till I saw him on his feet—said, " Oh, ay," in a northern accent. He said it so casually that for an instant neither Tom nor I got the message. Then Tom said, " You're joking, of course?"

" It's no joking matter," said Frink. He was handsome in a haggard sort of way, very black and white, not, I thought, the type I'd care to meet in a dark lane if he thought he had a grudge against me. " When I was a lad more than once I'd hear tell of men who'd been born—into this planet—thirty or thirty-five years old. Just appeared, hadn't travelled, no past, hadn't come from the south or any place you can name, one day they weren't in this world, and the next day there they were."

" You should have called the police," said Tom, trying to play it light.

But it was clear that Frink was in deadly earnest. He could be a maniac, of course, fanatics mostly are and he was a fanatic on this point if on no other, regular King

Charles's Head to him. But he believed every word he spoke. After a bit I began to get the feeling he could have pointed out the men he had in mind and proved they were creatures with no human past. It was eerie. He admitted that himself.

"Gave me the shivers sometimes. I mean, if you start on this earth thirty years old, say, what's happened to the years you never lived? Someone has to have 'em."

He had a real Highland voice. I swear the temperature dropped a couple of degrees when he spoke.

"And you get thinking," he went on, "if that could happen to him why not to me?"

"But it hasn't," I pointed out, urgently. "I know who my Mum and Dad were, and where they were born. I don't doubt you could say the same."

"Ah, but that's now," said Frink in his deep voice that contrived to be melancholy and musical at one and the same time. "You could wake one morning and find yourself a grown man in some other sphere of activity. Maybe some of the other planets are further ahead with research than we are, these—strangers—could come from a world we haven't explored yet. When I came south I was glad, everything seemed so ordinary. Now I wish I'd been older at the time, had the nerve to ask questions, what they remembered, if they remembered . . ."

This was so unlike the normal pub talk I couldn't find anything to say, but there flashed back into my mind the consideration I'd discovered there earlier in the evening, the two Simons, one of them (I'd said) only born two weeks ago. The coincidence was nearer home than I liked; I actually felt myself shiver. It was a relief when the barman called, Last orders, gentlemen, please, and I could say, This is on me, and go up and stand among normal chaps who'd never met Frink's strangers and wouldn't believe in them if they did.

When we parted Tom said he'd let me know about Lefty; the price was a bit more than he'd anticipated, but if Doggett would come down a bit . . . I said he wouldn't. Doggett's Yea was Yea and his Nay Nay, and he'd forgotten more about dogs than a lot of chaps (I meant Tom) would ever know. Frink and I walked part of the way back together. We didn't mention dogs—to this day I don't know if he really took any interest in them—and he did most of the talking. Stalking along beside me, he might have been the ghost of one of his own Highland ancestors, gifted with second sight and not the least disconcerted by it. It was a fascinating experience in a way, but it seemed to throw up a barrier between me and the real world, and I wasn't sorry when our ways parted. I don't think I should have been surprised if he'd dissolved into the evening mist and never been seen again.

::   ::

Even now the excitements of the day weren't over. I hadn't been back ten minutes before my phone rang. I rushed to it, thinking it might be Barbie, but, as in a saner moment I might have anticipated, it was Doggett. And Doggett in a killer's mood, and I soon knew why. He asked if I'd done anything about Lefty, and I said he could anticipate hearing from Tom Fraser within twenty-four hours.

"You can tell him to save the price of the call," Doggett growled—living more or less in his kennels he'd developed a number of canine attributes, I once heard

him take off a barking dog to the life in a manner that
sent an intruder scurrying for police protection—" the
dog's not for sale."

" You mean, he's disposed of?" I asked, and Doggett
gave a sort of yelp.

" That's just what I mean. He's dead. He's been
poisoned."

While I was digesting this Doggett filled me in with
some of the details. He hadn't, he said, a shred of doubt
who was responsible. There was a chap named Wright,
who had been in partnership with him once, and whom
Doggett had knocked down for abusing one of his greyhounds. Well, my friend was certain he was the responsible agency. Doggett had taken over the greyhound and
smashed the partnership; animals always mattered to
him more than humans.

" He's gone in with a fellow called Parnell, and he's
a crook if ever I saw one. He's never forgiven me for
buying that dog off him (he was talking about Wright
now), he's been waiting for his chance to get his own
back."

Only a moron believes that, because a man indulges
in a sport, he's what is technically known as a sportsman.
We've all heard about doped horses and that goes for
dogs, too, and no one questions that boxers can be
bought, and even footballers bribed to let the other side
win. I've never heard of a similar corruption on the
cricket field, though sometimes when you see how the
experts put down even dolly catches, you begin to wonder if the rot isn't starting there, too.

I let Doggett blow his top for a minute, then I said,
" Have you got any proof it was Wright?"

Dogget said, " I know. And pretty soon he'll know I know."

I began to feel anxious. Doggett's a tough proposition, he's taken some pretty hard pastings in his time, but he's only a small man and I don't just mean physically. Wright and Parnell were quite a team to have in opposition, and if a big gang decides to put a rival out of business, the little chap hasn't got a chance. Gangs haven't disappeared because flick-knives have taken the place of razors; I'd seen chaps who'd got themselves marked for life, and they hadn't been pretty. Of course, if Doggett had had the proof he could have gone to the police, but he'd have sunk like a stone if he had. Chaps in his walk of life don't have that respect for the boys in blue that the boys 'ud like. No, Doggett had to paddle his own canoe, and if he wasn't careful he was going to be sunk without trace. Mind you, I knew he wasn't above a bit of sharp practice himself, it was all in the day's work to him, but his enemy was always the man, never the animal.

After Doggett had hung up, I felt more ill at ease than ever. I'd picked up an evening paper in the pub and now I opened it. Mickey Rooney was still being tipped for to-morrow's race, there'd been a daylight raid on a fags factory, five men being taken unawares as they ate their lunch, overpowered and tied up. The paper kept referring to the raiders as the robbers, which showed how little the writer was in touch with contemporary thinking. Thieves, perhaps, but not robbers, who are only the rich who grind the faces of the poor, and if anyone thinks there aren't any in the affluent society he should get himself a pair of National Health glasses. There was a little paragraph tucked away at the bottom of the page about an elderly actress getting knocked down by a motorbike and carted off to hospital with a broken ankle. It appeared she'd just been going to make a come-back in a film, and she regarded the man responsible as worse than a murder. She actually used the word, it seemed to be cropping up everywhere—Crook, Doggett and now Lady Vere de Vere. On my sam, when I looked up I almost expected to see a chap with an axe or something come bursting through the wall.

And I was going to hear it again in the course of the next day or two.

:: :: ::

I have to admit I didn't relish having to break the news about Lefty to Tom Fraser. I didn't get a chance to try and contact him during the day but when I looked in at the Horse and Mariner fairly early in the evening there he was. No sign of Frink, though, and, in fact, I never saw him again. It wouldn't even surprise me to know he was now one of his own mysterious ghosts floating into the earth's atmosphere and (seemingly not liking it much) floating out again. Tom took the news in a most disconcerting way. He put back his head, he's what's called bullet-headed, with thick hair like fur, and he roared with laughter. He laughed so much that chaps all round us started to turn their heads.

" Good old Sim!" he gasped. " You know all the answers, don't you? Mind you, I wondered how you were going to wriggle out of it. I didn't think you'd kill the dog, though."

" I didn't kill him," I said. " It's Doggett . . ."

He put up a hand and with the other wiped some tears

from his eyes. " Don't tell me, it's Doggett as did it. Don't tell me," he repeated, " that's a made-up name if ever I heard one."

" Why don't you telephone him yourself?" I said, and he asked, " I suppose you've installed an electronic brain to take calls. What's the idea, Sim? New way of fiddling the income-tax?"

Though yesterday he hadn't been half-sure he wanted to buy Lefty, he now put on an act of being done down. I didn't stop long. I went to the Admiral, which I'd avoided for a few days, but when I got there it was a case of out of the frying-pan into the fire. There seemed an unusual amount of noise going on, and Ted was looking as black as the famous tar-barrel. Up at the counter I espied Sherry, waving his arms and declaiming like a Lord Mayor. When Ted saw me he said, " For goodness' sake, Mr. Crete, try and get him to lay off. I don't want any more trouble. I've got my reputation to consider." He was always talking about his reputation, it made you wonder why it was more delicate than the next man's, but ever since Madge's death he had been on tenterhooks. I thought I knew why. Macraes are a lot of self-righteous old baskets, who'd somehow manage to hold Ted responsible for their precious house being involved in a murder scandal.

I took my pint and moved along the bar to where Sherry was creating quite a disturbance. A few people were listening to him, but mostly they looked put out by the row. I'd noticed before to-night that Madge was now not mentioned at the Admiral, even by those who'd known her. Life goes on so fast, tides turn and rivers race by a particular spot on the bank, even if it happens to be the one where a woman was found murdered. In a word, she was no longer news; if Crook hadn't taken over the case she'd hardly be remembered at all. Sherry's diatribe had nothing to do with that affair. It appeared that he had been grossly insulted, mistreated, short-changed and actually robbed. One thing was obvious, he'd been in the wars; he had a great plaster above one eye and a wacky-looking bandage.

"What's up?" I asked. "You haven't been fighting the rozzers, I suppose?"

I thought he was going to put his whisky-glass through the big gilt-edged mirror. It cost me the price of a double to stop him.

"Now do give over," Ted besought him when he brought the glass. "We all know by this time what you think of our police, and that's your privilege. It's a free country and you're entitled to your opinion, but for Pete's sake keep it to yourself. Chaps come here for a bit of peace and quiet, if we're going to have all this barney they might just as well stop at home and listen to the wife. And that wouldn't do me any good."

His blooming reputation again.

"What have the police been doing to you, Sherry?" I coaxed him. It was my night for fireworks all right.

"That stupid old fool!" foamed Sherry. "She should be in a home, in a—what is the word you say?—a nut-house. Running in front of a bus right under my wheel, and then the police, they say it was my fault."

I could see in a minute we were going to have another explosion, and I felt I'd had enough for one evening. It's a funny thing, when I looked at the paper last night the incident that interested me least was the one concerning the middle-aged actress who'd broken her ankle; I couldn't guess it was going to tie up with Sherry Cox, sitting in the bar of the Admiral. But it turned out that his was the motor-bike that had mown her down. Have I mentioned anywhere that Sherry loved his bike as Crook loved his old car, and of the casualties inflicted during the encounter all his feelings were for the machine. It was obvious he'd already told the story at least once to-night, but that didn't prevent him telling it all over again for my benefit. It appeared he'd been going down to Windsor and, traffic being very thick and congested, he'd discovered an alternative route for part of the way. The fact that this involved using a one way street in the direction not intended by the authorities didn't cut any ice with him at all. There had been, he said, no traffic in the street at all, he had harmed no one as he came galumphing into the main stream of traffic just beyond the Broadway. Here the cars and buses were ranged in two lines, stationary behind a red bus that had pulled up at a request stop to take on an old boy on sticks. Practically parallel with the bus, but just too large to pass it, was an oil lorry, and behind these two the impatient drivers fidgeted and hooted and put their heads out of windows to call questions and give advice. Sherry decided that, though a car couldn't get past the front vehicles, a motor-bike could, so he came up on the right of the outside line. The way he told it he was going about 25 miles an hour, but you don't have to believe everything you're told. Jehu, who drove dangerously, would have made an admirable patron saint for him, if he'd ever made the grade. Just as he was swinging out to bypass the lorry an old girl stepped off the pavement in front of the bus, which was taking its time getting the old boy aboard. I suppose the traffic concealed him from her and he didn't see her because of the bus. There was a safety drive going on in the neighbourhood at the time, and the police were very down on bad drivers and jay-walkers.

" That is what they say," fumed Sherry, " but she was the jay-walker, and what happens to her ?"

" She broke her ankle, went to hospital and lost her chance of a come-back," I said. It seemed quite a lot for one injudicious step.

Sherry did his best to avoid her, and was it his fault, he demanded, if in doing so he had to cross the white line that had just been renewed down the centre of the road ? If she'd kept her head all would have been well, but as soon as she realised he was there she let out a yelp and tried to run. Of course, she ran straight into the bike, which knocked her down and toppled Sherry off the saddle in one movement. His crash helmet was jolted over his eyes, hence the cut and the plaster. Of course, all the cars started hooting like mad, the driver of the oil lorry climbed out and picked the old lady up, remarking at the same time to the unfortunate Sherry, " You're dead lucky, mate. If she wasn't as tough as the joint my missus served up last Sunday they'd be having you for manslaughter."

" It was her own fault," Sherry protested. " She ran under my wheel." He seems to have given the impression that nothing but his skill prevented her being a corpse at this moment, and personally he regretted it.

" You know what you can do with your skill," said the lorry-driver. " Your sort should stick to prams."

Confusion reigned everywhere. Drivers at the back

who couldn't see what had happened were hooting like lunatics, a woman on the opposite pavement shrieked to her dog to " Come away, Prince, away from the horrid glass."

" Glass?" I said, feeling a bit bewildered, and by an association of ideas got both ours refilled.

" My new headlamp," explained Sherry furiously, not even making a play of paying for the round, which showed you how upset he was. " Broken to shivereens." It was a new word to me, and I thought it rather an expressive one. "And my mudguard dented and the paint scratched—and my insurance will pay nothing of the first five pounds."

" What happened to the lady?" I asked. She seemed to be getting a bit overlooked in all this frenzy of self-righteousness.

" She was all right. Someone took her into a shop and made her a cup of tea. No one gave me a cup of tea." A policeman appeared with his little book, examined the skid marks, and apparently paid no attention whatsoever to the impatient queue who must by now have resembled a presidential guard in the Soviet Union. The lorry driver talked louder than anyone, pointed to Sherry and said it was his kind that were a menace on the road. Sherry hadn't even had the wit to try and get any of the drivers on his side. Eventually he was told he'd be charged with dangerous driving and would have to appear before the magistrate at a time of which he would be informed.

Sherry was livid. He knew in advance that the magistrate would be prejudiced, and would be dead in favour of the old woman. I was rather inclined to agree with him, though I was less sure about the prejudice.

When I said as much I thought Sherry was going to do his nut. He went into a long diatribe about Blind Justice, a cock-eyed old woman (he hinted that England was full of them) wearing her bandage askew, so that she could see precisely what she wanted to see.

" I have been riding my motor-bike all this time and never once have I found myself in trouble," he declared.

" You're dead lucky, mate," Ted told him. He wasn't eavesdropping, there was no need.

" And now they will fine me," Sherry declared.

" Lucky if the old girl doesn't bring an action," Ted told him. It wasn't the wisest thing he could have said in the circumstances, but he was justifiably fed up.

" An action! Against me? When she was in the wrong, rushing out under my wheels like a wicked fairy?" It conjured up a delightful picture, though I prudently didn't say so. " Who cares that I am hurt? I could be blinded, both my legs could be broken—and what would happen to me?"

" You'd be patched up under the National Health," Ted told him unsympathetically.

Sherry nodded like a mandarin. " We will see what Mr. Crook has to say to this."

" Lumme!" ejaculated Ted, and I exclaimed, " You're never going to drag Crook into this. He'll tell you the same as us, it's an open-and-shut case. Going down a one way street, crossing the white line. Lucky for you it is a first offence. Otherwise you might get your licence suspended."

" I am not speaking of my case now," Sherry informed us grandly. " It is perhaps true what you say, it is open-and-shut. Since I am not rich enough to bribe. . . ."

"That'll do from you," Ted told him. "For your information, the police can't be bought and sold like something in Woolworth's, not in this country. If you don't believe me, go on and try. Then it won't matter to you about your precious bike. You won't be wanting it for a couple of years."

Sherry chose to ignore him and turned wholly to me. "But the case about Madge Gardiner, that is—what is your word?—wide open. Oh, Mr. Crook may have a red face, but it will not be nearly so red as that of the Inspector Scott when I have told Mr. Crook what I know."

Ted and I exchanged glances. "Bluff?" he telegraphed, but I wasn't so sure.

"How does Madge come into this?" I asked.

Sherry smiled in a way that made me want to black his beautiful eyes for him. The smile demoted me and Ted to the Cretin Class.

"When I come to England," said Sherry, "my father, a wise man, tells me— Beware of bad women, steer clear of men who prefer little boys, but above all, keep away from the police. Never mind what happens, keep away."

Light began to burst in my brain, though I still didn't believe it. "For the Lord's sake, Sherry," I said, "you haven't been holding out on the police about Madge's murder? Suppressing evidence could get you a verdict of accessory after the fact."

"Why should they believe me then when they do not believe me now?" Sherry demanded. "But Mr. Crook is different. He will be glad." He told us why. You'll recall that when, that night, he went bursting out of the

Admiral in pursuit of the two hussies, he found that, like better-known men than he, he'd missed the bus. There was no sign of either girl, only a car vanishing up the road. And, of course, the girls were in the car.

"Did you see them?" I inquired.

"There was no need to see them, where else could they be? Had they wings that they could fly?" He hadn't fancied the idea of coming back to the Admiral to be laughed at, so he'd got his motor-bike and cruised round looking for some pub where he could finish the evening. Unfortunately he went in the direction of the river—if he'd gone the other way he could have had his pick—but the only place he found was a dingy little ale-house where, he said, he was regarded with hostility and where someone, he swore, tried to pick his pocket. Someone put on a juke-box which played Ten Little Niggers, and he came ramping out to find some louts tinkering with his machine. When he tried to drive them off they jeered and called him Smokey; and one of them said, Don't call him that, our cat's name's Smokey. When he came chugging back past the Admiral the doors were locked, though he could still see a light inside; he tried the door, but no joy there, so he got back on the motor-bike, taking the road that ran past the end of the lane leading to Mayflower Mansions. And—this was the crux of an overlong story—looking up the street he distinctly saw a man lurking in the shadows, half-concealed by a tree. The man, he swore, was alone. That, he said, was what he was going to tell Crook.

"He will thank me," said Sherry, simply.

"What a load of old rubbish!" said Ted. "You say you saw a man, you never mentioned him till to-night, it was raining, remember, you couldn't identify him, even if he was there . . ."

" He was there," cried Sherry, furiously. " I do not say he was the one who killed her, perhaps he had only stopped to light his cigarette, but—he was there."

" How are you going to explain to the police you've only just remembered him?"

" I did not say I had only just remembered him," insisted Sherry. " Only—why should I make trouble for myself for a rude old woman?"

Madge's rejection of the proffered drink still rankled.

" But this was murder, Sherry," I said. " There may be countries where you can play fast and loose with that kind of thing, but this isn't one of them." I hesitated a minute, then I asked him, " Look, don't go right up the wall, but—you're dead sure you did see someone there? I sympathise with you wanting to get even with the police . . ."

I wasn't allowed to finish. Sherry turned on me dramatically, throwing out his long fine hands. " You see? You are the same as them. You do not believe me. But Mr. Crook is different. He will not say You wish to have the lamplight, you wish to make a pony out of me."

" A monkey," I murmured. I'd noticed before that Sherry was dead nuts on British slang and sometimes he came out with a real beaut. " Did you happen to mention to anyone else that you saw this fellow lurking?"

Well, of course he hadn't. Hadn't thought about it at the time, he said, and afterwards, when it might be important, he'd decided it was no part of his job to do the police's work for them. Anyway, the news about Madge hadn't broken for some days. And, he pointed out, the so-wonderful British policeman had said Bruce was responsible, and who was he to say the police were wrong? They might even suggest it was peculiar his being there himself at that particular hour—and someone might recall that he and Madge had had a bit of an argument—though the most truculent policeman would hardly dare put that little spat forward as sufficient motive for murder. Anyway, there was nothing to prove he even knew where she lived. I fancy it was as clear to Ted as it was to me that Sherry really didn't give a dump who had killed Madge, he wasn't worried on Bruce's account or concerned with Barbie's anxiety, he simply wanted to wipe the police's eye and here was an opportunity. He had too much sense to suppose he could accomplish much on his own, but here was Crook, like a gift from on high, and Crook could produce rabbits out of the least promising hat.

" You know what the police are going to ask you," said Ted. " What was he like?"

" It was raining, not a great deal but a little, the light was bad, I was not very close and I was on my motor-bike. I can tell them it was a man, not tall, not short, you, Mr. Crete, anyone. But he was there."

He had sufficient grasp of English law to realise that, if he clung to his statement and refused to be shaken, there was a good chance, with Crook at the helm, of Bruce getting the benefit of the doubt. When Ted put a second question—Why should a strange man be there?—he answered very sensibly that that was no concern of his.

" Perhaps he needs money, he sees she is—what do you say?—loaded, he follows her. Now, me, I do not require any one's money." He pulled out a fat wallet and ex-

hibited for the benefit of everyone in the bar. Some
chaps never learn, I reflected, if he really supposed
Madge had been slugged for her money wasn't that a
first-class reason for keeping his own wallet where it belonged, in his inside pocket? I'd often wondered how he
got his living. His story was that Daddy was making him
an allowance while he gathered copy for his book on the
English at Home or whatever he proposed to call it, but
it sounded a thin yarn to me. There's a tidy living to be
made selling Indian hemp, particularly to layabouts
and chaps from overseas, and to some of these types it's
incredible that this traffic should be considered a crime.

"I shall tell him to-night," he announced. I realised
we were attracting attention. A voice from behind me
murmured, "Sleep on it, son" but I didn't see the
speaker, not to identify him, I mean, which, as it turned
out, was rather a pity.

"I've heard worse advice," I told him. "Anyway,
it's gone ten, I don't say he'd have gone to bed, sometimes I wonder if he even owns one, but he most likely
won't be home, whereas in the morning . . ."

"You think by morning I shall have changed my
mind."

"No, why should you?" asked Ted. "Only, like Mr.
Crete says, he may not be home."

"Why not ring him?" I suggested. "He might come
down here."

"Oh, no, Mr. Crete," said Ted, decisively. "I've got
nothing against Mr. Crook, but I've had enough upset
in my bar for one night."

Then he moved along the counter to attend to a customer, and I said to Sherry, "You do realise Crook will

have to pass the information to the police?" Actually, I wasn't certain if this was *de rigeur* or not, seeing they'd arrested a man in connection with the murder. " Is there nothing you can remember that would help Crook to identify him? Most likely he was in the Admiral that night—I do appreciate you weren't close enough to see him in detail . . ." If he could have remembered an unusual tie-pin, cuff-links, any special physical detail, that would have helped. " Was he wearing a hat?" I inquired.

Sherry considered, then said Yes, pulled over his face, but that sounded to me remarkably like second thoughts; it would explain his inability to give any sort of description of the fellow. Still, however claptrap it might sound to me, I knew Crook's reputation well enough to realise it might look very different by the time Crook was through with it.

Ted came back and Sherry inquired largely of me, " What will you take?" I said, " Nothing for the moment, and don't you take offence. It's worse than cold pizen." Luckily he decided to treat that as a joke. Ted leaned forward to say, " Are you sure this chap you noticed loitering wasn't Bruce coming *away* from the Mansions?"

But I knew that wasn't going to be the answer. Sherry had already told us that. There was, of course, the man in the blue car, but Crook had disposed of him. He was a resident and he had an irrefutable alibi. Ted asked, rather feebly this time, why a man intending murder should have made himself conspicuous by hanging about in such weather, why not wait under cover, but the answer to that was so obvious that neither Sherry nor I considered it. There was a light in the hall of the Mansions, and anyone (like the blue car driver, for instance) might come in (or even go out) at any moment.

I had another shot at trying to dissuade Sherry from bolting up to Brandon Street that night. He said he didn't care if Crook was out, he'd wait on the step for his return.

"You'll be arrested for loitering," Ted warned him, and that set Sherry off again against British conceptions of justice. I decided I'd stayed long enough.

"See you," I said to Sherry, moving along the bar.

Ted tackled me as I got near the door. "How's Mr. Crook making out?" he asked.

"He's on the ball," I told him, "but he's never above accepting a bit of help. One thing you can be sure of, whoever stands trial for the murder of Madge Gardiner it won't be Colin Bruce."

I was surprised by my own vehemence.

As I turned in the doorway for a final glance, I saw some chap had come up and was standing beside Sherry, talking. Sherry was leaning forward with his arms on the bar, so I couldn't see the man's face, and probably it wouldn't have helped if I had, since I recognised practically no one there. The streets were more or less deserted when I left the Admiral and walked by the cul-de-sac where Sherry kept his cherished motor-bike. Some road-hog had parked an enormous monstrosity, all salmon paint and cromium fins in the mouth; if anyone wanted a quiet snog farther down, in the shadow of the fountain, say, it was almost as good as having a gate set up. But I didn't hear a footstep or a voice, and as usual, the fountain ran dry.

Coming past the Horse and Mariner some time later I felt a touch on my arm; a voice in my ear said, " Hey, Simon, got any more dead dogs to sell?" It seemed the last straw to round off an exhausting evening. It was Tom Fraser, of course, and it occurred to me he'd had one or two more than usual. It was nearly closing time, and he'd been there, I presumed, since about six. I suppose it was creditable that he could proceed under his own steam.

I shook him off and watched him go, not too straight, over the road.

A gull came flying inland, a sure sign of bad weather. It practically dive-bombed me, screaming its peculiar unmelodious cry.

" Go and find yourself a girl," I told it, and to my surprise it sheered off. I wished I could follow my own advice, assuming, of course, that the girl was Barbie Hunter. But to-night she seemed a million miles away.

When I came back to my house it was quite silent; even Miss Muffet had put up her shutters. I sat in my room for a little debating whether to ring Crook or not, and tell him what Sherry had told me, but in the end I didn't. I decided to call him in the morning, and ask him then if Sherry had made it the night before.

CHAPTER VII

IN THE EVENT I didn't do that either, because, before 1 got round to it, Crook had called me.

" You were at the Admiral last night?" he said, and it was a statement not a question.

" That's right. Did Sherry tell you?"

" No," said Crook.

" He was all for coming round," I explained. " There's a box of dynamite for you. Bats are flying in his belfry, in his bonnet hums a bee. Well, you'll be seeing him this morning. He can tell you then."

" I'll be seeing him," Crook agreed, " but he won't be able to tell me anything. Not seen your paper yet?"

My paper is delivered to the house, but I have to go down and fetch it myself. I hadn't been down yet, and for once I'd overslept, so I hadn't even had the news on the radio.

" Came a cropper on Burford Hill," amplified Crook. " Both Sherry and his bike are write-offs. What d'you make of that?"

I waited a minute before I replied. Burford Hill would be on the way to Crook's house; it was, I knew, under repair at the moment, and there were danger notices at the top.

" What happened?" I said. " Or doesn't anyone know?"

" Bike appears to have crashed into some apparatus left on the site, carried off a few road lamps, Sherry came off even worse. So now," he wound up, "we'll never get his story of the Invisible Man."

"He rang you, then?" I said. Because, otherwise, how did Crook know there was an Invisible Man?

"Not Sherry. Ted. Just to say he might be on his way. When he didn't turn up I decided he'd thought better of it. Then I saw this piece in the paper, foot of a column, well, why should he rate more? No one knew he was coming to see me. Any notion why he didn't open his trap before this?"

"Wanted to stay out of trouble, I suppose. Still, plenty of people heard what he was saying. Ted was trying to quiet him down."

"What the soldier said ain't evidence," Crook reminded me. "Oh, I daresay they heard and I don't doubt he said it, but what we want is proof. Not that the rozzers had to accept his story," he added.

"Still, it might have made them think again. And anyway we now know there was someone else there."

"We knew that from the start," said Crook, grumpily. "Well, there had to be, seeing Bruce can't be guilty. I only work for the innocent, remember. There'll be an inquest, of course. You might be called."

"How can I help them?" I demurred.

"That'll be for the police to decide, won't it?"

He rang off.

I could see, of course, that Crook was going to try and make something out of Sherry's sudden death; I didn't blame him, it was second nature for him to find a criminal explanation to every fatality, if it helped his book. As for how he did it, that was his worry.

I had a busy day, and when I got in that evening old

Miss Muffett was hanging about the hall in no end of a tizz. I decided she'd been watching through her Nottingham lace curtains for my return.

" Oh, Mr. Crete," she bleated, " the police have been here looking for you."

I felt a bit of a jolt, but all I said was, " They must have time on their hands."

" They asked me what time you'd be back. I said I didn't know, but try again about seven."

" It's after that now," I said.

" Yes. I expect they'll be round any minute."

" They'll have to hurry up, won't they? I'm going out to dinner. Did they say why they wanted me?"

" Oh no." She looked smug. " The police never tell you anything, they're as bad as relations, always so secretive." She put her little pug nose in the air, as if she was sniffing on a relative's trail, and not much caring for the smell. " I do hope it doesn't mean trouble," she wound up, with her false white smile.

" I never knew them mean anything else," I assured her, making my getaway. I hadn't been upstairs five minutes when my bell rang; they operate the automatic porter system here, so I didn't have to go down. It was the police, of course, with instructions to attend Sherry Cox's inquest.

" I shan't be able to help you," I said, " but have it your own way."

I might as well have saved my breath; I knew I'd have to go. I had dinner at the Chicken Parlour, and went on to the Admiral. Crook was there already, talking to Ted, who looked about as cheerful as the unmarried elder sister at a wedding.

"No," he was saying, doggedly, "I don't know who he was, Mr. Crook. I don't know if he ever came here before, and I wouldn't be remembering him now if it wasn't for the Irish whiskey."

Crook saw me and waved and bought me a pint, which I suppose went down to expenses. He was asking Ted about the chap who'd been talking to Sherry after I left the pub.

"Did you see him, Simon?" he asked.

And I said I only saw there was someone there, but I wouldn't know him again. "But you know what Sherry was like," I said. "The friendliest chap when the chip was off his shoulder. He'd have chatted to a black beetle."

"Which is what he appears to have been doing." acknowledged Crook, dryly. "Why doesn't anyone teach the young that silence is golden? Not that you can blame them really, seeing they never set eyes on the stuff except as a band round a fountain pen and then it's only 9 carat. Come on, Ted, you can do better than that. Tall, short, fat, thin . . ."

But Ted was adamant. "I remember him because he asked for Irish whiskey and I don't get much call for that. I had to go and look for the bottle. All I was interested in was getting that young chap calmed down. He was creating a disturbance. And, like I said, I've got my reputation to consider."

"You sound like a Victorian deb," said Crook, brutally. "One breath of scandal and they're ruined, condemned to spend the rest of their lives keeping house for unmarried uncles and spoiling perfectly good china at hand-painting classes every other Wednesday. Well, did

you get the impression Sherry had ever seen him before?
All right, all right. I know about him and the black
beetle. So far as either of us is concerned it could have
been a beetle. Don't you ever look a chap in the face?"

" I've got my work cut out looking at his money to
make sure it's not dud. You'd be surprised the number
of chaps who try and pass foreign coinage and once it's
over the counter you've had it. That's not what I gave
you, they say. Mine was the real McCoy."

" One of these days," threatened Crook, " they'll do
the whole job by remote control—robots, see. Sure this
was the first Irish whiskey you were asked for?"

" I told you, there's no call for it."

" Chaps don't know what they're missing. Now, why
should a stranger go up and start talking to Sherry,
specially when he'd just announced he was comin' along
to see me?"

" Could be a parson wearing his collar the right way
round for once," Ted offered.

" It could be someone who wanted to stop him coming
to see you," I suggested.

" If he was a do-gooder," pursued Crook, " why ain't
he surfaced? And if he wasn't a do-gooder, what was he
doin' buttin' in? Who paid for the whisky?" he added
to Ted.

" This chap did. For both of them."

" You mean, they both had Irish?"

" No. Sherry had his usual Scotch. If he'd been buying it himself he wouldn't have got it from me. He'd had
more than his normal ration as it was. I never did see a
young chap who could put it away as he could," he
added, admiringly.

" So, whoever this chap was, he thought it was worth the price of two whiskies to keep Sherry where he was. How long did he stop?"

" They went and sat at one of those tables against the wall," Ted told him, looking harassed and no wonder. " Just before closing time I noticed Sherry was alone, but just when the other chap went out I couldn't say."

" Did he seem all right when he left, Sherry, I mean?"

" I didn't notice anything out of the way. You know how it is, Mr. Crook, the last few all go out together; I'm concerned with getting them off licensed premises in time. No one passed a remark . . ."

" And then you came and rang me?"

" Thought you should be warned. I'm sorry if I kept you up," he added, dryly.

He left us then to attend to some incoming clients. Crook jerked his head in the direction of a table some distance from the bar, and we carried our drinks over.

" Tell me something," I said, when we were settled. " Are you equating Daniels with this mysterious whisky-drinker?"

" Since I can't get any description of him, how can I?" Crook retorted. " I'll tell you this, though, if that chap had anything to do with Sherry's death he's no stranger. It's too late in the case for strangers to surface."

" You don't think it was an accident then?" I exclaimed.

" Well, do you? Sherry was crazy, he didn't even know what a speed limit was, but he rode like a veteran. If he was sober when he left the place and if there was nothing wrong with his machine—then—no, I don't think it was an accident."

" You heard about the incident at the Broadway?" I said, and he answered that Ted had told him something, " But you fill me in, Simon."

" His machine got damaged, he was complaining bitterly."

" That's what Ted said, a smashed lamp, a scratched mudguard. But if it was going wrong why didn't it go wrong on the way here? Besides, he wouldn't have been riding it without that lamp, and if he took it to a garage they wouldn't return it unless it was roadworthy. Still, that'll all come out at the inquest. You going?"

I told him Yes.

" Ted's got his orders, too. Very put out about it he is. Have to get someone to look after the bar. Mind you, I doubt if much that's useful will come out. I've been down to the mortuary. Ted'll be asked how much Sherry had to drink, and if he's got any sense he'll say the usual, you'll be asked if you noticed anything special."

" As far as I'm concerned he was perfectly capable of driving his machine," I said. " You were saying about the man responsible being in the picture from the start. Does that mean it could be anyone who comes here?"

" It could be anyone," agreed Crook. " Tell you something. According to Ted, Sherry was in an all-fired hurry to come along to Brandon Street, yet he stayed till closing time, drinking with a stranger and then apparently just sitting. Now why?"

" He took so much offence when Madge wouldn't drink with him it may be a part of his Courtesy Code not to refuse even from a man he doesn't know."

" But you left—what time?"

"About 10.5—10.10—I couldn't absolutely swear to it."

"So, even if Sherry wanted to do the polite, he could have been away by 10.20. If you want my opinion, I'd say someone was tooting anxious to see he didn't tell his story about the man of mystery and took steps."

"Such as?"

"Well, how does it look to you? A chap he don't know comes up, offers him a drink, persuades him to go and sit away from the bar, which he don't normally do, and then brought the glasses along. Ted was telling me that just as he handed them over he got a call from the other bar and—see what I mean?"

"I'm getting a glimmering," I said. "You think there might have been something besides whisky in the glass."

"Well, if Sherry was all right the fault must have been in the whisky or in the motor-bike. He'd been riding the motor-bike round most of the day without anything going wrong."

"Isn't it possible to tell if a man's been doped?" I asked, feeling a bit dazed.

"Sherry didn't choose his time well. I don't know if you went through your paper this morning, but there was a big punch-up between a van and a private car in the High Street, bells were going like mad, ambulances arriving and police swarming like a plague of blueflies. The constable who found Sherry phoned in his report, but said the man was dead as a doornail. As that Brides in the Bath chap observed, When you're dead you're done for. They had plenty of living casualties on their hands, no doctor saw Sherry for quite a while after he was found. Well, there's no cure for a broken neck and that's what he had. The bike was in smithereens . . ."

"Shivereens," I murmured. "That was Sherry's word. But, Mr. Crook, assuming you're right, how can you hope to identify this man?"

"All depends which man I'm after. And I know who he is, only I've got to put a name to him. Remember the story of the woman who lost one of her ten pieces of silver?"

He jumped about like a flea in a gale of wind. It was difficult to keep up with him.

"She found it, though," I recalled.

"Yes. But did you ever think you're never told where she found it? Oh, in the house, but whereabouts in the house? It wouldn't surprise me to know she'd pushed it behind Granny's photo on the mantelpiece, some place she thought 'ud be safe, and then forgot all about. Must have cursed herself for all that sweeping in the attic and down the garden path when there it was, under her nose all the time."

I looked at him rather suspiciously. Leg-pulling is one of his pet parlour games, but he looked as solemn as a judge. I knew, too, he wasn't just talking for effect.

"If ever I was to commit a murder," said Crook, "only I wouldn't, murder's a mug's game, I can't think of a better locale than a pub. No need to find an excuse to visit it, go in alone, go in couples. If business is heavy no one notices you, it's like Ted says, you're a hand taking the glass and putting down the spondulicks, you can talk to anyone you like, and it's all Lombard Street to a china orange if anyone remembers what you looked like by to-morrow morning. It's like that missing elephant that the hunter hid with a tribe of elephants."

I could only assume this was a variation on the missing leaf that a murderer hid in a forest. Crook caught Ted's eye and nodded and Ted came over with a refill.

" You think about it, Simon," Crook urged me. " You are here more often than I am, and nobody knows you. I mean, chaps might remember a pressin' engagement when they saw me come in, but all they'd have in their minds when you lined up at the counter was whether you were good for a round."

It wasn't complimentary, but I saw his point.

" Y'see, if a chap's had one over the eight—O.K., Ted, I didn't say he had, just if, then the cold night air 'ud either sober him, if he wasn't too far gone, or put him out like a light. But Sherry walked up the cul-de-sac to fetch his bike, he rode it as far as Burford Hill, no one's come forward to say they saw him weaving all over the road, it smells like Billingsgate to me."

" He was sober when he left," repeated Ted, " and that's what I'll say if I'm asked."

Just before I left I said to Crook, " You wouldn't feel like putting a card on the table, I suppose? Tell me who you've got in your eye."

He gave me a tremendous slap on the back, that nearly sent me flying.

" I don't mind a bit, Simon," he said. " My bet is that the chap responsible for Sherry Cox coming a purler is the same as the one who put out Madge Gardiner's light. And I can't say fairer than that."

: :   : :

The inquest was held the next day. The magistrate was a stuffed shirt who appeared to date from the days of the horse and cart, though perhaps his appearance belied him. At all events, he made it perfectly clear that he disapproved of all young men who rode motor-cycles to the disregard of public safety (he didn't go quite so far as to say they deserved to be killed, but I'm sure it was in his mind) and that set the temper of the court. There was a sheep-like jury who snuffed up everything he said, nodding like a lot of mandarins. There were no relatives to identify the dead man, but his landlady put in a good word, a model lodger, she said, and never tell her that colour made any difference, prompt with the rent, no girls after 10.30. She managed to get this far before the magistrate angrily shushed her, and she departed saying it was a queer thing when a young chap who was dead couldn't have someone to put in a good word. I thought it was a pity Crook wasn't there, he'd have loved her. Asked about his drinking habits, Mrs. Legge retorted she'd never seen him the worse for liquor . . . After she'd been got rid of, the policeman who'd found Sherry gave his evidence, a doctor said the man was deceased when he saw him and in his opinion death must have been instantaneous or nearly so, then it was Ted's turn. He looked pretty dour, as if he didn't think Macraes would take kindly to the notion of one of their chaps missing out on an hour's opening time because a silly young fellow had buckled up his machine and himself. When I saw Ted and heard him speak I was reminded of the Monument in the rain, grim wasn't the word for it. The magistrate, who was looking more disgruntled than ever, got precious little change out of Ted. Asked how much Sherry had

had to drink that night, Ted said he didn't keep count, he was there to serve his customers, probably about the same as usual. How many? Two? Three? More than three? What was he drinking? Whisky, the same as always. He came round most evenings, didn't seem to know a lot of people. Excited? Well, he'd taken exception to the way he'd been treated re an incident involving an old lady. Ted could supply details? Ted ruddy well could not. It 'ud be in the record.

Another policeman gave evidence about the accident near the Broadway, and a man called Marsh came forward to say that he'd overhauled the damaged machine the same afternoon said damage being very slight, and it had been A.1. when it left his garage. Someone else gave evidence that Sherry had ridden the bike down to Surrey during the day and it had behaved a treat. I was asked if I could add anything, but I simply supported Ted's evidence; Sherry had spoken of calling in to see a friend on his way back. Late? Well, not from the friend's point of view. I wondered if Crook's name would be mentioned. But it wasn't. Perhaps the police thought they had enough on their plate without further complicating matters. The sheep-faced jury brought in a verdict of death by misadventure, and if they could have added a censure motion one got the idea they would, no one expressed any sympathy for the dead youth, and his only relation appeared to be his father, to whom a cable had been sent. Later we heard that a return cable had been received; the father was coming by jet plane and wished to take his son's body back with him. That was almost the only human note about the whole proceedings.

As I came out of court I saw old Miss Muffett sitting

near the back, wielding a handkerchief with every impression of enjoyment. I almost expected her to tell me an inquest made a nice change. I telephoned Barbie a bit later and gave her the verdict. I could hear her snort right over the phone.

"How dumb can you be?" she said. "Things in life don't happen quite so conveniently. Here he was going to give Mr. Crook evidence . . ."

"Tell Crook a story," I murmured. "He couldn't have used it in court."

Still, not all the Heavenly Host could have persuaded Barbie that Sherry's death was due to misadventure.

So that made three of us.

CHAPTER VIII

THE FOLLOWING EVENING I took Barbie out to dinner.

The evening didn't begin well. Barbie was in a rather carping mood.

"I'm beginning to wonder if we haven't over-rated Mr. Crook," she said, disagreeably. "Time's rushing past and how far has he got us? He thinks Daniels may be mixed up in this. He wonders about the whisky-man (I'd told her about him) but he's no idea how he can be traced and even then he probably couldn't show that he was involved."

"He has an idea—mind you, at the moment it's no more than an idea—that Sherry may have been doped, and that's why he came to grief."

Barbie scoffed openly. "You mean this man, X let's call him, knew Sherry was going to be in the Admiral, knew he was going to come out with this story and bring it to Mr. Crook, and had the stuff in his pocket?"

"We don't know anything about him," I protested, "except that he moved in pretty smartly when I moved out. Sherry's idea was to finish the drink he'd got and then set out for Brandon Street. This chap stopped him. No one recognised him, no one's come forward to say I saw Smith, Brown or Robinson talking to the deceased. I know the one about speaking no evil of the dead, but I've wondered sometimes how he made a living. Sherry, I mean. And then, considering he didn't seem to have any close friends, why come so often to the Admiral?"

Barbie caught on at once. " You mean it was a rendezvous? But . . ."

" There's another thing. He was waving a wallet stuffed with notes. He was never short of cash, but this was something a bit showy just to bring out for a few drinks. And, though he never seemed to know anyone intimately, he was hail-fellow-well-met with everyone, the little friend of all the world. If he was involved in anything—illegal—he couldn't have a better front. A man who talks to everyone makes no one conspicuous. This man bought the drinks, persuaded Sherry to sit some distance from the counter while he brought them, it was simple enough . . ."

" Always assuming he had the stuff on him. I thought it was very hard to get hold of drugs."

" Not if you know where to look for the stuff." I remembered Doggett saying once that he could lay hands on enough dope between Charing Cross Station and the Circus to put out half London. He was dressing it up, of course, but there was some foundation in what he said.

" A dose of chloral would do it," I pointed out, " it wouldn't be fatal, just enough to make him feel dizzy and then when he came to a hill like Burford, where you have to go carefully at the best of times, you could be pretty sure he'd run into trouble."

" It seems pretty risky to me," demurred Barbie.

" You could call it aftermath of a murder," I pointed out. " I'll tell you something else. Crook suspects, if he doesn't know, more than he's letting on. He was positively cryptic to-night. Talking about the woman and the lost piece of silver . . ."

" Which one's that?"

" It's one of the parables. About a woman who lost something precious and wouldn't give up until she found it. Crook's idea was that it was probably under her nose all the time—Barbie, what is it?"

She had turned quite pale. "Who heard him say that?"

"There weren't many of us there. Just he and I and Ted."

"And you were meant to think he was talking about the whisky-drinker. But—we don't know he was ever there before that night, we've no link at all to join him to Mrs. Gardiner. But—who's been on the spot from Chapter One, before Chapter One, the prologue, who could move perfectly freely and never be suspected, and yet be able to follow every step of the way? Think, Simon, one little word, three letters."

It was my turn to look staggered. "You're up the creek," I told her bluntly, "if you think Ted was involved. Ted was her friend, her confidante."

"Who says so?"

"He told us so himself."

"Yes. He told you."

"You weren't at the Admiral that night," I insisted. "You could see she trusted him absolutely."

"I never said she didn't. Mr. Crook said it was quite likely she wouldn't know her enemy by sight. And there are two of them in this, remember. Say one is the husband . . ."

"Who you think may be identical with the whisky-drinker?"

"I didn't see the whisky-drinker; and if I had I don't suppose I'd recognise him. But I'd tell you who might have known him, and that's Mrs. Costello. She saw this man snuffing round Madge's flat, she'd know him again, why hasn't Crook invited her to the Admiral to have a drink, and told her to keep a weather eye open. Wouldn't that help?"

" It might help if this man came in, only it wouldn't help Lizzie. Hasn't there been enough death already in this case? Remember, angel, Sherry announced to all and sundry he was coming to see Crook, and someone saw to it he didn't get there. Say Lizzie recognises someone, do you suppose the same mysterious agency won't intervene to see she never gets as far as the courts?"

" Even Daniels, if that's the man we want, can't go round committing murder like—like the Grand Chain," Barbie protested.

" Why not?" I asked. " What's he got to lose? Besides, Crook may be keeping Lizzie up his sleeve for some future date." It seemed improbable that so simple a procedure should have escaped him, when it occurred at once to Barbie, though I admit it hadn't occurred to me.

" Well, then, let's get back to Ted. Think, Simon, how much do we know about him?"

" Why should we know anything? He's just the barman at the Admiral. And remember, he was amazed to hear that Madge had a grown-up daughter and a son-in-law. They may have been friends, but he didn't know the most important things about her."

" He says he didn't know. But what would you say in his place? And he's one of the few people who could have persuaded her to open her door to him at 11 p.m."

" He'd have to find a pretty good reason for bolting round from the pub."

" He could say, Let me in, Madge, there's something you should know, I didn't get a chance to-night at the Admiral—oh, she'd open the door all right. You said she was all of a dither . . . And then who else is so advantageously placed to see the whole game, the invisible man?" She looked at me eagerly for agreement; she was looking quite incredibly lovely. I knew at that instant she hardly saw me, even Crook was only a name to her. She just considered two men—Bruce and Ted. I began to see what kind of a pattern her suspicions would make. He'd been there, of course, on the night Madge was killed; I'd made him a present of the fact that the money wasn't forthcoming; he had known about Sherry and he had made the third in the conversation with me and Crook. Lay those facts out and see what you could make of them. The answer, of course, was whatever you chose. There was no proof he wasn't completely sincere, an old friend of Madge's . . .

" Not very old," interrupted Barbie, to whom I was outlining the position. " He'd only been at the Admiral about two years. Where was he before that?"

" In the country. Wait a minute, he told us the name of the place." I thought. " Beacon Heath," I recalled. " The Angel, Beacon Heath."

" Why did he leave? He doesn't give the impression of being a Londoner."

" I don't think he is." I remembered an occasion when we were talking about dogs, and Ted had said, " I don't know anything about them. Fishing's my line."

" Fishing!" said Barbie, scornfully. " How much do you suppose he gets of that in London?"

I thought of the little band you see standing along the

river's edge of a Sunday all the way to Richmond. It didn't seem much of an exchange for the real article. Beacon Heath was true country, though the authorities were doing their best to make it one more urban district. Still, the Admiral seemed a poor exchange for a man who loved the countryside. It wasn't as if Ted had children to go to school or a demanding wife who wanted something a bit gayer than a country pub.

"Do we even know there was another man that night?" Barbie went on.

"Who bought a couple of whiskies, one of them Irish? Yes, I saw him."

"Did you see him buy the whiskies?"

"Well, no, but there was someone talking to Sherry, and he didn't leave the Admiral till closing-time."

"That's only Ted again. And why didn't the other man come forward?"

"Half-a-dozen reasons," I told her. "Perhaps he'd told his wife he'd be at a business conference, perhaps she's like Lizzie's husband who regards a glass of beer as the entrance ticket to hell; perhaps he got himself knocked over by a bus and is now in hospital suffering from loss of memory. Perhaps he was catching a night plane, perhaps he just doesn't read the papers . . . There's no earthly way of tying him up with Madge."

"Unless he's the husband and was afraid Sherry might help to get him identified."

"He didn't see this man well enough to offer identification," I urged. "The night of the murder, I mean."

"That's what he told you, but after he'd had a session with Mr. Crook it's wonderful what he might have remembered."

I couldn't deny that; the thought had been in my own mind, too.

" And if it comes to opening doors, Madge would be much more likely to admit Ted than her long lost husband. After all, husbands don't seem to have loomed very large in her life."

" Are you calling her a tart?" I said. " Because, if so, you'd be wrong. She liked a bit of fun, who doesn't? But she never sold her favours, I'd go bail on that."

" She seems to have sold herself to you all right," was Barbie's cool comment. " Never mind about that, though, let's stick to facts. We know X was expecting money from her, we know she hadn't got it, Ted knows because you told him about the odd message that came to you on the crossed line. Well, say Ted is in the plot, all he has to do when he's locked up the Admiral is put a call through to X. X says, Go round and have a word, he goes round, not with murder in mind, I grant you that, because Madge couldn't be any use to him . . ."

" Look," I said, " we're doing one hell of a lot of speculating. We're like a train that has left the rails and can topple over an unseen embankment at any minute. You can make out this feature and that in the dark, but you can't see a clear landscape."

" And you'd rather wait till morning? Well, I don't think we've got the time to wait. We don't know anything about Ted before he came to London."

" If you'd ever tried to get a publican's licence you'd know it's easier to go through the eye of a needle. If Ted had ever so much as sold a drink out of hours he'd never have made the grade with Macraes."

"He could be in this other man's power in some way," Barbie urged.

"You need to be pretty deep in someone's power to commit a murder, let alone two."

"But surely, Simon, you can see that the second murder was inevitable, given the fact of the first. And I think Mr. Crook's probably right when he says the first murder was an accident, it was never part of the plan."

"There's one point you've overlooked," I said. "He'd need a motive."

"He could be in his partner's power. Suppose this man knew something about Ted that would cost him his licence if it came to Macrae's ears. He wouldn't be likely to get another, would he?"

I had to admit that was true. "You're not suggesting Madge was blackmailing him, I suppose?"

"I never met her. You and Mr. Crook don't seem to think she was the blackmailing type, but suppose she was threatened through the daughter, that would make her desperate. She might have said something that alarmed her visitor . . ."

"Well, we never thought it was a pleasant after-dinner chat," I reminded her frostily. "Barbie, you've engaged Crook to attend to this, for pity's sake keep yourself out of trouble."

"I'm in trouble," she reminded me. "Until Colin is cleared I'm in as deep as he. All I'm saying is it can't do any harm to find out a little about Ted. Why, that might clear him completely. You think I'm bone-headed . . ."

"Pig-headed."

"But I'm not an absolute fool. Ted may have had the best of all possible reasons for wanting to leave the

Angel, perhaps this was a better offer, perhaps he was sick of a small community, perhaps some woman was after him, he may have had some private local trouble. If we knew we could dismiss him from the case. I'm only suggesting making a few inquiries."

"You're not suggesting hiring someone else in addition to Crook? You haven't a hope. No private eye would dare take the job on for a king's ransom, not with Crook already in the field."

"I'm not suggesting anything of the sort and you know it. I just thought I'd take a day's holiday and cruise round Beacon Heath."

"Barbara Hunter, Private Investigator. Of course, you're insane, you know that. I didn't know you were so anxious for an early death."

"You said yourself this man can't conduct a massacre."

"I wasn't thinking of him," I said. "I was thinking of Crook."

But I knew that if she was set on this crazy plan I should go along with her.

"But he'll have your skin for a lampshade if he finds out you're monkeying in his affairs," I warned her. "Remember his advice about the Tar Baby."

"I never thought of the Tar Baby as amounting to much," was her scornful retort. "Anyway, it 'ud be much safer for us to put a few questions than for Crook. No one who's set eyes on him once is going to forget him. You and I are just a couple going round asking a few aimless questions."

"Don't imagine that anyone who's set eyes on you is going to forget you either," I warned her.

"They aren't going to see me more than once, that's

the point. Oh, Simon, how can you be so—desultory?
For all we know, Crook's being trailed already, his telephone tapped . . ."

" Not unless X has got an ally with the C.I.D."

" Besides, he's important. We can't afford too many
chances with him, he's really all Colin's got."

The inference was obvious. If there were going to be
any more bloody sacrifices what was wrong with the chap
now sitting at her right hand?

" I'm not asking or expecting you to take unnecessary
risks," said Barbie. " If there is a chance of bloodshed,
why should you be involved?"

" Say that somewhere private and I'll give you the
juiciest black eye you ever saw," I promised her. " Well,
let's have it, the plan of campaign."

This time it was she who hesitated. " I mean that,
Simon. Really, I shall be all right . . ."

" In a pig's ear you will," I told her, rudely. " If
you're so set on your Lady-Molly-of-Scotland-Yard act,
count me in."

" How about to-morrow?" she suggested in brisk tones.
"I don't have to be at the studio till the evening. It's one
of these quiz programmes that you play off the cuff, so
you don't need rehearsals. We've done it often enough
to know the drill. Mother's going away for a long week-
end to her sister at Leamington Spa. Her train goes soon
after 9, and she never lets me see her off, so if you come
about 9.30 say—have you a car?"

" I was going to ask you that," I said.

" It would cost me about five pounds a week in fines
for illegal parking. I can get to my headquarters by

underground, and there's a very convenient Green Line if I had to go farther afield."

"I'll get a car," I said. "I'm like you, I find it more trouble than it's worth in London, so I hire one when I need it. A better plan really, because then if anyone should take an interest in our movements the number of the car won't help them."

"It's like Puss in the Corner, isn't it?" Barbie agreed, pleasantly. "You have to watch all four corners at once. Still, with two of us the vigilance will be halved."

"Which of us watches the road?" I asked.

When we said good-night I told her, "Watch your step and don't take sweets off any old gentlemen." But so far as the first injunction was concerned I knew I might as well be Canute ordering the sea to recede.

As I made my way home it occurred to me to wonder, for the first time, just why Ted wanted to chuck up a country pub and come to the Admiral. It didn't seem to make sense.

:: ::

The next day was one of those brilliant mornings you sometimes get during a rainy season. Quite early there were a few tatters of mist, but these soon blew away and the sun came struggling through. There was a kind of buoyancy in the air, and the garage hired me a Baker-Boxer. I hadn't driven such a splendid car since I could remember, I usually go for one of the smaller kinds, but nothing was too good for Barbie. I picked her up at her gate, and as we moved off I saw a curtain stir in the flat above. The Hunters had the ground floor. I suppose I couldn't expect Miss Muffett to be the only Miss Pry in the city, but at the same time I felt I'd like to grab the creature round her scrawny throat—I took for granted it would be scrawny—and shake her black in the face. It was a delightful ride once we were clear of bricks and mortar. I'd looked up the road on a county map the night before, and marked all the diversions we could take. Time wasn't of great import, I didn't really expect to learn anything much, but it didn't matter. What mattered was that I had Barbie to myself for a whole day. Her spirits seemed to have risen to match the temperature. Just to be doing something, she explained, not just walking up and down and waiting for a miracle. If nothing whatever eventuates at least I shall feel we tried.

As we neared Beacon Heath the dread hand of the progressive builder became clearer and clearer. I think we had both imagined Beacon Heath as an old-world village with a green in front of the Angel, a bench *in situ* equipped with besmocked yokels quaffing pints, ducks on a pond, the lot. The reality was a minor new town that could have been lifted straight out of any suburb, rows of bright synchronised little shops with big windows, and two supermarkets. There was no Angel Inn, but an immense tatty bright roadhouse called The Archangel, with a chromium bar and a menu card as big as a sheet. We stopped to look at it; it stamped the place as Expenses Accounts Only.

" I can't see Ted here," I murmured. " Perhaps that's why he left." Because the place was being transformed and they'd want sideburns and foreign accents to give the authentic touch. We'd passed two less spectacular pubs but they were called The Black Horse and The Red

Cow, set in surroundings that couldn't have pastured either.

"Wait a minute," said Barbie. She slipped across the road into a stationer's shop where they sold postcards.

"Isn't there a rather famous church here?" she asked the languid young lady who glanced in her direction but made no further move to effect a sale. "The only one we can find looks like a swimming pool."

"Contemp'ry," said the young woman, examining her chipped nail polish.

"And an inn—the Angel?"

"You want the old town," said the girl, scornfully. "Three-quarters of a mile past the Model Village. That's worth a stop if you're interested. Ever so realistic really." For the first time she showed a grain of enthusiasm. "There's a race-course with a policeman chasing a chap carrying a bag marked Swag. There's a model of the old church there, but it's been closed for years."

"And that's where we shall find the Angel?"

"That's right. Potty little place really. When they built the New Town they wanted something a bit more class but to remind people—don't ask me why—so they built the Archangel. Got an old staircase or something a king once trod on"—she rummaged in a box—"might have a card of that."

She found it, a rather tatty sepia reproduction, but we bought it. It belonged, as we had suspected, to the Angel, not to the monstrosity over the road. When we came out, the manager of the Archangel, a dusky Mixo-Lydian type, had emerged from his establishment, and was scanning the road for possible clients. His attention was clearly focused on our Baker-Boxer. The only other car in sight was a little grey Hooper, and the driver of that came out of a tobacconist shop and got in and drove away. I don't think the Mixo-Lydian could have had much hope of him in any case. But we were another matter. A grin split his unpleasant face. He started to say something about a car park for patrons.

"Do you take trading stamps?" I asked.

I think he'd have spat at me if the pavement hadn't been so clean. As it was he disdainfully pointed to a café that accepted luncheon vouchers, but we hadn't got those either, so we got back into the car and drove away.

"I had a word with the girl while I was getting my change," Barbie said, "she told me the Angel doesn't do lunches, but there's Mrs. Wilson's Caff, a set lunch, but no licence."

"My vote goes to the Angel," I said. And brooded, "The Archangel, indeed! How are the mighty fallen! Or do you prefer Mrs. Wilson's stewed steak?"

"I'm starving," said Barbie, candidly. "Let's have a drink at the Angel and see what they offer, and if we don't learn anything we'll go on to Mrs. Wilson. She probably knows all the gossip. Provided, of course, she hasn't opened her caff since Ted left."

The Angel was oddly reminiscent of the Admiral; it had the same slightly gloomy interior and was much the same size. But in place of the rather subdued Ted there was a big gay-looking woman behind the bar, who reminded me of Madge. Barbie pleased me by preferring beer to a short drink; she and Mrs. Tewkes got on like a house on fire; she was just what we'd been hoping for, like a geyser no one's discovered how to turn off.

Barbie started the ball rolling. " We know the licensee who was here before you," she said.

Mrs. Tewkes looked startled. " Mr. James? Shocking, that accident. They've put up a notice now about the beach being dangerous for bathers, but it's like everything else Governments do, they're always too late."

" We didn't mean Mr. James," said Barbie. " Ted Farrer."

" Oh him! Well, that was some time back. Where is he now?"

" He's got a pub by London's riverside."

" Shouldn't have thought that would have suited him very well. Still, p'raps he didn't have much choice. And it 'ud be better than being barman at the Archangel, which was the best he could get after the trouble."

" I think he still regrets his time here," I put in.

" Yes. I'll lay." She nodded, and a big blue chain danced on her bosom. " That was a bad business for Ted. Mind you, my husband says he should have kept his eyes open a bit wider. It's not enough to keep the law, you have to be sure everyone knows you're keeping it. Funny thing was Ted's not a betting man himself. Fish, fish, fish, that's all he ever cared for. Not married, I suppose?"

We said, No, Ted wasn't married.

" Pity," said Mrs. Tewkes. " Brewers prefer a married man. Like a curate," she added, with one of her big infectious laughs. " Free assistance. No one pays a brewer's wife. Ted was lucky really to get that offer from Macrae."

I'd tumbled by this time. " Betting slips in the bar?"

177

I pushed my tankard across for another drink.

"That's about the size of it. Mind you, Ted says he didn't know it was going on and I believe him. You need four times the usual number of eyes in this line. Anyway, Frodsham's said he was paid to see the law was kept. Silly really, seeing nowadays there isn't the temptation. All these betting shops."

"Who stopped him?" I asked

"Well!" Mrs. Tewkes smoothed a high chestnut-coloured erection that did credit to the local hairdresser. "It was a dirty business. Ted wouldn't sell drinks to a minor, said he had his licence to consider. Boy swore he was eighteen and Ted asked if he could prove it. Pity was the boy's father was a big man roundabout, behind one of the New Town Supermarkets, and he said he wasn't going to have his son insulted."

"Was he eighteen?" asked Barbie.

"As a matter of fact, dear, he was, that very day. But when Ted asked him for proof he turned nasty. Mr. Romer swore to have Ted's blood. I've sometimes wondered if it wasn't a put-up job, but whichever way it was there was a stink and the brewers don't stand for that, as you know, so when the question of renewing Ted's licence came up old Mr. Hardcastle vetoed it. Mind you, they did say Romer was pinning the old man's ears back, and I wouldn't be surprised to know it was true, but Frodsham didn't back their man, and the long and the short of it was Ted went as barman to the Archangel."

"How long ago was this then?"

"Must be about five years. Mr. James came and he was here two years before he got himself drowned, and then Mr. Tewkes got the offer. You want to be careful, I told him, that's an unlucky pub but he doesn't go for superstitions, women's intuition he calls it, and says he wouldn't risk a penny stamp on it. Mind you, Ted tried for several other inns but no one would have him, not even to serve in the bar. Then young Mr. Macrae put in a word for him—there's no love lost between Frodsham and Macrae and he thought Ted had got the dirty end of the stick. The long and the short of it was he got his licence renewed and went up to London. Doesn't write, never comes back. How's he doing?"

I remembered chaps in the war who had been what we called bomb-carriers. Wherever they went the bombs came with them; if they shacked up in a country cottage you could be sure some Messerschmitt would unload a stray egg in the neighbourhood when it was being chased back across the Channel. I began to wonder if Ted was one of that lot. First the Angel, then the Admiral. I even began to wonder where he'd been before the Angel.

"Mind you," Mrs. Tewkes rippled on, "he was well-liked in these parts. Been here a long while, understood the people. He never took to the Archangel. I wouldn't have some of that lot in a zoo, he said. Not fair to the apes. He could be outspoken, could Ted. Wonder what he does about his fishing now."

"There is the Thames," I murmured, but I don't think she heard me.

"Up at four of a morning he'd be, and then standing all day by the water, never seemed to worry him whether he caught much or not. Daft I call it, but that's men for you." She looked across to Barbie and winked.

"He seems to have settled," I said, and invited Barbie

to have another drink. But she said No, and we ought to be getting along, and how pleased you must be to be at the Angel and not the Archangel.

" Did you see those sandwiches at the far end of the bar?" I asked her, when we were outside. "About a quarter-pound of home-cooked ham between each two slices of bread."

"I know," she agreed, fervently. "If I'd stayed another minute I should have succumbed, but I think we ought to try and find out more now we are here. I mean, why should anyone think he could blackmail Ted because of the trouble with Frodsham? Macrae knew about that. There must be something else."

"Remember," I warned her, "we haven't any actual proof that Ted is concerned in this affair at all."

"I know," said Barbie. "That's why we must ask some more questions." We began to walk down the High Street, looking for Mrs. Wilson's Caff.

When we found it it was very much what I'd anticipated, and pretty crowded, too. We managed to get a tiny table pushed up against the wall that we didn't have to share. There wasn't much else to be said for it. The choice was between steak pie and Irish stew, and I wouldn't care to recommend either. Mrs. Wilson didn't offer to send out for drinks, and her arty-crafty maidens disguised as waitresses probably wouldn't have demeaned themselves to go into a pub anyway. We'd reached the coffee stage and were practically the last people in the place before Barbie got a chance to ask questions. The coffee was on a par with everything else—made from Instant and much too weak. A waitress was ostentatiously spreading triangular pink-fringed table napkins over the white tablecloths, a concession to the greater delicacy of afternoon tea, and another had got a finicky tall dustpan and brush and was sweeping crumbs off the floor. I noticed a good proportion of them missed the pan.

"Are you closing?" inquired Barbie innocently, to Mrs. Wilson, who had come down in person to speed our departure.

"The staff need a little time for their lunch before we start serving teas," Mrs. W. pointed out stiffly.

"We were recommended to come to you," Barbie told her. "We'd come to look up someone who used to be at The Angel, but he's gone to London. He used to be the landlord there."

"Not Mr. James? But he was drowned in that shocking accident."

I reflected there seemed to be an awful lot of death connected with this case, and I didn't flatter myself we'd got to the end of the list yet.

"No. A man called Ted Farrer. Do you remember him?"

"Yes, of course. He lost his licence, you know, for permitting betting on his premises. So fortunate he wasn't a married man. And that wasn't all there was to it," she added, darkly.

"No?" Barbie looked surprised. "What on earth could people find to say about Ted? He seems such a quiet sort of person."

"Still waters run deep," retorted Mrs. Wilson, as I'd known she would. "And he had some very funny friends. You can't be too careful in his position. Tinkers, poachers, I don't know what, hob-nobbing with them and letting them come into the Angel."

"I didn't know you could stop them," ejaculated Barbie. " Not so long as they don't create a disturbance."

"It's not very nice for other people who want a quiet drink. And sensible people recognise which side their bread's buttered. I hear that when Lord Learmouth's gamekeeper went into the Angel and saw Harry Potter drinking at the bar as cool as you please, he nearly broke a blood-vessel. Harry Potter was known to poach game from the Learmouth Estate, and Binns, the game-keeper, said he watched like a lynx but he never saw Ted take anything in exchange for the beer Potter was drinking."

" Perhaps he was standing him one on the house," I said.

" Tit for tat, that was what most people thought," returned Mrs. Wilson. She pulled out a pad and started making out our bill.

Barbie, who, like most women, tripped lightly in where angels would fear to tread, inquired, " What exactly did you mean, Mrs. Wilson? That Ted accepted poached game in exchange for free drinks."

Mrs. Wilson slammed down the bill. Suddenly she looked angry. " I'll tell you this. Someone set on Binns one night, knocked him about shocking, he's never been the same man since. Of course everyone knew it was Potter, but Ted Farrer came forward and swore Harry had been with him at the time. No one could shake him."

" Presumably because it was true," said Barbie.

" It showed very little sense of what was fitting that he should have stopped on in the neighbourhood after he lost the Angel," insisted Mrs. Wilson.

" But if he'd cleared out everyone would have said he was running away."

If Barbie had come down to try and establish Ted's complicity in the double London murder it seemed to me she was going a remarkably funny way about it.

" I'm glad to know he's settled all right," said Mrs. Wilson spitefully. " Let's hope he's learned his lesson."

I paid the bill and she pretended not to notice the silver I left on the rose-bordered plate. As we walked into the street I heard the key of the shop turn behind us.

" What a beldam!" said Barbie. " I almost feel sympathy for Ted Farrer. I wonder if it's true that he was shielding the old poacher."

" It's just a lot of gossip," I said.

" Mr. Crook mightn't think so."

I gasped. " You haven't got the nerve to tell Crook we've been muscling in on his preserve?"

" There's no sense our making inquiries unless we're going to pass on anything we can find."

" We haven't found anything," I said.

" There was that alibi. Suppose it was false? And suppose someone knows it?"

" It's all supposition," I said.

" Suppose Madge knew? Don't ask me how, but suppose she did?"

" She wasn't the blackmailing type."

" She was being blackmailed herself."

This wasn't the way in which I'd imagined we should spend our day together, and when you came to add up what we'd found it amounted to damn all. Ted had made a mistake and paid pretty heavily for it. He'd given an unpopular character an alibi. I know women can work miracles, but if anyone was going to span the gulf between a faked abili, even allowing it was faked, and murder, he was going to be a lot cleverer than I was.

" What happened to Daniels after he came out of prison?"

" We don't know," I reminded her.

" Perhaps that's the answer."

I said, scandalised, " You've absolutely nothing to go on. He's probably never met the man."

" He's got a past, Ted, I mean, and people with a past are always fair game. I wonder what happened to Harry Potter."

That was one question to which we did find the answer. At a little sweet and tobacco store where we bought a packet of chocolate we learned that Harry Potter was dead.

CHAPTER IX

WE HAD to start back earlier than I'd anticipated. Barbie's show was on television, which meant she had to change into a suitable dress and decorations. She couldn't, it seemed, appear in the suit she'd been wearing all day. She had had the sense to bring a case with her containing her clothes, and she could change at the studio, but we had a fair distance to go, and as the evening came on the traffic began to thicken up. I was at a loss to realise what we'd gained, but Barbie never lost heart for an instant. She insisted that Crook would be interested at least to learn what we had discovered. Precisely what that was, as I've said, I wasn't sure.

" And in any case," I told her, " has it occurred to you that, if Crook has the smallest suspicion of Ted he'll have made his own inquiries by now?"

" He hasn't," said Barbie, simply. " Did you wonder why I asked at so many places? I wanted to know whether anyone else had been going round, and not a single person said, That's funny, you're the second to ask about Ted, though it's five years since his trouble." And before I could think of a suitable answer she went on, " Does it occur to you that there's something odd about this man Macrae taking so much trouble to get Ted a berth?"

" Perhaps he's a public-spirited person who believed Ted's version and thought he'd had a raw deal."

" Of course," said Barbie simply, " or it could be that his arm was twisted a little."

" I believe," I told her, " if a Martian popped up in front of the car at this instant you'd suggest he was somehow involved."

We were both quiet for a bit after that; Barbie was doubtless thinking along the same lines as myself. Suspicion wasn't enough. How could we set about *proving* that he was involved?

Presently I saw her look surreptitiously at her watch. We were coming back at the worst possible time. The side roads that had proved so helpful that morning did very little for us now. We ran into a factory neighbourhood where everyone knocked off at five o'clock, and every other worker seemed to own a car. It was like finding yourself in a procession of vari-coloured beetles.

" I'll get you back in time," I promised her, cutting in a bit adroitly and turning a deaf ear to a driver who objected to my skill.

" Just so long as you get me there in one piece," agreed Barbie, good-naturedly.

I worried a bit about the time factor, and then something happened that worried me a lot more. As I've said, we were in a fairly solid line of traffic, but glancing in my driving mirror I began to notice one car in particular that seemed to be following us fairly persistently. It was a small grey Hooper. Now as everyone knows, Hoopers are a very popular make of car, economical on petrol and not too expensive to buy. So clearly there'd be a good proportion of them on the road, and of these a reasonable number would be grey. But I found myself remembering the grey Hooper that had been parked out-

side the Archangel on our arrival. I told myself it was
fantastic, no one could know we were coming; only
there had been no secrecy about it. Anyone could have
followed Barbie, or me for that matter. If my monstrous
suspicion was right it had been pretty clever, because the
only time I'd glimpsed it had been in Beacon Halt, New
Town. But then I hadn't been in a good mood to notice
any other vehicle. I repeatedly told myself we were as
right as rain, since no one would dare to try and engineer
an accident with so much stuff on the road, but it was
cold comfort. Then I told myself I was getting fanciful,
it was just good old coincidence again, and to prove it I
took a sudden left-hand turn into what the map called a
second-class road, and I should have said was a country
lane. The light was fading and there were no lamps here;
if the car came after us that would be proof positive.

"Keep your eye on the driving mirror," I told Barbie,
"tell me if you see a grey car."

After a minute or so she said, "Looking like a snail?
An Archer?"

"A Hooper," I said. The cars aren't dissimilar if
you're an amateur.

"It's following us," said Barbie, in puzzled tones.

"Or the owner lives up this lane."

"Do you happen to know where the lane leads?" she
asked me. "It doesn't look to me as if anything more
civilised than a hedgehog would be living here."

"Can you see the driver?" I asked. She said it was a
man she thought, with a hat pulled over his eyes. These
Hoopers are rather low on the ground, and the Boxers
are high; in the failing light it would be hard to make
anything of his face. I began to regret my decision to

leave the main road; the going here was very stiff, and I hardly dared take my eyes off the stony surface. It seemed to me he was drawing slightly closer. Then a wooden door opened somewhere—it looked like the middle of a hedge and a motor-cycle shot out; we just scraped past, but the Hooper got held up. I put on speed.

" Hold your hat!" I said.

The voices behind us grew fainter; a turning revealed itself on our right and I made half a U-turn and we bounced through. I wasn't sure if we'd brought all the Baker-Boxer's paint with us, though.

" Have you any idea where we're heading?" asked Barbie, and I said, " There are telegraph poles over there, we must be near the main road," and a minute or two later we hit it. The traffic here was less dense and we made quite good progress. Though we both kept a sharp look-out there was no sign of the Hooper until we drew near to the Old Kent Road. Then a dark spot appeared in the driving mirror and I knew our old enemy had caught up with us.

" He can't try any brigandage in this crowded street," I told her, but I knew that was sheer wishful-thinking. He could bump the car, he could even come up alongside and block us. I hadn't any doubt now that he was on our tail. I accelerated and managed to get a Green Line coach behind us, close to one of its compulsory stops. That would hold up the Hooper, and then we had a bit more luck and shaved past on the amber, while our pursuer was held up by lights.

" There's a new large garage in Spiller Street," I murmured, " I'm going to run us into that."

We found the corner and took it; there was a ramp running up and luckily no queue and so we found ourselves under cover and out of sight of the road.

" Do you think he saw us?" Barbie panted, and I said I hoped not, but she'd better go and powder her nose, I'd turn the car in for an hour, and we'd go on by subway.

"Oh, dear," sighed Barbie with feminine inconsistency, " the one time I might have impressed everyone by arriving in a millionaire's car and this has to happen."

But she went off meekly enough, while I explained to the attendant that I'd be leaving the car for a couple of hours, say. I hauled Barbie's suit-case out from the boot and said something about the density of the traffic.

" I sometimes think I'd like a helicopter," the attendant agreed, " but I suppose by that time the traffic aloft 'ull be as bad as the traffic on the road, and it 'ull be a lot farther to fall."

" A chap scraped me coming along," I murmured, going round to examine the paintwork, but the damage was infinitesimal. That relieved me a bit; if you get a bit of damage to a hire-car you usually find you could practically have bought a new one by the time the owner's satisfied with the repair. Then Barbie came back, and I went ahead to make sure the Hooper wasn't lurking, but there was no sign of it, so I caught her by the arm and ran her across to the subway station.

" Keep a weather-eye open when we get there," I warned her. " This chap may have done his homework and know you're on the wide screen to-night."

But there was no sign of him anywhere.

" You take care of yourself, too," said Barbie.

I wanted to come and collect her when her show was over, but she wouldn't hear of it.

"We may be kept hanging about for ages," she explained. "We have to discuss next week, and there could be something for me in a play. One lives in hope."

"Well, ring me when you get back," I besought her, and she said, "It all depends on the time. Don't fuss so, Simon, I shall be all right. I'll tell you what, you ring me in the morning, not too early, and then I shall know you haven't come to grief either."

On that not particularly satisfactory arrangement we parted.

I went back to the garage and collected the car. "Has anyone been asking about her?" I wanted to know.

The attendant took fright at once. "Why should they?" he demanded. "She's not hot, is she?"

"Of course she's not hot," I said. "I only hired her from Jack's Garage this morning."

I pulled the hire card out of my pocket.

"In any case it wouldn't be the car this chap could be interested in."

A sly look passed over his weaselly face. "Husbands are inclined to be unreasonable," he agreed, with a smirk.

I'd have liked to knock his block off. Anyway, he said, no one had come.

"If they should you haven't seen her," I told him, though I didn't anticipate any development after this long pause. He nodded and said that 'ud be all right, Guv., so I gave him what would presumably be a co-respondent's tip and drove away. I kept a fairly sharp look-out all the way to Lucas Street but no grey Hooper surfaced. I told the man at the garage I might be wanting the car again, though I wouldn't book it definitely, and then I went out. It was getting latish by now, and I decided to look in at the Admiral before I had something to eat. It wasn't likely Crook would be there, but no harm making sure. I saw one or two faces I recognised, but no one special. Presently I asked Ted if I might use his phone. He didn't have a pay phone as a lot of pubs do, but he could be prevailed upon to let clients put through a call on his private line. He said Yes, he supposed so, not much sweetness and light anywhere in the world that evening, and I went through to his private room behind the bar. It was a typical bachelor's room, whose lack of comfort would have made a woman weep, but I don't suppose he ever noticed it. There were four Victorian type arm-chairs set diamond-wise in the four corners, a round table, a shabby desk he didn't even bother to lock, a book-case, a lot of fishing-rods piled in the corner. There was a stuffed fish in a case, and I wondered if he'd found it there on arrival or if he'd brought it with him. I dialled my number and heard the bell ringing away like mad, but no one answered it, and presently I hung up.

" No luck," I told him. He was busy and just nodded and I oiled out. It was getting a bit late for the Chicken Parlour so I turned into an Italian restaurant that had been newly-opened and I'd heard well-spoken-of. It had the usual rather dark interior, small tables with a Chianti bottle on each, but nothing else bogus. The food was first-class, though the service was incredibly slow. I'd heard that time doesn't matter a lot to the Eyeties, and now I believed it. I had plenty of time to look around me between the courses, and presently I got the idea that a chap dining on the farther side of the room was taking a rather unusual interest in me. At all events he kept looking across; there were big gilt mirrors on the wall, so he could watch my movements in the glass, too. I shifted my chair so that I got an oblique view of him. It wasn't too easy to see, but I was quite convinced I'd never set eyes on him before. He was thin and dark, with big bony features. He could have been almost anyone. He could, of course, have been the driver of the grey Hooper. My sole consolation was that if he was watching me he couldn't simultaneously be spying on Barbie. I was absolutely certain there'd only been one person in the car. Then it occurred to me that if he was that chap the grey Hooper must be parked somewhere alongside. I'd realised vaguely there were a few cars outside, but I hadn't paid any particular attention to them. The restaurant stood on a corner and the cars were mostly parked in a narrow street running off the main one. I asked my waiter if they had a telephone on the premises, and **he** indicated a door leading to some stairs. I ostentatiously **left** my coat and gloves by my table, in case he thought I was trying to make a getaway by the window, or something, and went through the door. My suspect was looking dreamily in the glass, you could make what you liked of that. I dialled my own number—it occurred to me to wonder what I'd do if someone answered, but of course no one did. The telephone was in a narrow passage with a window looking over the lane. Leaving the receiver swinging I tiptoed as far as the window and pushed it up. There was a light outside and I could easily distinguish the five or six parked cars, but the

Hooper wasn't among them. I was drawing my head back when I heard a sound behind me; it was my waiter, watching me with intense suspicion.

" Not that way, sare," he said. " There is a door."

" I know there is," I said. " I came in by it. I just wanted to make sure my car was safe."

I don't know whether he believed me; he picked up the swinging phone and put it back on its rest.

" Too bad about my friend," I told him. " I wanted him to join me for coffee and liqueurs, but there's no reply."

He escorted me back to my table without comment. My suspect was on his feet, talking with great animation to the manager and using rather more gestures than are common among Englishmen. I caught a word or two and realised he was talking in Italian, and all my suspicions were nonsense. How dumb can you get?

I ordered coffee and a liqueur and stayed for a while, somehow I didn't fancy my quiet room where I knew the phone wouldn't ring. When I came out it was to find a clear night, the stars being particularly brilliant. A wind had sprung up that had swept away the casual twilight mistiness, the moon blazed in the dark sky, there was an air of magic abroad. It wasn't a night to spend alone, but I couldn't go back to the Admiral, and I didn't fancy visiting the Horse and Mariner. Tom Fraser was still sore about Lefty and still dubious about Doggett's existence. So I went home. It passed through my mind that Barbie might ring up from her studio—not that I really believed that, but I was in a mood when one catches at straws. I found some letters on the hall-table and pushed them into my pocket. As I went up the stairs Miss Muffett's door opened a crack, and she said, " There have been two telephone calls for you, Mr. Crete."

" Have there?" I murmured. " Well, if it's important they'll ring again, won't they?"

I opened my letters, made a phone-call, drew a couple of cheques, and then tried to settle down to a detective story. But it was no good. The worst of books is they will prettify everything, not necessarily the crime, they don't seem to mind buckets of blood there, but the hero always gets his girl. I suppose after so much treachery and gloom the public demands a cheerful ending. I had a vision of Crook bursting his great face in a gigantic grin and exploding, " You call *that* a happy ending? Chum, you don't know you're born," but I wasn't in a mood for Crook's pleasantries to-night. Thinking about him, though, made me wonder how he was going to take our story, because even if I tried to suppress our activities I knew Barbie wouldn't. I found a cross-word I hadn't touched and that occupied me for some time, but from 11 o'clock onwards my ear was cocked for the sound of the telephone. And it didn't ring. That is, it rang once, and a youthful cockney voice said, " Do you do short time?"

" You'll be doing long time if you go on putting through calls like that," I told the chap tartly, and he rang off with a clang that nearly shattered my ear-drum. There was a lot of that sort of thing going on just then, particularly round my neighbourhood. I wondered if Barbie had had any. Women of all ages got them, and there was nothing the police or the Post Office could do about it. I thought that's one result of driving the girls off the game. I wondered if the police had considered that. The calls mostly came from boxes, and so, naturally couldn't be traced. I waited up till one o'clock, but it didn't ring again, and at last I went to bed.

I rang Barbie at half-past eight next morning. Not too early, she'd said, and I hoped she wouldn't think this an impossible hour. But no one answered, so I hung up and tried again later. I tried twice, and when there was no reply to my third call I began to get the wind up. The telephone probably was not in her room, but she must be awake by this time, I thought. I wished I'd stuck to my original notion of going back to the studio and insisting on bringing her home. My feelings of disquietude sprang up like the soldiery who leaped out of the ground where the dragons-teeth were sown. I couldn't wait any longer. A taxi was setting down an old lady on the other side of the street, and I chased after it and gave Barbie's address. I could have walked it in about fifteen minutes, but that sense of urgency wouldn't let me take it the easy way. When I reached the house I saw a bottle of milk and a newspaper on the step; I opened the gate and walked in. The newspaper had Hunter scrawled along the edge. The blinds—curtains, rather—hadn't been drawn in the two front rooms; I couldn't get round by the back and see what was happening there. I heard a sound above my head and looked up to see the ancient spy at the upstairs window. She pushed back the curtains and pulled up the sash.

"They're away," she hissed, like the first cousin to Cleopatra's asp.

"I know Mrs. Hunter is away," I said, "but Miss

Hunter was expecting me. You don't happen to know what time she came back?"

The old witch shook her head. " She didn't come in at all. I sleep in the front and that gate creaks when you open it. I should have heard her. She always wakes me."

She displayed that secret pleasure in giving bad news that actuates people whose own lives are uneventful.

" Her letters are still on the table," she added. " The postman will put them all in one box, though they're labelled as you can see."

" She said she might go back with a friend if she was kept late at the studio," I said, in the most careless voice I could assume. But I didn't believe it. If Barbie were with some companions she would have telephoned me to let me know her change of plan, bearing in mind her injunction to me to ring her. I couldn't rest: I thought of ringing Crook, but I was too unsure of my reception. Who appointed you nursemaid? he might say. In desperation I took the underground to her studio and walked in through the gate. The place hummed with activity, though it was Saturday morning, but I suppose Saturday doesn't make the same difference in broadcasting. A number of people were waiting in the hall, hoping for last-minute tickets for a live show, waiting for appointments, trying to get interviews. I could pick out the authors and actors without much difficulty. There was something about them, a studied disinterest imperfectly covering an inward apprehension, a sort of dogged eagerness, as though they were prepared to wait there till the end of the world and catch their prey in a butterfly net when they assembled for the final roll-call. At any other time I should have enjoyed watching them, but to-day I couldn't think of anyone but Barbie. I asked a girl at a desk if Miss Hunter was on the set and she looked at me in surprise and then consulted a paper in front of her.

" I don't think so," she said calmly.

" I thought she was rehearsing in this play," I ventured. (Because where else *could* she be?)

" What play?" asked the girl. " She was on the quiz programme last night. Perhaps you've got your dates muddled."

She was as exquisitely turned out, as cool, as smooth as if she were made out of enamel. I longed for a rough hair, a smudged lipstick, anything human.

" I suppose I have," was all I could find to say. But I knew, of course, that something had gone fearfully wrong. Only why to Barbie? Why not to me?

As I came away I caught sight of the same man at the studio car park as I'd noticed the night before. I crossed over to him. He was a brisk-looking type, appeared reliable, if you can ever go on looks.

" You know Miss Hunter?" I said, and he answered Yes, he did.

" She was here last night," I told him, and he said Yes, she was. Then he added, " It was you brought her, wasn't it?"

" That's right. I was going to call back for her, but I got delayed, and—keep this under your hat *pro tem* but—well, I've been round to the house and she didn't get back last night. It just occurred to me there might have been some accident on the set. I daresay," I added desperately, " this sounds just cops and robbers to you, but her lawyer won't think so."

" Lawyer?" That made him prick up his ears.

" That's what I said." Though somehow I couldn't really think of Crook as a lawyer. " The truth is she had an anonymous letter, probably some lunatic, but you can never be quite sure, can you?"

His expression changed, he looked sly and immensely knowing. " Keep this under *your* hat," he said, " but she was all right when she left last night. Met by a friend."

" Oh!" I murmured. And he nodded.

I put my hand in my trouser pocket and meditatively clinked some coins. It might not work, but, on the other hand, it might.

" Chap in a grey Hooper," my companion went on. " Noticed it specially because it's the kind of car I'm trying to pick up myself. Trouble with a second-hand job is you can't get a really good guarantee . . ."

I must have heard all this, to be able to set it down, but none of it really registered after grey Hooper. I wondered what the driver had told her, that her mother had been sick, that he had a message from Crook, it must have been something pretty convincing for her to have gone with him. Unless, of course, she had no choice. I had a ghastly vision of her getting into the car with a knife-blade at her throat, or a gun in her ribs; and if that sounds fantastic it's no more fantastic than the yarns you can read every morning in the Press. Then I realised the chap was staring at me, so I threw up my head, gave a semblance of a laugh and said in would-be relieved tones, " Of course, I know who that would be! How crazy can you get! Seeing too much TV, I suppose."

I pushed some coins into his hand, told him I was much obliged and heard him say it was always nice to know you had friends. Then I sauntered away towards the exit.

Up till now I hadn't allowed myself to believe actual misfortune had overtaken her; now I knew I couldn't kid myself any longer. I turned into a station telephone-booth and called Crook; I called him on both numbers, but there was no reply from either. I thought it would just put the tin lid on the situation if he'd decided to take a week-end out of town. There didn't seem much point going to the police; they'd only tell me the young lady had a right to go pleasure-riding with anyone she pleased, she was free, white and twenty-one. Though I was convinced it was a waste of time I went back by way of her flat. Nothing had changed; the newspaper was still on the step, flanked by the milk-bottle; the curtains on the floor above fluttered, and I saw two fingers come stealing round to separate them. I went through the farce of calling her number from a nearby post office, but, of course, no one replied.

When I got back to my flat the postman was just coming away. We only have two postal deliveries on Saturdays, the second one just before lunch. Then the postal staff can put up their feet till Monday morning, I suppose. I knew this particular man by sight; he was a tall, elderly bony chap, with remarkably light blue eyes. He must have had the stamina of a mountain goat; I saw him bouncing down steep basement flights and running up again as fleet as a deer. When he saw me he grinned.

"You've got some nice friends," he said. He passed the next two doors and vanished down an area. I got out my key and let myself in. There were a couple of letters in my box, and for once I'd beaten Miss Muffett to it. I saw at once which of the two had engaged his interest. If I hadn't seen this particular envelope before, I'd seen its twin. Cheap, off-white, addressed in straggling capital letters. The message inside was composed of words cut from newspapers and stuck together to make a sentence—two sentences actually. It ran:

You were warned. Take no steps.

This time there was no signature.

The postmark was the same as before. Posted in the district it had missed the last collection on Friday and been picked up, sorted and delivered in a matter of hours. It seemed quick work, but I'm told they don't bother with commercial mail on Friday nights, most of the business houses being shut till Monday, so presumably the residents get extra slick service. I didn't stop to open my other letter, I hurled myself at the phone. This time, when I dialled Crook's number, I heard his voice instantly. I forgot about his possible indignation at our private inquiry and I told him bluntly, "They've got Barbie. She's disappeared."

"Voluntary or the other thing?" he inquired, as cool as an ice cornet.

"Not voluntary. Listen." I told him about the previous day's excursion, our attempt to make out a solid case against Ted, the grey Hooper following us and finally catching up with Barbie.

"And I've just found a letter," I said. I realised I was breathing as though I'd been racing uphill.

"Quite the little Sherlock Holmes," was Crook's comment. He sounded positively affable and not in the least dismayed. I didn't know him very well, but I had the uncomfortable feeling that when he was aping the gentleman, that's when he was really dangerous.

"I've never understood the point of keeping a dog and barking yourself," he went on. "It's the sort of thing that makes any self-respecting dog put its hackles up and bare its teeth. And then it can be as dangerous as a charging bull. Ever thought of that?"

"We simply wanted to help," I said.

"Ever thought of the amount of harm done by do-gooders in this wicked world?" Crook went on, and I found myself thinking, This is it. *Après moi*, the deluge. I knew any second now it was going to come down upon me, tons and tons of storm-water, to drown, to flatten, to sweep me out of sight.

"Too bad you should have given yourself so much trouble," Crook went on. "If you'd wanted the gen. on Ted I could have given it to you."

I felt the breath go out of my body in a sort of whoosh. "You mean, you knew . . ."

"That's what you're paying me for," said Crook. "At least, what Mrs. Hunter's paying me for. A grey Hooper, you said. Didn't get the number, I suppose?"

"No. I thought we'd thrown it off the trail, but it

must have known about Barbie being at the studio last night—the driver must have known, I mean. What I don't understand is why Barbie went with him."

"Could be she had no choice," said Crook. "Chap don't have to drive a Rolls to have a persuasive way with him. Anyway, there's more than one grey Hooper in the world."

I hadn't thought of that possibility, and I didn't entertain the idea now.

"She must have been told some cock-and-bull story. If she thought there was anything wrong with her mother she'd go like a shot."

"Funny," mused Crook. "She don't sound to me like a nitwit. Female—yes, but the intelligent type. Hadn't gone through your mind she went with this chap because she wanted to go?"

"No, it hadn't," I said, furiously.

"This chap at the studio—any suggestion of force there?"

"He didn't notice any. But—she could be held as a hostage, couldn't she?"

"*Cui bono?*" asked Crook. He pronounced it kwee bonno.

"If you've got hold of an incriminating document they might offer her in exchange . . ."

"This ain't a Western," Crook protested, "and even a criminal daft enough to try and abduct one of my clients would have the wit to know that I wouldn't part with a document till I'd got it Photostatted. I'm no Mr. Muggins. And I don't think much of your idea, Simon. I don't believe that girl would sell Bruce down the river, even for Mum. And Mum wouldn't thank her if she did. Now, listen. You want to help?"

" You know I want to help. If Barbie's in danger . . ."

" Listen," said Crook again. " I ain't running a matrimonial agency, and it's nothing to me who the lady weds or if she weds you both. My only job is to get young Bruce out of clink, and I tell you candidly, Simon, I'd feel safer with you somewhere out in the long grass."

" You mean . . ."

. ." Get lost," said Crook, brutally. " Go into the wild wood, go to the North Pole, look for that house under the sea that fish merchant built. Only—keep away from sugar's flat and keep away from Harpoint. (That was the prison where Bruce was being held.) If you like to send me your address on a postcard I'll file it for reference. Understood?"

" You don't realise," I began in desperation, and at that his wrath finally broke.

" God in Heaven," he cried, " haven't you done enough harm as it is? Chasing round, arousing suspicions, making trouble for me all along the line? This ain't a paper-chase you're playing at, it's a double murder, and if I don't watch out it'll be a triple one. And I don't intend to feature as Corpse Number Three, nor I don't want sugar to feature either. What you do with your own carcass is your own affair. You know the old law, that a householder had the right to shoot a trespasser on suspicion? Well, I ain't such a bad shot myself when amateurs come poaching on my preserves. Why not start a new trail, give 'em a run for their money, then perhaps they'll come after you."

" That 'ud suit you fine, wouldn't it?" I said, fiercely.

" Too true it would," he agreed. " Oh, by the way," his voice changed as if he'd taken off one record and put on another, " one little development that might interest you. Some Nosy Parker going through Ted's possessions found a tube of chloral at the back of a desk drawer— just the job for doping and no after-effects. Now you see what you can find out by staying on the spot and keeping your peepers open."

And on that exit line he rang off.

CHAPTER X

AFTER SOME TIME I remembered to look at the other letter I had brought up. I knew the hand-writing at once. At any other time the contents would have seemed to me top priority, something I must take action on immediately; but to-day only Barbie seemed to have real significance. Doggett wrote that he had now had proof, to his own satisfaction if not that of the authorities, that Wright and Parnell had been in a conspiracy to poison his dog, Lefty. I knew, of course, that he wouldn't approach the police, however favourably the circumstances might support his contention. Men in his shoes settle their differences in their own way, and the police are regarded as spoilsports by a good many citizens. Ted hadn't wanted them at the Admiral, they might give him confidence but they wouldn't arouse it in others. I knew, then, that Doggett was, as they say, on the boil, and prepared to take matters into his own hands. And he wouldn't consider Wright deserving of any mercy. He would peg him out on an ant-hill, leave him locked in a burning house—nothing was too strong. His letter was that of a man lost to reason. It might already be too late to intervene, but I could hear Crook's voice—Get lost, you're nothing but a liability. And I felt I might be better employed trying to control Doggett, if time hadn't already run out, than sit about on my backside in my flat waiting for news of Barbie. I found a postcard and scrawled an address on it, then remembered the next day would be Sunday, and in any case the final Saturday collection had been taken up. I threw the card in my waste-paper-basket, threw some things into a case and left the house. I went by a devious route to Wimbledon—my train left from Waterloo, but on Saturday afternoons it was a stopping one and I knew I could pick it up in the suburbs. If the driver of the grey Hooper was on my trail he might not expect me to follow this course. There were not many people travelling, and though I walked through a number of carriages my presence didn't appear to arouse any interest. Passengers alighted and boarded the train at every stop but none of them aroused my suspicion, though I knew, of course, you can never be a hundred per cent sure. I wished I'd been able to let Crook know where I was, though in the mood he was at present I doubt if he'd have turned a hair if he'd read in the Sunday Press that my body with half-a-dozen knife stabs in it, had been found at the foot of some embankment.

Doggett seemed surprised to see me. " There was nothing for me to do in London," I explained, " Crook had pushed me out of the nest like a discarded fledgeling, I thought for both our sakes it might be wiser to come down here."

" Wiser?" said Doggett in the same suspicious voice.

I told him about Barbie.

" Are you sure it's not you they're after?" he said. " I warned you to stay away from that girl."

" I can't," I told him, simply.

" Look where it's landed you."

I looked about me. " I could be in a worse place."

"You've got Crook on the warpath. Anyone who thinks he can take on Crook must be a maniac."

"She could be in danger."

"And not the only one. What happens to me if they follow you here? Didn't think of that, I suppose?"

"Chap must have done his homework," I brooded. "He knew where he'd find her."

"He'd only have to be able to read to do that." Suddenly he chuckled in a humourless sort of way. "Could be he didn't think you were her best escort," he grinned. "You ain't in too healthy a spot yourself. Does she know anything that could harm you?"

"What could she know?" I asked. "My own idea is she's being held as hostage on Bruce's account."

"I don't know anything about that," said Doggett. "Only if anyone thinks Crook would give in to blackmail he's madder than I thought. Why, he'd let you and the girl go overboard to save his client."

"If anything happens to Barbie," I began, and was pulled up short by his incredulous furious gaze.

"Of all the sodding fools!" he ejaculated, softly. "My God!"

"You're so full of good advice," I taunted him, "it mightn't do you any harm to take some of it yourself. All this yap about taking the law into your own hands . . ."

"What am I supposed to do? Call the rozzers?"

"Well, no," I agreed, "you'd hardly do that." There are quite a lot of tricks in the trade, and Doggett knew them all; the police knew a number and what they knew they didn't appreciate. "Why don't you cut your losses?" I urged. "You can't get the dog back, your chance will come sooner or later . . ."

"It's against my principles," said Doggett. "Besides, Wright could have an accident, couldn't he? Anyone could have an accident. Someone's got to teach him a lesson."

"All right," I said. "So he has an accident. And how long before you have an accident? Remember, God's on the side of the big battalions, and Wright's battalions could eat yours for breakfast."

We went down to the Fishermen's Arms as soon as it opened. Doggett knew a number of people there, one or two mentioned Lefty, others talked about the night's racing. No one mentioned Bruce or Barbie or even Madge Gardiner. I got the impression that if I'd spoken any of those three names my answer would have been a blank stare. Murder's happening all the time, Madge was a silly old totty asking for trouble. Doggett was in his element here, various chaps came over to ask his opinion, one man wanted to buy a dog if my friend could give him a tip. In a way it was like being in a club; the rounds were taken up by everyone in turn, I was accepted along with the rest. Even strangers seemed to know Doggett. One man came over from the bar and asked if Sir Lancelot was a good bet.

"As good a way as any of losing your stake," Doggett told him. "You'd do better to spend it on beer."

The chap took the hint and bought a round. As he moved back to the bar to give the order I asked Doggett, "Who's that character?"

Doggett shrugged, but I felt uneasy. "You're too free with your tongue," I said. "He could be in cahoots with Wright."

" So what? But I'll ask him, if it's worrying you."

The stranger—he said his name was Tharp—had just said Here's health and taken up his glass when Doggett inquired, " Ever met a man called Wright? Operates hereabouts?"

Tharp slowly put down his glass. " You pulling my leg?"

" No," said Doggett. " Should I?"

" You mean, you haven't heard?"

" Heard what?"

" Wright was found shot about two hours ago. The police are asking questions."

One of the men with us turned sharply. " Police? Are you . . .?"

" I'd have to tell you if I was, wouldn't I? No. Did you know him, though?"

" We were in partnership at one time," said Doggett. " Quite a while back, though."

" Didn't see eye to eye?"

The colour came boiling into Doggett's face. " Chap like that's got no right to keep kennels," he declared. " And so I told him."

" Any idea why . . .?"

" Someone 'ud want to murder him? I could guess."

Tharp said abruptly, " Who's talking about murder?"

That gave most of us a jolt. " Why, you . . ." Doggett began.

" I said shot. They found the gun beside him. Any idea why he should want to take his own life?"

" Perhaps someone poisoned his kennels," one of the men suggested.

"Well, would you kill yourself because someone wrecked your business? Wouldn't you stay alive and see he got what was coming to him?"

"I'd take him with me," Doggett allowed. He put down his empty glass; I don't think he'd tasted a drop. Tharp nodded to the barman who was going round clearing the tables.

"Same again," he said. He looked at me. "You ready? And by the time you've brought those I daresay the other gentlemen wouldn't say No to a refill."

He spoke blandly enough, but I didn't like it, and I could see the others didn't like it either. He was down here for a purpose, sounding us out.

"Wright a friend of yours?" I exploded.

"I didn't really know him. Maybe the tax chaps were after him."

"How did you happen to hear then?"

"Some chaps were talking." The barman came back with some drinks on a tray. "You'd heard about Wright?"

The barman nodded. "Had the police round before opening-time. I can't tell you anything, I said, though I had heard a rumour. Got into the hands of money-lenders, could be something worse, I wouldn't know. I suppose he did do it himself?"

It was the question I'd been inwardly debating ever since I heard the news. I thought it was a good thing for Doggett I had come down this afternoon. I could give him an unshakeable alibi.

"That's the tale that's going round. Why, would anyone want to do it for him?"

To my horror Doggett said, " Ever heard of a dog called Lefty?"

Tharp considered, then shook his head.

" He was a winner if ever I saw one. But—no, you wouldn't recognise the name. Wright poisoned him just before his first race."

" For crying out loud, Joe!" I said.

" It's the truth."

" Who are you?" I asked Tharp, outright.

He looked a bit surprised. " Charlie Wright was my brother-in-law. I don't say he was a good husband to Maud, but he was in the family."

Doggett picked up his tankard. " Please yourself!" he said ungraciously. " Don't look to me for a wreath, though. Not that I'd have let him out so easy," he added in a voice that would have convinced the Lord High Advocate. " Strychnine, that's what he used on my dog."

" There was talk of doping," Tharp told us, slowly. " Could be he only meant to slow up your dog, what's its name—Lefty, and he overdid it."

" You don't dope with strychnine," retorted Joe. " And he meant it all right. Said I'd played a trick on him and he'd get his own back."

" And had you? Played a trick, I mean?"

" If he can't get up in time to stay abreast of the rest of us he shouldn't be in the game at all," Doggett said, fiercely. " Fact is, he lost his nerve and chose the easy way out."

Two other chaps came up to join us. They were talking about Charlie Wright.

" What's the latest?" Tharp inquired. The two men

looked at him silently, someone said, " This is Charlie's brother-in-law, come down for the funeral."

" Whose funeral?" said one of the new-comers. " You don't get rid of old Charlie that easy."

" You mean, he's not dead?" Doggett sounded furious. He turned on Tharp.

" I didn't say he was," Tharp protested. " I just said he was shot." He finished his drink, nodded and went off.

" What's his game?" Doggett demanded, staring after him.

" If you're asking me," I said, " he was smelling out the ground. This chap Parnall, do you know what he's like?"

" That's not Parnall." But he sounded uneasy.

" You hadn't been threatening him?" I asked. The group was beginning to break up and I wasn't sorry to see them go.

" Threats!" said Doggett, but there wasn't his usual fire in his voice.

" Come on," I said. " Let's have it."

" I wrote him a letter, that's all."

" Signed?"

" Not exactly."

" Well, are they likely to be able to trace it to you?"

" Don't see why they should. It didn't have an automatic bullet in it, if that's what you have in mind; besides, he shot himself, didn't he?"

" Could have been the smart thing to do," I suggested. " I wouldn't like to have you agin me, Joe. Now he'll be nicely tucked up in hospital for a while, give you a chance to simmer down."

" If that's what he's thinking he'd better start asking for emigration papers," said Doggett, grimly. " Mind you, if I was the police I might start by asking Parnall how he spent his afternoon."

On my sam, I half-wished it had been Doggett who'd got the bullet and was safely out of harm's way.

"You never heard of finesse, I suppose," I said. "You've made everyone within hearing distance (and in the circumstances that was quite a crowd), know how you feel about him."

"As I said, if it had been me behind the gun he wouldn't be lying snug and pampered at my expense in hospital; he'd be lining up for his pauper's grave. I promise you that."

There was a quality in his voice that chilled my blood, and I don't chill easy.

"I've got to go back to-morrow night," I said. "For Pete's sake, take a hold of yourself. It's not worth it, not even for a dog like Lefty."

I'd have suggested his coming with me, but I knew that 'ud be madness. I fidgeted round, longing for news of Barbie, but sure it would be asking for little short of death to ring Crook in his present mood. He's the sort that could blow a private atom bomb down the line. All the same I swore nothing should prevent my returning to the Smoke next day.

And nothing did.

After we left the Arms, and we didn't stay much longer, we went back home.

The rest of the evening passed pretty silently. Doggett usually went to the track on Saturday nights he told me, but for once he wasn't in the mood. He pulled out a

great batch of papers and occupied himself with those.
I put on the television. Doggett had the more profitable
evening.

Next morning he took me round his kennels. When
you saw him with his animals he was as different from
last night's brooder as Jekyll from Hyde. Mind you, he
hadn't got a womanish sentimentality about them, they
were his partners and they were expected to do their
job and help earn his board and keep as well as their
own, but he evinced a sort of consideration for them
you'd never have dreamed he possessed for any living
thing. One of the dogs was a bit under the weather, and
he made more fuss of her than if he'd broken his own leg.
Later we went over to inspect a bitch he was thinking of
acquiring for breeding purposes. It was Sunday, but
every day of the week was the same to him. It was fascinating to watch the two men completing their deal,
like seeing two razors sparring. I listened absorbed until
Doggett had completed his bargain, a pretty sharp one,
and agreed to come round and collect the beast the next
day. Just as he was leaving this chap said, "Anything
fresh on Charlie Wright?" and Doggett answered, "He'll
live from what I hear."

"To stand his trial for attempted suicide, I suppose."

"For more than that if I had my way," Doggett told
him. "The chap's as crooked as a corkscrew."

He didn't see anything funny in saying that, though
I knew he'd pulled a few fast ones himself. I even
wondered if he knew more about the "accident" than
he'd admit, though how he could have pulled a trigger
by remote control was something I couldn't explain.

"Not a pal of yours?" said the chap.

214

" He poisoned my dog."

" Got any proof?"

" I don't need proof. I know."

The chap—I never did learn his name—sent me a significant glance, but I wasn't in a noticing mood that morning.

When we got back to his rooms Doggett opened some beer. " We'll go along to the Arms later," he said. He was like Crook, he always kept a supply on the premises. He went back to his paper-work, it was staggering how much there was, he said he always did it on Sundays, and I sat around reading *The People* and the *News of the World,* always expecting to see Barbie's name leap out of the page, but for some reason the Press hadn't got hold of the story. The Hunters' Mrs. Mopp wasn't a patch on mine. Miss Muffett would have been round at the station long before this. I tried to remember if Barbie had told me when her mother was coming back. She'd set things in motion all right, I thought Crook better hold on to his hat with Mrs. Hunter on the trail. However, I thought it probable he knew the exact lie of the land. Africans in villages passing the tale down the grape-vine have nothing on Arthur Crook.

All this time the wireless had been playing a vociferous musical programme from some foreign station. Doggett said the sound helped him to calculate; I thought it was calculated to split anyone else's ear-drum. And sure enough after a time someone started banging on the door. Well, you wouldn't have heard a normal knock above that concatenation of sound. It wasn't a self-contained flat, just a couple of rooms and a bath. I don't think he could have cooked an egg on a gas-ring if he'd had one, though I'd noticed a battered old stove on the landing that, I suppose, was common to the floor. Anyway, Doggett didn't like eggs, he said they were constipating.

He let whoever it was bang for at least a minute; what with the wireless and the thumping and other doors opening and other voices yelling to give it a rest and put a sock in it, it sounded like the start of a battle.

I touched Doggett on the arm. "Someone seems to want you," I bawled. You had to bawl to be heard above that row. I said it twice before it seemed to sink in.

"What's that you say?" he demanded. "Can't you see I'm busy? Turn that damn' thing down if it's that important."

I lowered the volume and the comparative silence nearly bowled me over. The knocking, that had halted for an instant, when the knocker heard me yelling, I suppose, began again. Doggett didn't look in the least concerned.

"That'll be the old cow from below," he said. "Always on the grouse about something. Known hereabouts as the big F.F. Fault-Finder, see? You don't want to bother about her. Turn that thing up again, I can't think." He added something about quiet reminding him of graveyards.

"You'll have the whole house in here in another minute," I protested. "Anyway, perhaps it isn't her."

"You think it might be Charlie Wright's ghost? O.K., open the door, and tell him Hallo from me."

I said uneasily, "It could be Tharp," and Doggett retorted, "There's one bastard I don't want to see again."

Now even above the banging, voices could be heard, someone ran up the stairs yelling like a banshee. Doggett flung down his pen and hurled himself across the room.

" I'll tell her," he said. " Serve her right if she got herself raped. Not that a man wouldn't need to be blind . . ."

He tore the door open.

" Began to think you must be deaf," roared a voice I'd heard before, and Crook came marching into the room.

I spoke before Doggett could find his tongue.

" Is there news?"

" News? I'll say there's news."

" Of Barbie? How is she? Where is she? She's not with you?"

I tried to look over his shoulder.

" Well, of course she's not with me," said Crook. " She decided to join Mummy for a couple of nights. As simple as that."

I fell back against the wall, unbelieving. " She wouldn't—not without telling me."

" A snap decision," said Crook, blandly. He put out his huge hand and switched off the radio. " It's not that I'm hard of hearing," he explained, " but I never see why I should play second fiddle to a machine."

I was experiencing the sensation of a man running up a flight of stairs and putting his foot on the tread that isn't there.

" Because of the man in the grey Hooper?"

" Got it in one," beamed Crook.

" But—she went off with him," I stammered.

" That's right. He drove her down. Just keeping an eye on her. Sugar may be one hell of a good actress, but she's like all the dames under fifty, she don't know when to come in out of the rain."

" She'd have been safe enough with me," I said. " I wouldn't have let her come to harm." Then the full force of what he'd told us struck me like a tide. " You mean, you know who the driver of the Hooper car is?"

" It's like I told you," said Crook, " I don't aim to lose my clients. Nor I don't aim to end up the third corp in the case. I don't say you wouldn't defend Sugar with your life-blood, but how if someone came gunning for you?"

" So you set him on the trail?" I still couldn't take it in. " But the letter?" I jabbered. " The anonymous letter in my box—*you* sent it?"

" You didn't leave me any alternative," Crook explained, as calm as you please. " We couldn't risk you coming to look for her; somehow I had to get you out of my hair."

There was a movement beside me; during the exchanges of the past minute or so I'd forgotten we weren't alone. Doggett said, " So now you've got all the answers, how about introducing your friend?"

" Of course. You've gathered, I suppose, this is Arthur Crook." I turned to Crook. " This . . ." I began.

" Let me guess," suggested he, beaming like the aurora borealis. " Mr. Joseph Daniels, I believe, late of H.M. Prison, Foxville, and widower of the late Madge Daniels. I have to admit you've given us a good run for our money, but the Old Superb and me, we keep up with the legend, and we run our man to earth with all the rest."

CHAPTER XI

THERE WAS the kind of silence that may be expected to precede the Day of Doom. For myself, I felt as if the bottom had fallen out of the world, and I was dropping down, down into the pit. Then Doggett, turning his head slightly, said, " Why don't you tell him, Simon, he's made a mistake? Doggett's the name—who is this chap, Daniels, he's talking about anyway?"

" That's a rum thing to ask when you see his face every time you look in a mirror. Next thing, you're going to tell me you never went snooping round Mayflower Mansions."

" I don't even know where they are," Doggett told him. " Any reason why I should?"

Crook leaned back and pulled the door open. " Come in, sugar," he said.

I whirled, heart going like a trip-hammer, but it wasn't Barbie who came in. Instead Lizzie Costello, that little black beetle of a woman, came bustling over the threshold. She didn't hesitate. Marching up to Doggett she declared, " That's him. Told him I'd know him again. Big 'ands like a butcher and nice shining black hair out of a bottle."

" I don't know what you're talking about," said Doggett, playing it as cool as a snowflake. " Only you've got it wrong."

" Meaning you never saw this lady before?"

219

" Meaning just that," agreed Doggett, " and no loss neither."

" No call to be rude," said Lizzie, pertly. " Asking for Mrs. Gardiner he was. And was Mrs Gardiner at home."

" That's a new name, isn't it," said Doggett. He turned to Crook. " I thought Simon said you were a lawyer. You must know you can't take a story like that into court."

" You'd be surprised," said Crook. " Thanks, sugar. You know you'll have to give this evidence in court—on oath?"

" And glad of the chance," Lizzie assured him, suddenly vindictive. If she'd been a scorpion she'd have dispatched Doggett there and then. " Poor Madge! One of the kindest souls that ever drew breath."

" I suppose you've got the date all lined up, the date you saw me, I mean," Doggett sneered.

" Mr. Costello 'ull know that. It was the night they were demonstrating outside the local Pally—ante-chamber of hell Mr. Costello calls it. If this is the ante-chamber, one chap said to him, lead on to the palace. I can't wait. He'll be able to fix a date for that. Three of the disciples got picked up by the police," she added, proudly.

" Who's paying your bill?" Doggett asked Crook. " Must be costing you a packet, suborning witnesses and all that."

Crook didn't turn a hair. " Well, who usually pays?" he inquired. " The poor bloody taxpayer. Not that you could expect to know about that," he added, getting in a neat stab. " You wouldn't know one if you met him at your own dinner-table."

Crook's got the reputation of being a dirty fighter, no objection to kicking a man when he's down, and he was enjoying himself putting the boot in. " Thanks, love," he said to Lizzie. " You've been a big help."

" You really mean to put that totty in the box and hear her say she recognised me on the unlighted staircase of Mayflower Mansions, and that proves my name's Joe Daniels?" Doggett's voice throbbed with an incredulous contempt.

" Never heard of the law of slander?" asked Crook. " You're right, of course. And all Lizzie is going to testify is that you were the chap she saw snouting round Madge's flat on a date specified. And then I'm goin' to put another witness in the box to swear that your real name is Joseph Daniels. Y'see, there's one thing you can't disguise. You can change the shape of your nose and the colour of your hair, you can have your teeth fixed, you can grow a moustache or take one off, but you can't alter your finger-prints, not without you cut off your hands, and that's not a solution any murderers consider."

" Who are you calling a murderer?" Doggett demanded.

" Just throwing out the idea. Now, my friend—where are you, Jim?——" He looked round and a second figure materialised out of the gloom. He was the man who'd introduced himself to us as Tharp and I've never had any reason to suppose that wasn't his real name. " Come in, no need to be shy. Now Tharp had a word with the landlord of the Fishermen's Arms last night and he got the loan of two tankards you'd been using; and later we turned 'em over to the authorities for their comments—and does it surprise you to know that the dabs on one of them are identical with those of a chap called Joe Daniels, who was found guilty of murder about twenty years ago?"

Doggett didn't speak, I didn't speak. For a moment we all stood there, tongue-tied. Lizzie seemed to have vanished downstairs where I didn't doubt she was having a magnificent seance with the inevitable ground-floor witch. So it was left to Crook to say, " No harm gathering up those two mugs, too." Indicating the two glasses we'd been using. They were a very striking design; Doggett had bought five at a local market, and each had an engraving of a different kind of sporting dog on it. Tharp came forward and picked up the two glasses, putting two fingers in the mouth of each so as to leave no prints.

" Do you mind?" said Doggett, and he made a sudden savage rush forward. " Those happen to be private property."

I don't know how he did it, seeing he's as bulky as a rock, but Crook was half-way across the room in a breath and Doggett fell over a Number Ten shoe while Tharp whisked the glasses out of reach. I'd seen him do just the same trick at the Admiral.

" You'll get 'em back," he promised, " though whether you'll have any use for 'em is another matter. And even if your lawyer could persuade a jury that the two we got from the Arms weren't yours and Simon's here, there'll be no mistake about these. A very tasty design," he commented, turning to look at the three others on a shelf on the wall.

" O.K.," said Doggett, when he'd got his breath back. " So you can show I'm Joe Daniels. What are you trying to make out of that? There's no law says a man can't change his name. And if you try and run me in for Madge's murder you're going to make a laughing-stock of yourself from here to Moscow. I wasn't even in London the week she died."

" And I expect you can prove it, too," agreed Crook.

" You bloody well bet I can. Never been married yourself, I understand?"

" Oh, the girls don't fall for me," said Crook. " One glance and they decide they could do better for themselves in the zoo."

" What I mean," Doggett ploughed on, " is sixteen years' separation is better than any divorce. I didn't even know Madge was alive till I saw her picture in the paper. According to what I was told she was killed by a flying bomb in '44."

" And it was just coincidence you were seen hanging about outside her flat."

Doggett shrugged. " You're not going to make that one stick."

" And I seem to recall the name in the paper was Gardiner."

" She could have called herself Lady Himucamuck and it wouldn't have made any difference. It was Madge all right. People like her don't change, not without they get scarred or burnt or something, they just grow older."

" That's a funny thing," remarked Crook, and Bristol Cream couldn't have been smoother. " That's just what

I said to Simon here, didn't I, Sim? So when you met
up with her again that must have been the great re-union.
Hands across the Great Divide . . ."

I know Crook has the reputation of taking the most
daredevil risks, but I thought if he got himself murdered
now he'd have no one but himself to thank.

Then he dropped his second bomb. "There's one
more point I didn't mention," he said. "When the
police were going over those glasses they found a second
set of finger-prints they were able to identify, and whose
do you think they were? A con-man called Samuel
Osborn, also in Foxville, for three years, came out in '57.
Name doesn't ring a bell?"

I shook my head. "I never had a call to be a prison
visitor."

"Strictly involuntary," said Crook. "That's where
you met up with each other, of course. When Simon
came out he was to get a place for the pair of you, and
I suppose you've been running a racket together."

"Say it's all true," said Doggett, "you still got
nothing on either of us. We changed our names—natch
—you know what it's like for men just out of the pen.
You try and pin anything illegal on either of us. Or are
you going to spring another surprise, say you found
finger-prints in the flat where Madge was killed?"

"It wouldn't be me finding them," said Crook. "It
'ud be the police. And we know they didn't."

"We've been going straight," Doggett insisted . . .

"Till you met up with your lady wife, and I'll say that
was a shock. How come, Daniels? Or was it just little
Lord Chance? You said yourself you couldn't fail to

know her again. After that it 'ud be simple to follow her home, find out where she lived, hang around and get the gen on her. Who was Gardiner? Were they married? or just in the sight of God? Then you found there wasn't any Mr. G., which left the field wide open for you. And, of course, you remembered your little girl."

" She was my kid, wasn't she?"

" Not any more. You'd signed away your rights."

" A lot of choice I had, didn't I? With her mother ready to sell her to the highest bidder. Anyway, I reckon a woman who's not prepared to work for her own child doesn't deserve to keep her. But I did wonder what the figure was."

" The figure?" For the first time Crook looked flummoxed.

" Well, of course. I wouldn't let one of my dogs go for free, and I reckon a kid 'ud fetch more than a dog."

" I wonder Madge's ghost don't rise up and petrify you," said Crook, and though his voice sounded almost amiable it had a quality that made my blood freeze and set me thinking of the Medusa, who turned men into stone by a single glance. I could actually feel my blood chill. " Didn't you know it's agin the law in this country at least to sell a child, even if she is your own daughter?" He waited a minute, then said, " Is that what you asked Madge? If so, it's not surprising she picked up the candlestick and lammed out."

" I don't know anything about a candlestick. I wasn't there that night. And I can prove it. Anyway, what value to me was Madge dead?"

" Oh, I don't think murder was ever in mind," Crook

reassured him. " Only things don't always go according to plan. We learnt that to our cost in the First World War. A lot of men died learning it."

Joe said, " There was a big race on at Rampington that day. I had a dog running, Tudor Rose. Chaps will remember. No, the one responsible for knocking Madge out is the young chap the police have got under lock and key. I don't say I always agree with them, but this time they've picked the right boy. I tell you, he's as guilty as hell."

" Now that's a funny thing," said Crook, appearing to notice me for the first time since this shattering conversation opened, " your pal here, Simon?—Sammy?— which do you prefer?—he don't agree with you. He's been working like the proverbial black to get our boy off the hook. Don't mind who he pins the responsibility on —Ted Farrer, for instance—and no holds barred. Eh, Simon?"

" You told me yourself on the phone you'd found chloral tablets in his desk." But my voice sounded rusty, unreal, even to myself.

" Not me. It wasn't me that found them. It was Ted; and knowing they hadn't been there twenty-four hours earlier he rang me to give me the gen."

The room went whirling round me, darkness put out my eyes.

" Ted rang?" I repeated when I was able to speak.

" That's right. Got the idea someone was trying to frame him, goodness knows why."

" Perhaps he realised someone knew he had them and was getting in on the ground floor," was all I could think

of to say. " He could easily have known you suspected
him . . ."

" *I* suspected him?" Crook's astonishment sounded
genuine, but he's such an actor there's never any telling.

" Why couldn't he have been the man in the alley, the
man Sherry saw?" I demanded.

" Well, I always knew that couldn't be Ted. He didn't
smoke—remember?"

Time rolled back. I saw Chapple handing round his
cigarette-case, heard Ted say, Thanks, I don't use them.
I hadn't remembered that till now.

" Well," I said, " seeing you were so sure, why did you
let Barbie and me go on a wild goose chase? Or did you
think that was damned humorous?"

" How was I to know where you were going? Neither
of you thought of putting me in the picture. Anyhow,
if you want a chap to hang himself you have to give him
plenty of rope. Bruce would have my blood if he knew
the chance I let his girl take, only it wasn't such a big
chance really. You were under surveillance as they say
all the time, even in the Angel. No reason why you
should recognise that, of course. Or him. Just another
fellow having a quick pint."

" And you sent him to the studio to collect her after
the show?" The bricks were falling into place at last.
Any minute an outsize one was going to fall on my head
and crush me flat. " But—you're madder than a March
hare if you suppose I'd have hurt a hair of her head."

" I don't believe you would," Crook agreed. " But
you weren't in this on your owney-oh, and your partner
here has summary ways of dealing with difficult young

women. Remember Maud Winter." That was the name of the W.A.A.C. Joe had strangled. " Mind you, when we told her what we knew she didn't believe it at first. But he's on Colin's side, she said. Still, there's some risks even I don't take. Besides, we needed you to lead us to your partner. Once you thought the girl had been kidnapped you were bound to get in touch, and so you did, coming for him like a homing pigeon. Rum to reflect it was you who told us at the outset there were two chaps involved. Of course, the phone call—I haven't got it, tell him he'll have to wait, I haven't got it—that was meant for you all along, no twisted lines there. I've been wondering, what made you tell us? Your way of playing for safety, I suppose, put you in the middle of the picture, so you wouldn't be caught short. Funny how chaps will do it, play for safety, I mean. Only—did you know even then you were going to kill Madge?"

I felt as if an iron hand was clamped on my shoulder. I shook and tried to wriggle myself free.

" I don't know what you're talking about. I never saw Madge Gardiner till that evening, never heard her voice till it came over the wires that night . . ."

"And never came to the Admiral before that evening, though you'd been living in the district for months. I suppose that was just another coincidence? Or could it be that, after you got Madge's message, you rang the boss, and said, Go round and tell her second thoughts are often best."

" If that's all the evidence you've got . . ."

" Joe's on a trunk call from London, ain't you, Joe? And trunk dialling ain't come our way yet, so you'd have to get the number through the operator. And there'd be a record. Greenline 1070. And the record shows a call to that number on the night Madge died. So—round you come and there Madge is—flashing a wad of notes in a way that dazzled the eye. Not surprising if you thought she was trying to hold out on you, and anyway, yours not to reason why, yours but to do and die, only this time it was Madge did the dying."

" It was Bruce who went home with her," I said.

" And someone played sentinel in the alley. Not Ted, because he don't smoke, not Bruce having come out double-quick, because he don't smoke either. And what were you doing hanging around there fifteen minutes after the Admiral closed?"

" Who says it was me—besides you, of course?"

" You saw a chap in a little blue car drive up and alight. That was 10.45. We've got the sort of proof a jury 'ull accept. But it was only 10.32, say, when we parted at the mouth of the cul-de-sac. Why did you hang around for another fifteen minutes, if it wasn't that you were keeping your place in the queue to visit with Madge?"

" You're suggesting she'd let me in just because I rang the bell? A complete stranger, someone she'd never set eyes on till that night, and probably didn't even notice then?"

" Ah, but she mightn't think it was a stranger." His voice changed suddenly in that uncanny way of his, the words didn't seem to be spoken by him at all. It was Colin Bruce's voice that filled the room. " Oh, Mrs. Gardiner, I'm so sorry to disturb you again, but I think I must have dropped one of my gloves—could I just come in and look?" The voice changed back to Crook's normal boom. " Found it on the stairs, I suppose, or in the doorway? And a nice bit of luck it must have seemed to you. Here was your chance to load your violence on to another man's shoulders. And never tell me you weren't prepared to take the law into your own hands if Madge didn't come up to expectations. Murder starts in the mind, a man don't kill till he's prepared to kill. Mind you, I don't say you knew how the evening was going to end, but—you took the glove with you to be on the safe side. Then, when the body's found, the police are going to look cross-eyed at young Bruce. And out you come, like that chap in Shakespeare . . ." He looked interrogatively at Tharp, who'd been standing all this time, guarding the two glasses with the dogs engraved on them. Lizzie was having herself a ball with the old girl downstairs and, like the prophet, she'd go in the strength of that meat for weeks to come.

" Oh villain, smiling damned villain," corroborated Tharp.

" That's the one. You must tell me what I can do to help, Mr. Crook. I was there that night, oh yes, I saw them go off together, but if sugar says he didn't do it, well, I'm on sugar's side. And, of course, if there's any chances to put a fresh knot in the rope they're weaving for young Bruce's neck, there you are, fresh as a daisy and willin' as Barkis, to lend a hand."

" Don't fall for any of this, Sim," Doggett told me. " He's trying to make you get your rag out. Toiling in the dark waiting for you to light his little lamp for him. Just remember it's for him to prove you were there, not for you to prove you weren't."

" You're confusing me with the police," Crook rebuked him. "They have to assume a chap's innocent till he's proved guilty, but me, I don't stand by their rules, to me everyone's guilty, from the Lord Chief Justice downward, everyone except my client. Mind you, some clients are more helpful than others. Bruce likes doing things the hard way. So our one chance was to find the chap who did put out Madge Gardiner's light. We had one or two pointers, of course, specially after Sherry Cox bought his. It had to be someone who was at the Admiral on both occasions, and that narrowed the field a lot, I mean it cut out the drunk with the scar, because Ted was tooting sure he wasn't there the second night; it more or less eliminated the Irish whisky-drinker, because why'd he want to call attention to himself by drinking something out of the ordinary, when he hadn't done it before? If he had, Ted would have remembered. But you were there both nights, we know you were hanging around the Mansions at 10.45 on the Wednesday, and you haven't explained yet what you were doing between 10.15 and 10.45 say on the night Sherry came to grief."

"Does he have to account for every spare minute?" asked Doggett derisively. "Maybe he was in the Gents."

"Ted saw him leave the Admiral by the front way before 10.15 and a chap called Tom Fraser saw him passing the Horse and Mariner just before closing time—that's eleven p.m. It 'ud take a cripple 12 minutes, say, to get from one house to the other, but a fine upstanding chap like Simon 'ud do in about six. And yet he took thirty. What was he doing the rest of the time?"

"You tell us," Doggett invited.

"I think he was in the cul-de-sac making sure Sherry 'ud never reach Brandon Street. He's quite a mechanic is Simon—ain't that true?—and he'd know that a man coming to see me 'ud go down Burford Hill. And he'd know the road was under repair and special care needed. But say Sherry, driving like Jehu, came to the top and started to put on the brakes and the brakes wouldn't work? He wouldn't need them till he got there, not that hour of the night; or the hand-brake 'ud serve. But that's a killer's hill, you need everything you've got even in daylight, with all those lamps and what not strewn around. We all know Sherry's kind of driving, full out, then whammo! slam on the brakes. Only—brakes have gone on strike, you're over the edge, keep your head and pray for a miracle and it could be you'll make it yet. Only—he didn't pray hard enough or his guardian angel was having a coffee-break. Why, going the rate he did, dirty great lamps all over the road and the kerb looking as if a bomb had hit it, poor chap never had a chance. And who's going to suspect that nice soft-spoken chap, Simon Crete?"

" A jury found it was accident," I said.

Crook said something that would have made every juryman's face turn red. Even Doggett gave a little jump and a characteristic growl.

"Not that you didn't work it very pretty," Crook allowed. "Murder by remote control. Only—ever wonder why murderers get caught? It's because they overlook some detail so small or so obvious they don't even notice it."

You could have heard a pin drop in the room by this time.

" Pardon me for breathing," said Doggett, " but this

happens to be my room, so if you haven't anything else to say . . ."

" Oh, don't stop him," I pleaded. " He was going to tell me my fatal mistake."

" Two actually, though they match up fine. It's wanting to play safe. Why couldn't you leave Ted out of this? If there was a case against him I'd make it, if I couldn't make it no one would."

" It was you who suggested he was involved," I pointed out.

" Me?" Once again he sounded genuinely astonished.

" The woman with the piece of silver," I reminded him.

" And you thought Ted was the missing piece of silver?" He shook his head. " You should look in the glass. And there's one more thing, one more question you're going to be asked. I'm giving you plenty warning, so you can think up a good answer. How do you explain the fact that Madge had your phone number written down in her flat?"

" I don't believe it," I told him bluntly. " Why on earth should she?"

" Because you were the one she was to ring that night and get instructions—after she told you she'd got the money, that is."

I glanced at Doggett. " Does this make any sense to you, Joe?"

" It's his story, not mine," Joe said.

" Maybe you were to go round and collect it. Or she was to leave it some place, one of the lockers at a main station, say. Easy and cheap and who's going to suspect there's anything unusual in a suit-case left by a middle-aged woman in a station locker?" He grinned in an unpleasant sort of way. " I daresay the police 'ud have some shocks if they opened all of them," he opined. " Still, she hadn't got the cash."

" You're trying to tie knots in me," I said. " Granted I was a fool to mention the phone call, but seeing I knew nothing of the woman who made it—well, it was a coincidence I should hear her voice within a couple of hours."

" Is that what you call it?" Crook said. " Oh, well, a rose by any other name is still a blooming rose. Care to explain how it was the chap who gave her the number got it wrong?"

" It's happening every day of the week," I told him, scornfully. " People get the figures transposed, probably wanted 76 instead of 67 . . ."

" Only it was 67 she got and 67 plus the rest that was written on the back of the photo."

" Back of what?" I exclaimed.

" She had to write it down somewhere where she wouldn't lose it, hadn't she?" Once again Crook's voice changed. " Ring 6700 and ask for Simon. Well, she had to write the number down somewhere and here was something she wouldn't throw away by accident. So, like I say, she wrote it on the back of the photo."

" Which photo was that?" I said.

" The unframed one of the little boy, you know, where he's sitting on a rug holding a toy train. Funny how it's the little things that give a chap away. If you'd turned it over—though I suppose there was no reason why you should—you'd have seen it. R.6700."

I began to laugh. I must have overdone it, because I

saw Joe watching me like that spotted beast—a lynx.
" You really had me worried for a minute," I said. " But
come, Mr. Crook, you'll have to do better than that.
You see, there wasn't any unframed photo of a little boy
holding a train. There were two pictures, both framed,
on the mantelpiece, one with his mother and the other
hanging on to a puppy." Crook just stared.

" Both framed, were they?" he said.

There was a choking sound beside me, and I caught
Doggett's eye. His glance would have felled an ox.

" And that's just what you've been, you great bloody
ape!" he exploded. " I told you to keep your mouth
shut."

" Now, come to think of it," said Crook, " the photo
wasn't in that room at all. The phone was by Madge's
bed, and when she got the number she wrote on the
nearest thing, and that was this picture. But, give you
my word, it exists, and it'll be produced in evidence.
Yes," he brooded. " It wasn't in the living-room, after
all. Only, if you'd never been inside the place, how the
hell did you know?"

He nodded to Tharp, who'd put the two glasses into a
handcase he'd brought with him. Tharp moved towards
the window, but, " No, you don't," cried Joe. He
snatched up one of the bottles we'd emptied, smashed off
the neck and stood there, lowering, like a bull, the jagged
glass held in front of him. There aren't many better
weapons for close fighting than a broken bottle, as plenty
of police have found to their cost. He was a short man,
but, as Lizzie had noticed, he had large hands and long
arms, which gave him a disproportionate reach. It
wouldn't be difficult for him to strike upwards and he

could easily cut into Tharp's jugular vein. And seeing how little he had to lose I didn't suppose he'd hesitate. Tharp stopped where he was. Joe said to Crook, " That goes for you, too. Get hold of the other bottle, Simon."

Tharp stuck out a long leg and kicked the bottle out of my reach. It was a real Hogarth scene; outside it was getting dark; they weren't very coming-along with street lights in this bit of the town, and there wasn't even a footstep on the pavement. I imagined Crook had got reinforcements of some sort laid on, and whoever it was was waiting for a sign from the window. At least I could see to it the signal wasn't given. If either of the men moved, Doggett would do his stuff without compunction and without delay; he'd look to me to deal with the second (unarmed) man. It went through my mind that Crook, who's said to be prepared for every emergency, might even have one of those miniature transistor cameras concealed in one of his enormous vulgar coat-buttons. It's happened before.

" Pass me that case," said Joe, indicating the one in Tharp's hand.

No one moved. I couldn't see what good he thought he was going to do, even if he ground the glasses to powder. There were still the two we'd used at the Fishermen's Arms, and, even supposing Crook was gilding the lily and no one had examined them for finger-prints, such prints could be duplicated and are as efficacious as a lie-detector.

" I said give me that case."

I knew that tone in Joe's voice. Another second and he'd rush his man, and to hell with the consequences, just as years and years ago he'd borne down on that black-mailing little slut, Maud Winter.

A new voice startled us all. Lizzie Costello had come to the end of her party with the old girl downstairs and, anxious not to miss a trick, had come beetling back up the stairs. Now she called, "Give him the case, dear. Can't you see he means what he says? All right then, I'll give it him." She made a dash forward and the next second the room was plunged in darkness. As she ran like a scuttering hen she'd switched off the electric light. "If you lived with Mr. Costello," I heard her disembodied voice say, "and heard him preaching about the hell we're all going to you wouldn't be in any hurry to get there."

The place was chaotic. I knew it was only a matter of seconds before someone got the light going again, but Lizzie was a match for the lot of us. Back on the landing she was yelling blue murder; doors were opening everywhere, feet tore down the stairs; voices called, someone mentioned the police. I heard a crash as someone went down, I still couldn't see who, then feet came surging, a torch glowed, the light came on. The room looked as if a tornado had swept through it; it also seemed remarkably full of people. A chap in a blue uniform had his hand firmly on Doggett's shoulder.

"For Christ's sake keep your trap shut," Doggett was saying to me. "Nothing that's been said at present can be used in evidence, not till you've been cautioned." The boy in blue—well, hardly a boy—stooped and gingerly picked up the jagged bottle-neck that Doggett had dropped during the mêlée.

237

" Let's be going," he said.

" You take us," Doggett told him. I could see the gleam in his eyes; he was planning how to get possession of that wicked weapon. Before the room emptied blood would flow. But Lizzie had one more shot in her locker. Crook always equips himself with allies, and they come all shapes and sizes. And, like him, they mostly don't give a hoot for the rules. Lizzie suddenly snatched a long rusty hat-pin out of the bird's-nest erection she had on her head, a kind of tartan deerstalker with a plume up the side, and said, " You heard the man. Get going. Or . . ." She waved the pin, and I swear she'd have run it to the head into either of us, and Crook wouldn't have stopped her. Either the bobby was fascinated or he had no more respect for the law than Crook, because he didn't stir an inch to stop her.

" What kind of an officer are you ?" Doggett demanded furiously, as we came pounding out of the room. The chap didn't answer until we reached the street. Quite a reception we had, considering that a few minutes earlier the world had seemed practically uninhabited. Lookers-on came tumbling out of their doors, peering out of windows, rising up through the pavement like souls in a Stanley Spencer canvas . . . In point of fact, he didn't answer even then. He left it to Crook.

" Oh, Bill ain't a rozzer at all," said Crook, lightly. " He happened to be going to a fancy dress party in the neighbourhood and he dropped in to borrow his taxi-fare. Quick change artists don't have anything on Bill. Sugar's chauffeur Friday night and now . . . That's the girl," he added, breaking off as Lizzie appeared driving a couple of policemen before her, the real article this time, like Bo-Peep on the rampage. We all swept down to the station, and here Crook took the wind out of everyone's sails by announcing that he intended to exercise his prerogative as a citizen and accuse me of wilful murder.

Doggett was another who knew all the answers.

"And after that there'll be the slander case against Arthur Crook, Esquire," he announced. "Hold it, chum, he's only bluffing."

"Always happy to learn," puffed Crook, looking like a demented alligator. "Anyway, I was always a gambler, so one bet more . . . And since we're on the subject of gambling," he'd got round to the police officer by this time, "anyone like to bet you'll find a sizeable supply of drugs in Sam Osborn's flat. Suitable for doping dogs. Ain't that right, chum?"

"Doping dogs?" I repeated.

"That's what I said. Infallible way of making certain your bet comes in first. Mind you, it's a bit chancy, but not too difficult once you know the ropes—or so my clients tell me. And it ain't in nature for one man's tips to be right all the time. Besides, where did the chloral come from that was found in Ted's drawer? It wasn't there on the Thursday, he'll take his Bible oath on that. Turned the place over, doing his nut to find some oil of cloves to put on a bad tooth. Then come Saturday he looks in the same drawer and there the little bottle tucked back nice and neat and—get this!—not a print on it. He knows his onions, does Ted Farrer, and he reckoned it had been planted, and who was the gardener? I give you three guesses. Ted don't entertain a lot, but on the Friday night he let one of the customers have a loan of his blower, and what was the customer's name? Sam Osborn, alias Simon Crete. Adds up as neat as one and one and one and one and one."

" Have you finished, Mr. Crook?" asked the station sergeant as dumb as a bunny. " Because if so I'll warn you both," and here he looked full at Joe and me—I never did like chaps with fat red faces and this one could have served as a sign for The Rising Sun Inn—" you don't have to make any statement or answer any questions till you've got your lawyer with you, but if you do, anything you say will be taken down and may be used in evidence."

" We've nothing to say," said Doggett. " How could we, seeing we don't know a thing."

" I'll tell you one thing you don't know," chimed in Crook the Irrepressible, " and that's how to take it easy. When I was a kid my Mum took me to Church—come to think of it, it must have been Lent, that's one of the Church seasons in case you didn't know—and there was a preacher and he said the trouble with Christians was they never took time off to breathe. So busy climbing the Mount of Virtue they fell over their own feet, and even if they reached the top they were likely to fall off because they never looked up. And the same goes for the Bad Lads' Brigade. Can't leave anything to chance, must be covered at every turn. That anonymous letter now," he added, darting from point to point like a dragon-fly. " The one you so conveniently lost. Talk about gilding the lily! Wanted to load this little bundle on to Ted, didn't you? Only if it was him, then he must be the one that wrote the letter. And how did he know your address? You were practically a stranger to him. And a chap with evidence don't push that evidence into his coat pocket and lose it within the hour, wears it next his heart, always assumin' he's got one. Neat, of course, to show it to sugar's Mum, because she's one of the Incorruptibles, and if she said she saw it, then see it she did. But you didn't dare risk letting me take a peek at it, let alone the rozzers—police, I mean. Pardon, I'm sure. Always the chance someone 'ud tumble, wasn't there?"

"Now," I said, ". you're going to explain what advantage it was to me to write myself an anonymous letter."

"Oh, it's an old trick," said Crook. "Chaps get the notion that if they can wear the martyr's robe, then they automatically join the Martyrs' Union. But it don't always come off. I've known husbands take a dose of weedkiller in the hope of getting their lady wives hauled off for attempted murder, only sometimes it acts like that thing—what is it, that you chuck away and it comes wheelin' back and prangs you on the boko. Hoist with their own petard. It's safer really to leave a little bit to chance. If you surface into the limelight too often even nice, innocent chaps like the police start gettin' suspicious. I mean who were *you* to rate anonymous letters?"

"That'll do, Mr. Crook," said the senior police officer present. "We take your point."

And at that he did shut up, but only because he'd no more to say. And couldn't, for an instant, think of any more damage he could do. I stole a glance at Doggett— I'd never thought of him as Daniels since he came out of Foxville. His face was like a block of wood and his mouth looked as if you'd need a vice to prise it open. But I knew he was like the police. He'd taken the point, too.

And suddenly I lost them all and only saw Barbie,

that wonderful, wonderful girl I met so much too late. It was like seeing her on the far side of an abyss even a Jet couldn't span. Oh, well, I heard myself say, I knew from the start there was no future in it.

And for once—seeing Crook was present—I had the last word.

CHAPTER XII

THEY TELL YOU British justice is the best in the world. All I can say is, I'm sorry for the rest of the world. The jury never even pretended to believe a word of my evidence, even when it was the immortal truth. Like the money I brought away from Madge's flat for instance. I didn't take that by force, she gave it me. Crook was right about me ringing Joe, and he said, " Probably stalling. No harm anyway giving the old girl a jolt." And he told me I'd probably find her at the Admiral, name of Gardiner. Mind you, I knew who she was. Crook was right again about Joe coming upon her by sheer chance. I think he hated her. When he was up for the death of Maud Winter his lawyer wanted Madge to testify on her husband's behalf, but she said, What's the use? Prosecuting Counsel 'ud tear me to pieces, I'd do him more harm than good. Joe was never cut out to be a husband, and she felt it badly that he'd never taken any interest in the child. Mind you, I think she was right, I think her evidence might have done him more harm than good, but he never forgave her. He was like that chap in the Old Testament who saw his enemy delivered into his hand. Not that he didn't want the money he expected to get from her; it would have enabled him to branch out in quite a big way, but first and foremost he saw a chance of getting even with her. I'd hoped Bruce would have some prior engagement which would leave the position wide open for me to carry her parcel home; but it didn't work out that way. Of course I was the chap Sherry saw smoking a fag in the byway. I remembered hearing a motor-bike go past, but at that stage I didn't even realise Sherry owned a motor-bike. Finding the glove was just a piece of luck; I shoved it in my pocket. I swear at that stage I had no more idea of murder than the Man in the Moon. Of course, I let on to Madge that I was Bruce, and by the time she saw I wasn't it was too late to try and bar me out. When she said, I haven't got it, I pointed to her bag and said, What's wrong with that for a first instalment? and she tore out the notes and threw them at me. Take them and get out, she said. There's no more on the premises, and you won't find any, not if you take the walls to pieces. I pulled open a few drawers but oddly enough I believed her. Still, her throwing the notes at me rankled, I didn't see why she shouldn't have to sweat a little.

" If you don't go right now I'll call the police," she told me.

That was a silly thing to say. Joe's right. Women who try to boss you about deserve all they get.

" Oh, I don't think you'd want to do that for your daughter's sake," I told her, and I picked up one of the photos. " Nice little chap," I said. " Be a pity to let him know his grandaddy was an old lag." And then, when she said nothing, I asked her if Joe had seen these. " Might be a good idea to take one along," I said. That's when she picked up the candlestick. She sprang into violent life, as though someone had turned on a 150 watt bulb inside her. It was quite a weapon, too, must have been made out of an old ship's bell or something. I knew that, being a woman and in the mood she was, she could reduce my face to a bloody pulp before she even realised what she was doing. She came at me yelling like a banshee; at all costs I wanted to stop that row. And I don't need Crook to tell me that seeing red isn't just a figure of speech. We had quite a hassle before I got it away from her, and I struck out, just once. As if I'd said Abracadabra, down she went on the hearth-rug, like a stone. There was hardly any blood, just one mark where her forehead had hit a chair or something. But she was dead, out like a light. I couldn't believe it. Then I knew this was the last chance I had of keeping my nose clean, for the police's benefit anyway. I went round wiping surfaces, I went into the bedroom and tore the clothes off the bed, being careful to touch nothing else—it's ironical to think the photo and the telephone number were under my hand—I rubbed the candlestick clean and put it back on the shelf. Then I remembered the glove in my pocket, and I stuffed it under the body. I took the money, I had to make it look like a break-in or just some fellow from the pub taking Madge for a ride. I realised later how lucky I was that Lizzie Costello chose that evening to take a bath, though even so she heard me go down. Still, she didn't have time to open the door and peek out.

When Bruce was arrested I didn't lose any sleep, and anyway I needed all I could get. When I told Joe about Madge, as I had to, I knew that if he could have dropped me into a bucket of acid and converted me into sludge, without attracting suspicion, he wouldn't have hesitated.

And then Barbie surfaced. Barbie changed everything. I'd never known a girl like her before. I'd never known the urge to settle down. Love 'em and leave 'em and never overstay your welcome, that was my motto. There are two kinds of men, the stayers and the goers, and I belonged to the last kind. Until I met Barbie. And even from the beginning I think I knew it was too late. To her I was Simon Crete, a nice kind of chap trying to help to prove her lover's innocence. She'd never heard of Sam Osborn and wouldn't have crossed the road to give him a good-day if she had. Because of her I got much more deeply involved than I'd intended. It wasn't only for safety's sake that I wanted to stay in the picture, though I admit the anonymous letter was a blob. Why should anyone suppose I was a source of danger? If any threats were flying around they'd be aimed at Crook. More than once I wished I could be standing on the pavement armed with a poisoned flit gun when he went bowling by in his absurd yellow contraption he calls a car.

No, the thing that really irks me is Sherry's death. He was a pleasant young chap and he didn't deserve to die. Only he was in the way and he had to be pushed out. It's the law of nature. Plants get too thick on the ground and start to suffocate each other; bushes have to be pruned, trees lopped; it's bad luck on the superfluous buds and boughs, I suppose, but that's all. As soon as I heard he was going to Crook with his story I knew I had to act and act fast. Mind you, I couldn't be certain he was a source of danger, but there are some risks only a fool will take. And it wasn't just Sherry, it was Sherry backed up by that unscrupulous monster, Crook. So I did what he later knew I must have done. I tinkered a bit with the brakes, tickled up the steering, but not enough to arouse his suspicions. Knowing him, I realised he probably wouldn't even touch the hand-brake till he got to Burford Hill, and most likely he never even knew what hit him. All the same, it's not fair to say I killed him. He was a victim of his own times. The world's overcrowded, competition's intense, even competition for sufficient air to breathe, let alone pure air. The history of our time is the history of the survival of the fittest, the most cunning, the most aware. Men confront men, and the weaker goes to the wall. Classes find themselves opposed and instead of merging for strength, they fight it out. It's the same with nations. Push or be pushed. Sherry, through no fault of his own, was one of the pushed. It was as simple as that.

I never told Joe about Sherry, that way he couldn't betray me even by accident. Just for the record, the whisky-drinking chap turned up; he had been sent abroad by his firm next day and didn't know about Sherry till his return. He wasn't any use; just one of the bossy kind who saw a young chap in a tizz and thought he'd shed sweetness and light. And everyone knows how much good he did.

I think that wraps everything up. Oh, the chloral. I really did think Crook had an eye on Ted, and a little bit of firm evidence might have clinched things. Naturally, if I'd remembered about him not smoking, I wouldn't have taken the trouble. He said he'd never had chloral in the house in his life, and no one could disprove that. Anyway, it wasn't important because Sherry hadn't been doped. As to when Crook started getting on to me, I suppose I'll never know. Perhaps it was the letter, but more likely it's just he'd suspect the Archangel Gabriel if he got in his way. Better hang wrong f'ler than no f'ler, that's Crook.

Joe used to say that, sooner than face another prison sentence, he'd chuck himself out of a window, and I used to agree. But now I know I'd sooner face a life sentence than stand where I stand to-day.

:: ::

" You know how it is at the end of an evening's viewing," said Crook. " You've had the late extra, you've had the weather report, and there's nothing left but the epilogue. And the more brief and to the point that is, the better."

He was talking to Mrs. Hunter and her daughter and Colin Bruce, lately released from prison and preparing (so the coarse-minded Crook put it) to lock himself into another sort of cage.

" What burns me up," said Barbie in her outspoken way, " is that Daniels gets off scot-free. Oh, I know he admitted under examination he was accessory after the fact, but no one seems to take that very seriously."

" It wouldn't have counted to him for virtue to have turned his partner in," Crook pointed out. " It's called Queen's Evidence, and is said to ameliorate your sentence, but Daniels has the sense he was born with, if that ain't saying a lot, and I daresay he didn't look forward to having his throat cut or his head kicked in *en route* for the dock. In our rough masculine world, sugar, it ain't looked on kindly, selling your mate down the river. And as for not paying his whack, I tell you, a leper with his bell won't be more shunned than Joe Daniels after this. He wasn't—isn't—precisely what's called a straight blade, and in his world a chap who's been marked by the police has only one place to go—and that's Coventry."

" And Mr. Crook doesn't think he intended Madge to be murdered," Mrs. Hunter put in.

Crook agreed. " He told his story from the box very nice, I thought. Here he was in a bit of trouble, his wife offers to lend a hand if she can raise the spondulicks. She's to get in touch with Simon Crete—she never heard of him as Osborn—and fix the details. Osborn goes round to find out when they can expect to collect, there's a bit of a rough house and she gets herself knocked out for the count. You know, it's a pity he couldn't have come to me, I could have swung a manslaughter verdict. Well, they'd have found her prints on the candlestick, the money would be intact—him taking it told heavily against him—he wouldn't have been the police's favourite man, but you can't have everything."

" Even if he didn't mean to kill her," said Barbie uncompromising, " he wouldn't have lifted a finger to stop Colin being found guilty. And there was that young Indian—what was his name?"

" Mr. Seringpatam Cox. I'm not holding any brief for him, sugar. I think he was about as healthy to have around as a mad dog."

Colin suddenly took a part in the conversation. " And that's the chap you allowed Barbie to go around with?"

" You know, it's a funny thing," said Crook, " but she was as safe with him as with the Archbishop of Canterbury. He wouldn't have lifted a finger to save your intended, but he wouldn't have lifted it to harm you either."

"Oh, nonsense," Barbie told him, "he was simply using me. I enabled him to stay in the picture and get all the gen. as it came along."

"You're shocking Mr. Crook," her mother said.

"Well, who's kidding who?" Crook inquired. "What's sauce for the goose . . . You were just making use of him, weren't you? You were Beatrice to his Dante, but you'd have let him fall over the cliff if it would have helped Romeo here. And—a word in your ear——" he added to the young man. "Easy to see you're not a Benedict. Come and have a drink with me a year hence and then we'll see if you're so glib about allowing women to go round with mad dogs. Women go round with who they like and every husband has to learn to put up with it. Why, the only person in this affair who hasn't been playing for his own hand has been Madge Gardiner, and she got herself murdered. Which shows you how the ungodly flourish."

"And even she helped to sign her own death-warrant." Crook caught Mrs. Hunter's eye, and his return glance said, "Sooner him than me." A wife who knows all the answers is batting on a very tricky wicket, though he didn't doubt she'd carry her bat for a century, being her mother's daughter and all. "I mean, if she hadn't hung around in bars and allowed comparative strangers to see her home, she might never have ended as she did."

"The lady always gets the last word," Crook agreed. "Still, she was my cup of tea. Her and Lizzie Costello . . ."

"Ah!" cried Barbie, and her eyes were glowing.

" Now you're talking. She was splendid. I envy her. If I'd been there that night . . ."

Crook leaned over and laid an enormous brown hand over her clasped ones.

" That's a dame all over. Always want to run before they can walk. You don't become a heroine overnight, sugar, any more than you become a murderer. Lizzie came up the hard way, thirty years of trouble and strife. It makes you or breaks you. It broke Madge in the end, but—know who I wouldn't be? The Recording Angel when Lizzie Costello breezes up on the Last Day. If he's got any sense he'll cover his eyes with his wings, and let her go through nice and quiet, without any argument."

When they got up to go Barbie observed, " It was a miracle for us that you should have been in the Admiral that night. A chance in a thousand . . ."

" No chance at all," Crook contradicted her. " I was there of set purpose to get an alibi for young Ron Taylor. But Ted was right, he warned me I was wasting my time. Only this morning Ron's Mum told me he'd been picked up with a couple of other lads on the stolen car racket. All that work and what's to show?"

" I've just told you," cried Barbie. " If you hadn't been there Colin might still be accused of murder. It makes you believe in a plan . . ."

" Oh, get away!" said Crook. He grinned at Bruce. " You can't win, can you? Ah, well, you'll learn. Not got much to say for yourself, have you?" he added candidly.

" Barbie's been doing overtime," Colin pointed out.

" And that's the way it'll go on," Crook confided to Bill Parsons when his visitors had departed. " And, seeing he's one of these Cloud Cuckoo chaps, whose work is practically his religion, I daresay it'll be a very happy marriage."

Saying which, he declared the office closed *pro tem* and he and Bill went over the road to the Currant and Bun and drank to Single Bliss.

>>> If you've enjoyed this book and would like to discover more great vintage crime and thriller titles, as well as the most exciting crime and thriller authors writing today, visit: >>>

The Murder Room
Where Criminal Minds Meet

themurderroom.com

9 781471 910265